PRASE FOR (

"Olivia Miles is an expert at creating a sweet romantic plot and setting endearing characters within it, which ultimately results in a delightful read." ~ *RT Book Reviews*

"A charming holiday tale of fresh starts, friendship and love with a heroine even Scrooge couldn't resist." ~Sheila Roberts, New York Times bestselling author, for THE WINTER WEDDING PLAN

"Sweet, tender, and burgeoning with Christmas spirit and New England appeal, this engaging reunion tale sees one couple blissfully together, artfully setting the stage for the next book in the series." ~Library Journal for MISTLETOE ON MAIN STREET

"Hope Springs on Main Street is a sweet and worthy addition to your romance collection." ~ *USA Today*

"Olivia Miles weaves a beautiful story of healing and second chances." ~RaeAnne Thayne, New York Times bestselling author for HOPE SPRINGS ON MAIN STREET

"Readers seeking a peppermint-filled, cozy Christmas contemporary will be satisfied…" ~*Publishers Weekly*, for CHRISTMAS COMES TO MAIN STREET

THIS Christmas

OLIVIA MILES

ALSO BY OLIVIA MILES

ISBN 979-8-9862624-3-7

THIS CHRISTMAS

First paperback edition, October 2019
Reissue edition, October 2022

THIS
Christmas

Chapter One

Carrie

This Christmas was going to be the best one ever.

Carrie Campbell was sure of this. Even more sure than the year she turned six and Santa had brought her the doll that ate and drank and wet its pants, and she'd been pretty sure then, because she'd written no less than twenty-four letters to the big guy, mailing a fresh list each morning in December, and making sure to bring it up in person when she sat on his knee in the Winter Lake town square gazebo at their annual visit to the Christmas Festival. This year, she was so sure, that she had splurged and bought herself an entirely new outfit for tonight's dinner, from the crimson red wrap dress to the lacy stockings to the rather impractical velvet kitten heels and matching clutch. After all, it wasn't every day that a woman got engaged, was it?

She'd told everyone she knew. She couldn't help herself. It was just bubbling within her, bursting to come out, from the very moment that Lucas had first suggested dinner tonight. It was their four-year dating anniversary. And only two weeks ago, she had found *the ring*.

She had been "cleaning" his apartment one evening, when he got held up at work, and there it was, the unmistakable Tiffany blue box sitting in his bedside drawer beside his extra set of keys and the silver cufflinks she'd given him for his birthday two years ago. At first, she didn't even know what to do. She'd stared at the box, in shock, in joy, in total surprise, and backed away as if it were a bomb about to detonate. Really, she told herself, she shouldn't take a peek. He'd spring it on her any day, she'd already blown the best part of her reaction, and she needed to save some of it for when he opened the box. With more willpower than she knew she possessed, she had closed that drawer, pressed her lips together to suppress her squeal, and went about her business for the rest of the night, well, other than the fact that every time Lucas left to go into his bedroom, her heart sped up a bit.

It wasn't until the next day that it occurred to her that it might not be a ring at all. That maybe it was a pair of earrings or a bracelet—a Christmas or anniversary gift that he hadn't yet wrapped. The decision was made. She had to check. She had to set her expectations. And so, the very next time she had access to the bedside table (when she'd excused herself to his room to grab a sweater, even though she was practically sweating from anxiety) while he whipped up one of his famous stir-fries in the tiny space you could almost call a kitchen by Manhattan standards, she'd yanked open the drawer, pulled out the box, and opened it before she had time to change her mind or he had reason to check on her. And there it was. Sparkly. Round. Practically winking at her.

It wasn't exactly the ring she had carefully hinted at starting at their two-year mark (she had hoped for a cushion cut on a pave band like her sister Tess's ring, and this was a brilliant, three-stone setting), but it was close enough, possibly even more beautiful than what she'd envisioned, and it was a ring nonetheless, as her best friend Melody was quick to point out when Carrie told her the next morning at the Upper West Side preschool where they both taught.

"A ring!" Melody had dramatically set her hand to her heart in mock relief. "Sure took him long enough!"

It was true, Carrie knew, that four years *was* a long time to be dating someone in your thirties, but it also confirmed to her that tonight was the night. It was Christmastime in New York. It was *snowing*. They were going to a cozy little restaurant in Little Italy—and it was their dating anniversary. And as of three o'clock this afternoon, she was officially on winter break.

She just had to get through the day.

A crash in the corner of the classroom pulled her from her daydream (and she was just getting to the best part, where Lucas got down on one knee and reached his hand into his pocket), and Carrie looked over to see that little Zachary Dean had dumped the contents of the dollhouse again. She counted to three, reminded herself that Zachary was only four, and that she only had one more hour left in her day before she was free for the next two weeks. Technically, her four-year-old class was only in attendance four days a week, and Fridays were a day reserved for meetings, cleanings, and lesson planning, but Carrie had cleared everything off her plate early this morning so that tomorrow she would be free to think of nothing but her upcoming wedding.

3

She closed her eyes and smiled. Told herself it was no big deal that Zachary was now upending the container of blocks. Nothing could destroy her happiness.

Besides, she loved children. She wouldn't have become a preschool teacher if she didn't. And now that she was getting married, it wouldn't be long before she and Lucas started a family. There would be logistics to figure out, of course. Raising kids in the city was obscenely expensive, after all. But she wasn't opposed to making the big move out to the burbs—Connecticut or New Jersey. She knew Lucas had scoffed at the idea any time she'd mentioned it before, said he hadn't moved to New York just to end up back in some small town, but surely he'd have to see the reality of it in time. Besides, he was older now. Nearly thirty-five; two years older than her and the same age as her sister, Tess, who had an eight-year-old child. Surely he'd see the benefit of spending weekends doing things like coaching baseball and going to the park instead of hitting the bars.

If they had a summer wedding, she could be pregnant by this time next year, she calculated, as she set the miniature table and chairs, beds and dressers into the wooden house. Maybe it would be a boy. A little Lucas Junior. Maybe he'd be sweet like Timothy—she cast a glance to the little boy with wire-framed glasses who was playing with some toy trucks, making engine noises as he pushed them around on the mat. (He was her favorite, of the boys, that was. Her favorite girl was Clementine, with her contagious giggle and blonde ringlets. Not that she'd be letting on.) Or maybe she'd end up with a spirited little boy, like Zach.

She practiced her patience.

"Time to pick up, Zachary," she warned, and he gave her a long, stern stare. He scowled as he began shoving the remaining pieces back into the dollhouse. Turning brightly to the rest of the room, Carrie sang out, "Clean-up time!"

At once, twelve little voices joined in chorus, the same song they sang every afternoon, Monday through Thursday, an hour before pickup. Next, they would have their snack. Then they would have a story. Then, because it was Thursday and the last day of their four-day school week, they would share their favorite and least favorite parts of the week (practicing turn-taking and listening skills!) and then...

Then she was going to get engaged.

With renewed energy, she picked up a plastic bin and began collecting all the toy horses that Jasmine had been playing with, hoping that she wouldn't have to pry the white one from her chubby hands, as she nearly had to do yesterday.

"You promise to keep him safe?" Jasmine asked today, holding the toy close to her chest.

"I promise." Carrie smiled. "He will be right here waiting for you after winter break. Nice and warm and toasty."

Jasmine looked uncertainly at the horse and then out the window where snow was still falling steadily and then chucked the toy into the bin before scampering off to join the others at the two rectangular tables where they would have their snack.

Carrie laughed and finished collecting the toys while her teacher's assistant began pouring water into paper cups. Tanya glanced at the door a few times, and then, with her finger pressed to her lips, and a long, telling glance at the children, opened it.

Carrie stared at Melody, who was balancing a large sheet cake as she strode into the room, the art and music teachers close behind.

"Congratulations!" they all cried out, and then, as if on cue, all the kids called it out too.

Tears prickled the back of her eyes when she realized that this had been planned all day. That her best friend, her coworkers, and her kids, even Zachary, who was now grinning proudly, had held onto the secret, waiting to surprise her.

It was the happiest day of her life, and she knew that there would be many more to come. Her wedding day. The birth of her children. Vacations. Anniversaries. The life she had been waiting for.

"You guys! You didn't have to do this!" After all, Melody knew that the proposal hadn't exactly happened yet.

"You don't expect us to wait two weeks to celebrate with you, do you?" Melody asked, and all the kids shook their heads in larger-than-life motion. "This is a big day and you've waited a long time for it. We're all just so happy for you."

Carrie waited until Melody had set the cake down before giving her a big hug. "Thank you."

"That's what friends are for," Melody said with a wink. "Remember that and be sure to call with all the details before I head home for the holidays."

Home for Melody was Tampa, Florida. She went every year, but everyone knew that Carrie stayed in the city for the holidays. She rarely left the island of Manhattan, unless Lucas made plans, which was less often than ever now that he was a partner at his law firm.

Carrie glanced over to see Clementine raising her hand. "Yes, Clemmy?"

"May we please have some cake now?" the little girl asked in her small voice, and Carrie burst out laughing.

"Of course! What's a party without cake?"

"A party!" a chorus of small voices called out.

It was, indeed, a party, Carrie thought joyfully, as one by one, the faculty popped in to congratulate her and a card, signed by everyone, even the children, in shaky letters, was presented.

Carrie felt her smile slip and she moved closer to Melody. "You don't think we're…jinxing anything, do you?"

Melody snorted as she sliced the knife through the cake, ignoring the cry of demands for the corner piece with the pink butter cream flowers and butterflies—a special touch; few people other than her sisters knew how much Carrie liked butterflies.

"Carrie, it's been four years. It had to happen eventually."

Melody was right. It had been four years ago to the day that she and Lucas had gone on their first date, at the very restaurant they would dine in tonight, after meeting five days earlier at a bar in the East Village. It had been the usual casual conversation. Name. Occupation. What had brought each of them to New York. At the end of the night, he'd put her number in his phone. She hadn't expected him to use it. Usually, these things ended when the bartender announced last call. But he did phone her. The very next day.

And now…he had bought a ring! There was certainly no reason to worry about superstitions, especially when she saw the joy on the children's round faces as they were handed their cake.

She could barely touch hers, so great was the anticipation,

and by the time the parents lined up in the hallway, she felt downright sick. She'd seen the ring. She'd never been much of an actress—that had been much more of her sister Julie's territory. Would she gasp? Bring her hands to her mouth? Both of the above?

"I hear that congratulations are in order!" Mrs. Fine smiled warmly at her as she helped shrug little Daphne into a pink puffer coat. "How did he propose?"

"Oh, he hasn't. Yet." Carrie realized her error the moment she saw the pinch of confusion between Mrs. Fine's brows. "It's happening tonight. We just wanted to celebrate with everyone, before the holidays."

"Oh! Well, good luck then," Mrs. Fine beamed, as she shuffled Daphne along the hallway.

Carrie pulled in a breath. She didn't need any luck. She was already the luckiest girl in the world.

Lucas was coming straight from the office, so they'd agreed to meet at the restaurant at seven. There was no point in him coming all the way uptown just to go all the way back downtown again, after all. Besides, she rather liked the idea of arriving separately for this date, just like they had four years ago. And just like four years ago, she took extra care in getting ready, carefully applying her makeup and brushing her hair, happy that she'd had the chance to snag a last-minute appointment at the nail salon on the corner after scrubbing away any evidence of finger paint.

After all, she didn't want to go showing off her sparkling ring with chipped nails and neglected cuticles!

The phone rang just as she was stuffing it into her new

clutch. She checked the caller ID: her younger sister. She swiped the screen, sending the call to voicemail. Jules was probably calling to see if she'd sent their niece a Christmas gift yet, so that she could wiggle her way onto the card like she did every year, with the promise to pay her back, which she never did. This year, Carrie had finished her Christmas shopping by the first of December, and Phoebe's gift—a knitting kit—had already been wrapped and mailed to Vermont.

Carrie sighed as she put on her coat. She'd call Jules tomorrow when she had news to share. Right now, she wanted to savor the moment, not be sidetracked by family drama.

The phone rang again—Jules could be persistent—but she smiled when she saw the name that appeared on the screen. "Lucas," she breathed.

"I'm running a few minutes late," he said, but his voice was muffled and there was a lot of noise in the background. Subway, she determined. "I had to swing by my place first and pick something up."

Excitement and nerves ripped through her stomach and she took a deep breath before replying calmly, "No problem. I'll still plan on meeting you there." Really, his apartment was only about eight blocks away, but she'd grown attached to the idea of not seeing each other before the big moment. It was like a wedding day. No need to jinx it.

She opted for a cab. The occasion seemed to call for it. It wove expertly through traffic, and she savored the sights of the city illuminated for the season. Even now, she still felt a thrill when she saw the city at night. It was so different from the small town where she'd grown up, and different was what she'd been searching for. And found. Here in New York, her life wasn't defined by her past, and her future…well, her future was about to start. Tonight.

When she arrived at the restaurant she was pleased to see that it was decorated for the holidays, with garland and lights and holiday music coming from a piano near the bar. A drink? She'd barely eaten today from the nerves, managing only half of a slice of that delicious cake. But one would be fine. It would give her something to do while she waited.

She ordered a glass of white wine, even though she did prefer a smooth Cabernet, especially on a cold winter night. But red made her teeth turn purple and tonight was certainly not the time for that. She took a small sip, and then a larger one. She was already halfway through the glass when she felt a tap on her shoulder.

She turned, smiling, to see Lucas. He was wearing his grey coat and the plaid scarf she'd given him last Christmas, and his dark brown hair was still wet with snow. She reached up to brush it away, but he moved his head and swept it off himself.

"Sorry I'm late," he said, frowning a little.

She frowned now too. This was hardly the greeting she was expecting on the night she would be engaged. Still, she told herself, he was harried. He'd had to change plans. And everyone knew what a hassle it was to get around this city on the best of days, much less with the snow coming down.

"The table's ready," she said, smiling brightly. She waited to see if he would kiss her, or hold her hand, but he just nodded.

"Is it possible to have something a little more…private?" Lucas asked the hostess when they reached a table for two in the center of the room.

"Of course," the woman said, and with a small smile, she led them toward the corner of the room.

Carrie's heart was ready to burst by now. He was nervous! Of course he was nervous! All men were when they were about to get down on one knee. But now, she was certain. More certain than ever. And she'd been fairly certain all day.

She took a seat and stared at him, wondering how she would suffer through an entire meal waiting for him to ask her to be his wife. Wife! Four long years had led up to this moment, four years of anxiety and worry that it would never happen. But it had. She was here. And he had a ring.

He opened his menu, scanned it quickly, and closed it again.

"You already know what you're having?" She had hoped they would start with the bruschetta, although, if he planned to, say, pop the ring into a slice of tiramisu, maybe it would be better to skip an appetizer and get on with things.

"The lasagna," he said, reaching for his water. Was that…sweat dotting his brow?

She hid her smile behind her menu. It was.

"I believe the lasagna is what you ordered the last time we came here. Four years ago." She smiled at him, but he just tipped his head in confusion. "This is where we came for our first date, don't you remember?"

He looked around the room, nodding as if suddenly remembering. "I thought it looked familiar."

Carrie took a sip of her wine. A long one. Yes, she had been the one to choose this place for tonight, but that was only because Lucas was always in meetings and it was easier for her to make the reservations, just as she always did.

11

"That wine looks good. I'll order a glass." He flagged down the waitress.

"Or a bottle?" It was, after all, a special occasion.

"A glass is fine," he said, placing the order.

"Another for me as well," she said, resisting the urge to frown. She perked herself up by reaching for the breadbasket, and then, remembering that he could pop the question at any moment and she didn't exactly want a cheek full of focaccia when she cried out her answer, she pulled her hand back.

The wine came quickly and she held her glass up in a toast. "To four years," she said before he could take a sip from his glass.

"Four years." Lucas's eyebrows shot up again at this and he took a long drink. When he came up for air, he seemed hesitant, as if he wanted to say something and didn't know where to begin.

She stiffened in panic. He wasn't going to do it now, was he? Before they'd even placed their orders? She wasn't ready! Well, she was ready. Technically she had been very ready for two years, maybe three, but all that didn't matter anymore. What mattered was that they were here. In their restaurant. And that they were about to commit to each other for the rest of their lives. Theirs was a relationship that could clearly endure the test of time.

"I'm excited about the holiday party tomorrow," she blurted. Her heart was racing, she wasn't sure why she had just done that, and Lucas looked startled, his expression frozen.

She smoothed the napkin in her lap and took another sip of her wine. Why rush such a blissful evening? They would want to look back on tonight and remember everything they had talked about, and eaten. And the waitress would be interrupting them at any moment to ask for their orders.

No, best to wait. She'd waited a lifetime. What were a few more minutes?

"About that." Lucas sighed heavily as the waiter appeared at the table. He ordered the lasagna. She asked for the penne.

No appetizer. No need to read into that.

Lucas looked sheepish. "You don't need to worry about coming this year. No one's bringing any dates, really, and it's just going to be a lot of shop talk. I'll probably make an appearance and cut out early."

Carrie stared at him. "But I bought a dress! And we always go to the party together and have a nice time. And most of your coworkers are married."

"Not most," Lucas said stiffly.

Carrie did a mental tally. Most.

"The thing is, Carrie, that I…I don't think I can do this anymore."

She felt her chin dip and her eyes locked on him. "Do what?"

"This." He waved a hand across the middle of the table. "You and me. I think…I don't think it's been working out."

"What?" Carrie saw the waitress approach their table and then, with wide eyes, scamper off again. Carrie blinked, trying to process what she had just heard. "But…we've been together for four years."

"Four years is a long time," Lucas said. He looked tired. "I'm ready for a change."

A change? Weren't marriage, children, and a family a…change?

"I don't understand," she said, as tears prickled the back of her eyes.

"I can't make you happy, Carrie," Lucas said, shaking his head. "And I think you know that."

She stared at him as her chest thudded with the knowledge that a part of her had always feared this exact moment. Lucas didn't want to move to the suburbs. Fine! She would stay in the city. Lucas didn't care about things like Christmas or Valentine's Day. She hadn't even bothered with a tree this year! She loved dogs, but Lucas was allergic. She'd resigned herself to going without one.

But those were little things. Trivial, really. Being together. Having a life together. That was what mattered.

"We have history. Four years."

He nodded. His mouth was set in a thin line. He didn't say anything.

Carrie knew she should exit this conversation now, and gracefully. She wasn't going to convince him of all the things they'd argued about in the past, sticking points that had made people in her circle ask her if she was sure he was worth it. But he was. Because she knew he would come around. He just needed time.

And he'd bought the ring.

"But…the ring."

He squinted. "What ring?"

"The ring in your bedroom." She didn't care if he accused her of snooping. She wanted answers.

He sighed, shaking his head. "That was for Dave," he said. "He asked me to hold onto it for him."

Of course. She had never even considered that it could be

for his brother—his younger brother—or that Dave might actually be willing to propose to his girlfriend after only one year of dating!

The napkin was a ball in her lap, and she released it slowly, feeling the cramp in her fingers. He was never going to propose. Not now. Not tomorrow. The ring hadn't been for her. It was never, ever going to happen.

"You're going to find everything you ever wanted," Lucas said, forcing a smile. "Just…not with me."

"But Christmas—" She shook her head. She couldn't even think about it. They'd been planning to go skiing next weekend "to get away from the hassle" as Lucas had phrased it. Lights and trees and holiday music weren't his thing.

"You have a family. And you know I've never been big on Christmas. Surely you'd want to spend the holiday with your sisters?" Lucas's tone was gentle, but it wasn't reassuring, and she resented how easy this was for him.

"In Winter Lake?" Carrie hadn't been back to her Vermont hometown in three and a half years, and she didn't like thinking of that visit any more than she liked thinking of the visits she had missed.

Spending Christmas with her sisters had never been part of the plan. The plan had been to get engaged and spend the holidays imagining the rest of their lives together.

So much for this being the best Christmas ever.

Chapter Two

Jules

Julie Campbell was on her third cup of coffee of the morning, mostly because it gave her an excuse to keep walking off her nervous energy, even if it was just from her desk to the office kitchen and back again, when her phone beeped. She looked down at the screen and smiled her first real smile of the day.

You've got this!

She glanced at her boss's door and quickly typed: I hope you're right.

Ye of little faith, came the reply. We'll celebrate tonight.

Jules didn't reply to that. No sense in getting ahead of herself here. Still, the promise of drinks with Aaron at their favorite corner bar lifted her spirits and gave her something to focus on until she got up for another refill. Technically, her five-o'clock deadline should be keeping her busy, but she couldn't keep her mind from wandering to the eleven-o'clock meeting with her boss.

Ten forty-nine. Eleven minutes to go. Her stomach fluttered and she regretted not eating that bagel she'd bought for herself this morning at the food truck parked outside her office building, but she was afraid she wouldn't be able to keep it down. Now, she was more afraid that she might faint.

She pulled open her top drawer, where she kept a bag of pretzels, and then remembered that she had polished them off yesterday, in another nervous fit, when Lynn had first suggested today's meeting.

She closed the drawer. Checked the clock in the bottom right corner of the computer screen, just as it ticked off another minute. Ten minutes. Lynn was nothing if not prompt.

She was also rather terrifying.

Still, this was not a meeting to be feared. She'd had plenty of those in the past, after all; she knew the warning signs: demanding executives with tempers to match their egos, micromanagers who would never be satisfied, and went through freelancers like ballpoint pens. She'd learned to jump ship before she was thrown overboard. Move on to the next gig—that was the beauty of freelance work. There were downsides, though. Enough of them to have finally prompted her to consider a—her stomach heaved—permanent position.

This was going to be a good meeting, she reminded herself. The meeting where her employment at Creative Design was confirmed. She'd been freelancing with the firm for six months and, after careful consideration, decided that this was a long-term fit. Sure, Lynn wasn't the easiest person to get along with, but Jules had managed. While others avoided her, Jules played the game. (You didn't have two older sisters and not learn a thing or two, after all.) Lynn was too busy for lunch? Jules was happy to fly and buy. Lynn was a stickler for deadlines? Jules had never missed one. (Others didn't either, but still, Jules prided herself on her effort these past few months.) Lynn liked to talk for hours about her baby? Jules was happy to listen, or pretend to, at least.

And now, all that was about to be rewarded. She'd go into the New Year as a permanent employee, with a health care plan and a savings plan. She felt like an adult. She felt giddy.

Lynn's door opened. Jules's eyes flicked to the corner of her screen and noted the time. This was it. She stood up, smoothed her skirt, and smiled at Lynn, who lifted her chin by way of invitation.

Lynn's office was a windowless, soulless box in the loft space where the marketing firm was housed, but it was, nevertheless an office, a rare gem, distributed to only six individuals of the forty employees. Jules sat in one of the two grey visitor chairs, focusing on the framed photo of Lynn's baby dressed up as a caterpillar for Halloween while Lynn closed the door. It was a cute baby, and just the mere fact that Lynn had a baby at all meant that she couldn't be all that bad. There was a soft side to her. It just wasn't always revealed at the office.

Still, Jules liked working here. She liked her coworkers, and she liked the work. She'd made a good friend in Callie who had the cubicle beside her, unlike some gigs she'd had, where there wasn't a soul her age, or she was sectioned off to some random underused conference room assigned for temp work, excluded from social opportunities. Here, she was one of the pack. There were Friday happy hours at the dive bar in the lobby. There were bagels every Monday morning.

It was an easy commute from her apartment, and the salaries were generous. It was the right fit for her, perfect really, and she was only mildly anxious at the prospect of giving up her freedom, signing away the comfort she had in working for the freelance agency, knowing that if something didn't work out, they could always find her another gig…eventually.

It was the *eventually* part that had made her decide to go for the permanent position—that and the makeshift family she'd found in her office mates.

Last time, after a three-month contract at a publicity firm was up, she'd been out of steady work for nearly two months, give or take two eight-hour temp shifts, which required answering phones, not writing copy. And she was terrible at answering phones; she always pressed the wrong button and disconnected the call instead of putting it through.

"So, Julie," Lynn said. She dragged out Jules's given name in a lazy fashion, as if she were deliberating what she might say next. She took her seat, resting her hands on her desk. "I know we discussed the permanent position."

Jules pulled in a breath and nodded her head. "That's right," she said. She smiled. "I like working here. It's been a really great six months."

"And we've enjoyed having you," Lynn said. She hesitated.

Jules had the uneasy feeling that there was a "but" coming on. She frowned, sensing a shift in the energy of the room.

"But I'm afraid we're not able to offer you a permanent position."

Jules felt her shoulders deflate. She was quiet for a long moment.

"Oh." She swallowed hard, hoping that the emotion wouldn't creep into her voice, but her cheeks felt warm, damn it. "So we'll just renew the contract then?"

It wouldn't be the worst thing in the world. After all, the freelance rate was better than an hourly breakdown as a permanent employee. Only, ever since she'd wrapped her head around being one of the team here, she couldn't help but feel disappointed.

"That's just the thing," Lynn said. "We only have room in the budget for one copywriter at this time. And we've decided to keep Ken on board."

Jules felt her eyes widen. Ken was another freelancer. He'd only been brought in a few weeks ago when they got hit with a big campaign.

"Have I done something wrong?" She felt childish asking this, desperate even, but she had to know; she couldn't understand.

Lynn shook her head. "There is only so much money in the budget, and Ken has more experience."

Jules swallowed hard. So even though she'd done her best, it hadn't been enough. That was almost worse than knowing she had screwed up and was facing consequences. She'd tried. Given it her all. And now she was out.

It felt like the story of her life. Only this time, she'd hoped for a better ending.

Her eyes were burning but she couldn't cry, not here. Not in front of Lynn. The woman had just fired her. She had known she would since last night. Planned it the entire time that Jules was preparing herself for the big news. She'd been so excited she'd almost jumped the gun and told her sister Carrie.

She snorted to herself. Good thing her sister hasn't bothered to pick up the phone or call her back. Normally it irked her that Carrie could be so distant. Now, she supposed she should be grateful.

"I know you're disappointed, and if we get busy and need to staff up, you'll be the first person we call."

As a freelancer, Jules understood this to mean, like hell.

"You can pack up now," Lynn said. Despite her smile, her tone was firm. The last thing they needed was a temporary employee doing something crazy between now and five o'clock, right? "We'll pay you through the day, of course."

Jules stood. For a moment, she didn't quite know what to do, what was protocol. Lynn didn't seem to know either, and finally, after a beat, she reached out her hand. Jules took it, fighting the urge to squeeze it really, really hard, just to show that she was in control here, that she wasn't going to let this knock her down, that she had plenty of other opportunities, that she actually preferred to be a free agent.

But that wasn't true at all, was it?

She hurried back to her desk and gathered up her belongings, wishing that she hadn't chosen today to bring her small handbag to work. Her mind was spinning and she couldn't think straight as she opened drawers and then closed them again.

"You heading to lunch?" asked one of the graphic designers, a guy they called Palmer because it was his last name and his first name was William, the same as half the other guys in the office. Sometimes Jules and Palmer grabbed sushi across the street and chatted about his love life and her lack of one. He was a good guy. She looked forward to those sushi lunches. And now, there wouldn't be another.

"No." Jules managed a tight smile. Her tone was breezy

enough, even though her throat felt like it was closing up. She had to get out of there. Before she started crying. "My contract's up."

"Ah, really?" Palmer looked so disappointed that Jules had to look away. They'd all go on, a big happy family. Soon, she'd be forgotten. Usually, she didn't mind that, coming and going, not leaving many marks. She was used to it. Preferred it up until now. Days like today were exactly the reason why it was better not to get too attached to a situation. Nothing was permanent. "The others are in a meeting. The tea campaign. They'll be upset they didn't get to say good-bye."

It was for the best, but Jules didn't say that.

"I'll stop by sometime. We can all go for drinks." It was a hollow promise, but it was the best she could do. She grabbed her cardigan, today's lunch, which she now had no desire to eat, and stepped away from her cubicle. She'd never finished the assignment due today, but she assumed that would be Ken's problem now.

Her eyes narrowed as they shifted to his workspace, but he must have been in the meeting with the others. Part of the team.

There was some hand lotion and a box of tissue that she didn't have room for in her bag. She set them on her friend Callie's desk, knowing that it wouldn't be long before she received a text from her expressing her confusion and outrage. She'd see Callie again. But it wouldn't be the same, and she was old enough to know that.

She made it outside before the tears fell and looked down at her phone to see the blue light flashing in the corner. Of course. Aaron.

How'd it go?

She blinked at the screen, her heart twisting when she considered what she would tell him. He'd been so excited for her! And now she had to let him down.

She sniffed, shaking off that feeling. This was Aaron she was talking about. Her best friend. Her biggest confidant. Her cheerleader. Her rock.

Aaron wouldn't be disappointed in her. He'd be disappointed for her. And that, well, that was a wonderful—and rare—feeling.

Aaron showed up at her apartment straight from work.

"I'm sorry," he said, pulling her into a hug. They always hugged when they met and parted, but this time, Jules let it go on a little longer than usual, and Aaron didn't try to stop her.

"I just can't believe it," Jules said when she pulled away. She searched his face, trying to find an answer there that she hadn't been able to reach all day. She walked over to the coffee table and picked up her glass of wine. It was her second, and the evening had barely started. She was in for a long night.

Aaron shrugged off his coat and left his boots on the mat. It had been snowing in Boston for at least five straight days and it felt like it would never stop. The first day had been pretty. The second day, not so much. By day three the commute to and from work felt like nothing short of a chore. Now, she almost hoped it went on for another couple of weeks. It would give her an excuse not to leave the apartment that had nothing to do with her unemployment status.

Almost reading her mind, Aaron said, "Let's go to the bar.

I promised drinks and drinks there will be. And some fries. And maybe some of those nachos we like, too."

"Extra peppers?" She managed a smile and decided that he was probably right. She'd been home since noon and she was already experiencing cabin fever. And eating her way through the fried food menu items at O'Malley's did sound pretty comforting.

"Okay then," she said. "Let me fix my face." She'd cried off her carefully applied makeup hours ago, much of it on the long, cold walk home. She rarely wore much more than a bit of lip gloss, but today… Well.

Aaron slipped on his shoes and handed her the big black parka that hung in her tiny front closet, currently overflowing with shoes, umbrellas, and seasonal clothes that didn't fit in her bedroom closet.

"You look beautiful just the way you are."

She knew that she shouldn't read into the compliment—this was Aaron, best friend since sophomore year at Boston University when they'd shared a table during first term exams in the library and gone for a pizza afterward. Aaron that had held her hair back when she'd been over-served on her twenty-first birthday. Aaron who was eager to get to the bar, where the hockey game would be playing on every screen.

But still, she accepted the coat and put it on without a trip to the bathroom first. And she did feel a little better already.

"You know you'll get another freelance job," Aaron assured her once they were seated at the end of the bar near the window of O'Malley's, a beer in front of him, a cider for her.

"I know." Jules knew this, logically. Except…She looked out the window at the falling snow as people rushed by, eager to get home after a long day. "But it's the holidays. No one will be hiring until January."

"Temp work?" He winced at her. He knew how she felt about that. "I'm sure that lots of places are short-staffed this time of year."

"It's a last resort," Jules said. "I already called my freelance agency. They promised they'd let me know as soon as something popped up."

"Well, that's good." Aaron grinned and glanced back up at the television that hung above the bar, just in time to see their team score a goal. It was their bar, their usual place. Nothing fancy, but comfortable, and conveniently located halfway between their buildings, only two and a half blocks from her small apartment, with one bedroom and a bathroom, on the top floor of a brownstone in the Beacon Hill neighborhood. She'd lived here since she'd graduated from college and had no plans to move. As long as she could continue to pay her rent, that was.

She took a long sip of cider. "It's just..." Jules shook her head. "I know this sounds crazy, but I actually wanted to stay there."

"That doesn't sound crazy," Aaron replied. He took another sip of his beer, and when their nachos arrived, ordered another round of drinks, even though her glass was still half full. Service here was always a little slow.

She gave him a look. "Please. You know that this isn't exactly characteristic of me. I'm not the kind of person who can settle down in one place." The apartment was an exception, and that was because she had no need for anything bigger.

Aaron took a sip of his beer and shrugged. "We all have to grow up some time."

"Nice." She gave him a rueful look, but the thought hit her hard, square in the chest. All her life she'd been accused of being flighty and fickle, of not knowing what she wanted, of not taking life seriously enough. Now she finally had, and look how it had ended up!

"There will be other jobs," Aaron said, and sure, he was probably right.

"But one I would want?" She frowned. "I liked it there. I liked the people. I saw myself staying there for a long time. It feels like...well, it feels like a loss."

"Cheer up, buttercup. You've still got me." He gave her a hundred-watt smile and nudged her with his elbow.

She grinned back. Yes, she still had him. On days like this, she didn't know what she would do without him. Luckily, she didn't have to.

"I know it didn't turn out the way you wanted, but I think it's a good thing that you went for the permanent position. And not getting it sort of proved to you how much you wanted it."

"I did." Jules nodded. "I liked the idea of having a health care plan. And a savings plan. Of knowing where I was going every day and who I would spend the day with. It doesn't feel good to not know where you stand."

Aaron grew quiet. He raised his eyebrows. "Tell me about it."

She frowned. "What does that mean?" After all, Aaron had a steady job at a commercial real estate firm. He'd been promoted three times in five years. His life was stable. While hers...

The bartender slid their drinks across the counter. Aaron

drained his first glass and reached for the fresh one. "Nothing. The beer's getting to my head."

Jules wasn't so sure about that, but she let it drop. "I had friends there…" she went on, feeling a tug in her chest when she thought of the happy hours she would miss, the sushi lunches, the bow ties that Norman always wore and that everyone always poked him about, even though they secretly loved it.

"Hey!" But Aaron grinned.

"You know what I mean…" Now it was Jules's turn to elbow him lightly. He felt solid, familiar, and right. So much better than sitting home alone, feeling sorry for herself. And who needed happy hours with the office crew when she had this bar and Aaron to keep her company?

"You and I are different, I know. We're more like…" He paused.

"Brother and sister," she said, at the same time that Aaron said, "Boyfriend and girlfriend."

Oops. She hadn't seen that one coming. Aaron stared at her, something awfully close to hurt creeping into his deep brown eyes, and for lack of anything else to say, Jules said, "Or…cousins?"

He frowned. Deeply.

Well, now she'd done it. She swallowed hard. Reached for her cider. He reached for his beer.

Really, they should just stop drinking. But this was only the second round. So what was going on here, exactly?

"You know what I meant," Aaron finally said. The game was back on, but he wasn't looking at the screen. "We do everything together. We eat dinner together. We go grocery

27

shopping together. We spend every weekend together." He paused. Jules felt her stomach lurch. "It's sort of like you're my girlfriend. I mean, you're a girl, and you're my friend, but you're like...my person."

Aaron was staring at her, a little frown knitting his brow, his brown eyes so earnest that she ached to reach out and hug him and never let him go. She loved Aaron.

But was she *in love* with him? And was he *in love* with her?

"You're my person, too," she said carefully.

"And there's no one else I'd rather spend my time with," Aaron continued.

"Me either," Jules said honestly. She studied Aaron carefully. His ash brown hair was rumpled from the snow and his glasses needed cleaning. He was cute. Very cute. And he'd had many girlfriends in the eight years that she had known him.

And she'd really never thought of any of this before. He was her friend. And she couldn't ever lose that friendship. She'd lost enough already.

They stared at the game, eating their nachos even though she barely tasted them, despite the jalapeños, and when the bartender asked if they wanted another round, it was Jules who called it a night.

"I need to go to bed and put this day behind me," she said. Every single part of it, she thought to herself.

Still, she didn't like leaving things like this. She pulled on her coat and wrapped her scarf around her neck. "Free tomorrow?"

Aaron's smile returned. "For you? Of course."

Jules's shoulders sank in relief. "Good, then we're going

Christmas shopping. And if you help me find something for my niece, I may just treat you to a hot chocolate in return."

"My kind of deal," Aaron said. "But you'd better get that thing mailed soon if you want it to arrive before Christmas."

She nodded. Christmas was a week from Sunday. Of course, the gift would likely arrive late, but it was better than no gift at all. And she wanted to make sure that this year the gift for Phoebe was extra special. That the little girl could feel her love from miles away. That she would know someone was thinking about her.

Jules pulled her scarf tighter, gave Aaron a quick hug good-bye, and escaped out into the winter night. She didn't know what had just happened back there, but she was too emotionally charged to process it all right now. It had been a long day. A bad one. And she needed to put it behind her.

She knew that there wouldn't be any job opportunities until after the holidays. Maybe she'd head back to Winter Lake. Hand deliver Phoebe's present to her instead. Give her a little Christmas surprise.

Some time away would be good, she thought. For her. And for Aaron.

She warmed up to the idea as she turned the key in the front door of her building and hurried up the stairs. She'd think about it. But not until tomorrow. Tomorrow everything would be clearer.

Chapter Three

Tess

Damn it! Tess cursed under her breath as she braked at yet another red light. It was the third since she had left the house, and she'd lived in Winter Lake long enough to know that by all reasonable calculations, she'd be lucky to get through the intersection of Main and Thatcher without having to come to a full stop again.

She glanced at the clock on the dashboard and sighed. Phoebe would be expecting her to be visible in the audience, front and center, like always, but tonight, she'd be lucky to get a seat at all. The elementary school holiday pageant was a ticketed event, but the PTA fell short of assigning seats. Even though the show didn't technically start for another twenty-five minutes, Tess knew that the difference between showing up forty-five minutes early and walking in ten minutes before the event started was the difference between having a view of her child or the back of a tall man's head.

The light turned and Tess pushed down Main Street, gritting her teeth when the car in front of her slowed to take in the lights from the big tree in the town square. They might have all the time in the world, but she had learned the hard way recently that there was no such thing. Time was fleeting. And right now, the last good seat in the auditorium was probably being taken.

She resisted the urge to honk her horn. She could practically hear Andrew's tsk of disapproval. But Andrew wasn't here. He didn't know what it was like. She was raising a young daughter on her own. Some days, she was fine. Others, she crawled back into bed after Phoebe had boarded the school bus. She needed a job but she didn't even know what she was qualified for anymore. She'd given up her whole life to make one with Andrew. And now Andrew was gone.

And that still didn't seem very real.

She pulled into the parking lot with fourteen minutes to spare, of course having to loop around until she resigned to a spot in the far corner, where the plows had dumped piles of snow. She grinned, thinking about how she and her sisters used to sled down similar banks during winter break when they were kids. Dangerous. Stupid. Lucky. They could have been hit by a car, coming down School Street. Their mother wouldn't have been any the wiser.

Tess grabbed the cupcake carrier from her backseat, bundled her scarf closer to her neck as the wind howled, and hurried across the slick pavement to the front door as quickly as one could with three dozen carefully frosted cupcakes in her hands. The school seemed to glow from within, even though it was only slightly past four. She dropped the cupcakes off with Jodi Swanson, head of the PTA, and former president of her twelfth-grade class, who was hovering outside the cafeteria doors. Jodi all but tapped her watch as Tess set the contribution on a table with the other baked goods. Tess stifled an eye roll, refusing to feed into it. She didn't have time to feed into it. She had bigger problems.

The auditorium was just to the right, and the entire room was alive with conversation. Tess stood back and scanned the rows, looking for two open spots until she remembered, of course, she only needed one this year. Surely someone had set a coat on a chair so they didn't have to sit hip to hip with a stranger? She was thin—depression beat any fad diet, it seemed. Maybe she could squeeze in.

She walked down the aisle, past parents clutching cameras and families jostling older or younger kids. Grandparents smiled dotingly. Christmas was a little over a week away, after all. The break had officially started. It was a busy time. A happy time.

For most.

Finally, she spotted a familiar face up ahead, her friend Natalie, waving to her. "I saved you a spot," she said as Tess approached.

Natalie had brought her entire family with her—husband, parents, brother, sister-in-law. Tess scooted past Natalie and her husband, who gave her a sympathetic smile, and the twin preschool-aged boys who each occupied a lap. Her seat was wedged between Natalie's father, who was already snoring, and Natalie's brother, who was tapping on his phone.

The lights dimmed almost immediately, and as soon as the curtain rose and the third-grade class crossed the stage in single-file order, Tess saw Phoebe's eyes go right to the chairs that she and Andrew always used to take. Today, Tess was on the other side of the aisle. She watched her little girl's brow furrow, and resisted the urge to call out to her, "I'm here, honey! I'm right here!" But all she could do was sit and wait and hope that Phoebe would spot her.

The song began, a rather messy rendition of "Jingle Bells," complete with bells, that kept getting shaken when they were not supposed to be. Normally this was something that she and Andrew would have elbowed each other over, but she couldn't find any amusement in it right now, not with her daughter's face looking so lost and worried.

The song ended, and Tess used the opportunity to cheer loudly, managing to catch Phoebe's attention. Her expression lifted into a brilliant smile and all at once, everything in Tess's heavy heart melted away.

She smiled. Smiled at Phoebe smiling as they launched into the next song, which was even more of a disaster than the first and had the people behind her snickering. Tess forgot where she was for a moment, and leaned in to whisper her own commentary, but she was jolted by a rather large snort from Natalie's father, who smacked his lips a few times and gave her a glass-eyed stare before nodding off again.

She glanced to her left to see if she and Natalie's brother might share a laugh about that, or at least a look, but he was still tapping at his phone. Tess could hear his wife murmuring to turn the device off.

Right, Tess thought, her heart feeling heavy again. Natalie was down at the end of the row, with her husband and children, where she belonged. And Tess…well, Tess was sitting in a room with hundreds of people, wedged hip to hip with two of them.

And she'd never felt more alone.

An hour later, Tess stood at the back of the cafeteria, nursing a plastic cup of punch, her eye on the door where the children were streaming in from backstage, one class at a time. Natalie was overwhelmed with her extended family and two now wailing four-year-olds. There were other parents she knew, of course—it was a small community and she'd seen the same parents at every event since Kindergarten, and gone to this very school with many of them—but it felt strange to intrude on their family time, like a third-wheel.

"Tess."

Tess was startled and pulled away from the wall she'd been leaning against. Lisa Sheehan wrestled a chubby baby to the other side of her hip. She had been in Carrie's grade growing up, of course. Now she had a child in Phoebe's grade and another in first. They'd all grown up.

And grown apart, Tess thought a little sadly.

"How's Carrie doing?"

"Oh, Carrie is fine. Fine!" Not that Tess would know, but she didn't let on. People didn't really want to know the answer to questions like this, she'd learned. After Andrew's accident, people would stop her at the playground or ballet class or grocery store and ask how she was doing, but when she started talking, answering honestly, admitting that she was barely sleeping or missed him terribly, their eyes would shift and they'd look uncomfortable. Soon, she realized it was best to just say, "Fine." She was just fine. It was all fine.

"She's still in New York," Tess added with a tight smile. Of this she was sure. Carrie never left New York. She'd come back exactly four times in fifteen years. She'd moved away and moved on. From Winter Lake. From her family.

Still, Tess fixed a well-rehearsed smile on her face. Her "going out in public" face, as she called it.

"Well, tell her I say hello!" Lisa smiled and moved away, where her husband was waiting for her with the kids' coats.

Tess looked away as a pang pierced through her, and right into the eyes of her smiling daughter coming through the door.

"Mommy!" Phoebe ran to her, arms outstretched as if she hadn't seen Tess in months. Or worried she would never see her again.

"You did great," Tess said, holding her tight until Phoebe pulled away. "What do you say we celebrate with some mac and cheese and ice cream?"

"At home?"

Home. Once, Tess had loved her home. It was a Victorian, within walking distance to the center of town and close to the lake. The three of them used to walk to the ice cream shop on hot, Sunday afternoons, and eat their cones on the way back: strawberry for Andrew and Phoebe, chocolate for her. She could sit on the wicker chairs on the front porch and watch Phoebe play in the front yard. Or she could sit in the back-yard and hear the leaves of the giant maple tree rustling in the wind. But lately, being home felt uncomfortable and empty. It was too quiet, especially when Phoebe was tucked in for the night.

"Why don't we head to Preston's instead?" Tess suggested,

sparking a big cry of approval from Phoebe, meaning it was too late to retract the statement. Not that she wanted to. Preston's was one of the few places in town where she felt comfortable these days, other than the lake and the small park out near her childhood home, and it wasn't because of its dark, rustic décor and blazing stone fireplace. It was the one place in town where she wasn't alone, or the only one feeling Andrew's loss.

With that decision made, she felt like she couldn't get out of the school building fast enough, past the happy, complete families, who didn't have broken hearts they had to hide. She gathered up her cupcake carrier, pleased to see that only one cupcake remained, which she set on a paper plate for whoever wanted it.

Outside, the wind was cold, and Phoebe shivered. "Can't you get the car and pick me up?" she asked.

Tess would have laughed if the thought of it didn't make her want to cry. That was something Andrew had always done—gone to fetch the car in the rain and the cold, while she and Phoebe waited inside, warm and dry, looking out the window for his car.

She closed her eyes, briefly.

"We'll hurry," she said, mustering up the enthusiasm that got her through her weekends, evenings, and morning hours, when Phoebe wasn't at school but instead, beside her. Sometimes Phoebe's company was just what she needed to snap herself out of her funk; other times it was downright exhausting having to hide her emotions. They scurried across the pavement, and Tess fought off the guilt of running late and having to park so far from the building. She should have known better than to schedule a job interview so close to the pageant, but she wasn't about to turn down an opportunity, especially when it was the first one to come along.

She checked her phone as soon as they were in the car, even though she knew that it would be pointless to expect a response this soon. Surely they needed to take their time and consider all their options.

But she hoped they wouldn't take too much time. As it was, it was going to be a lean Christmas if she wanted to be careful with their savings.

Preston's was in the center of town, right at the intersection of Main and Lake Streets. In the summer, the back deck was one of the hottest spots in town, with a waterfront location and a view of the mountains in the distance. Tess pulled to a stop in the lot around the back, bracing herself for a long wait but knowing that Jeff Preston would find a way to make it a little easier for them.

Sure enough, they barely wedged into the vestibule, and the smell of burgers made Tess's stomach rumble. It had been a couple of weeks since she'd been in, and in that time, the place had been transformed with colored lights and a wreath above the mantle and old-timey Christmas hits bleating over the speakers.

For a moment, Tess felt a sense of betrayal. Could this Christmas really be so easy for Jeff?

She pushed that thought immediately away. Of course, it wasn't easy for him. Andrew had been his best friend, his oldest friend. Andrew was an only child, and Jeff had grown up with three sisters, in the house next door to Andrew's family. They were more like brothers than friends. More like family.

"Tess!" From across the crowded waiting area, Jeff held up a hand. He grinned—he had such a great grin, the kind that made all your problems seem to drift away, at least for a little while, Christmas decorations and all.

She felt her shoulders sag in relief. Just the sight of him made her feel better. The smile proved they'd been right in coming here.

"Hi, Jeff!" Phoebe pushed ahead of her and bounded up to the bar, where Jeff was tending, a cloth slung over his shoulder, his green Henley pushed up at the sleeves.

"How's my favorite girl?" he asked, and then gave Tess a wink.

"I had a pageant tonight. I got to sing and dress up like an angel." Here, Phoebe turned to show off the white wings she had insisted on wearing over her pink puffer coat.

"That deserves a special treat. If your mother says it's okay," he added, his smile turning rueful. He glanced at her, raising an eyebrow in question.

"It's okay," Tess said. She sometimes feared she was spoiling Phoebe recently, but then she looked around her. It was Christmastime—the happiest time of the year. And Phoebe needed all the happiness she could find right about now.

They both did. It just wasn't so easy to find when you were thirty-five.

"A table's clearing over by the fireplace," Jeff said. "I'll set you up."

Tess's eyes drifted to the line of people, but Jeff was already coming around the bar. He patted her shoulder. His hand felt reassuring and solid. Across the bar, she could see the eyes of a few women, wearing barely there tops despite the weather, nursing glasses of white wine, and no doubt watching Jeff's every move, stationed right where they could chat him up or giggle at his jokes. She almost wanted to laugh, to pat their heads and say, "Nothing to worry about here, ladies." Absolutely no need to be jealous of a widowed single mother.

She took Phoebe's hand and followed him to the back of the room. "One of the perks of knowing the owner," Tess said, as she and Phoebe settled into their chairs.

"Not the only reason you stop by, I hope." Jeff grinned.

Tess held his gaze a beat, then, feeling her cheeks flush, looked away for a moment before looking back up. "No, we really come for the food."

"Just for that, I might have to make you clear your plate tonight," Jeff teased.

Tess rarely ate breakfast, and she'd been too busy getting ready for her job interview to have lunch. Now she watched as a waitress carried a tray with steaming heaps of pasta to a couple near the window. "I don't think you'll have to worry about that tonight. We're celebrating."

"Kiddie cocktail!" Phoebe reminded Jeff, and he laughed.

"Coming right up," he said. "But first... Have you finished your list for Santa?"

Tess tensed. She had kept a mental catalog of everything that Phoebe had mentioned, scratching the preposterous items from her list (A cell phone? At age eight?) and snagging everything else, well, except the dog that she was considering giving into come the spring. But now Christmas was barely more than a week away. If Phoebe decided to add to her list, which she was known to do, then Tess feared she risked disappointing her. And she didn't want to do that. As much as she dreaded this holiday, she needed it to be special.

Phoebe nodded firmly. "I sure did. I want a skating dress for my doll, a knitting kit, a new sled…" Tess silently checked off each item as Phoebe rattled them off. All accounted for. All tucked away in the attic where they wouldn't be found. "And a star necklace."

Tess frowned. A star necklace? This was the first time that Phoebe had ever mentioned such a thing! Where was Tess even supposed to find something like that?

Jeff must have sensed her alarm because he changed the subject. "Well, I'm sure Santa knows that you've been a good girl. That is if you finish all your homework tonight."

Phoebe giggled. "There's no homework tonight! It's winter break!"

"Winter break. Remember that?" He gave Tess a conspiratorial wink. Indeed, Tess did remember her breaks, because she counted down the days when she could return to the comforting routine of school. Her home life was unpredictable at best, at the mercy of her mother's moods, which shifted with the tides when their father walked out on them when Tess was nine, never to be heard from again. Still, she and her two younger sisters had kept busy, sledding, skiing, and attending all of Winter Lake's many festivities.

"What are you going to miss most about school these next few weeks? Let me guess!" Jeff feigned concentration for a moment, and Phoebe looked enraptured. Finally, he held up a finger. "I've got it. The homework!"

Now Phoebe was hiccupping she was giggling so hard, and Tess smiled as she watched her. "No, Jeff! Not homework! I'm going to miss the swings!"

"You go on the swings at this time of year?" Tess was amused. She assumed their outside recesses were filled with angel making and snowman building.

"Oh, yes. We have a contest to see who can go the highest."

Tess set a hand to her chest, her smile pulled from her face. Visions of Phoebe up in the air, her ponytail flying, her body slipping, and then—

Jeff was looking at her sternly. He shook his head and then gave her a little squeeze on the shoulder as he turned to go. "Relax, Tess," he whispered in her ear. "It's all going to be okay."

Tess watched him go and then opened her menu, even though she already knew the options by heart. Preston's had been their place long before Andrew had left their lives. It was one of the few constants in her world. One she hoped would never change.

"So," she said to Jeff when he returned shortly with the pink fizzy drink, complete with extra cherries. "You've decorated the place."

He shrugged. "It's Christmas."

Indeed, Tess thought heavily. It was Christmas. She'd been dreading it since Thanksgiving when she and Phoebe had gathered with Jeff's parents at their cozy house on Willow Street, nearly identical to the one beside it, aside from the paint colors, where Andrew had grown up, even though his parents had sold it years back before they'd moved to Arizona. A pity invite, she couldn't help but feel. It was a family event—a noisy affair with Jeff's sisters and their husbands and rowdy sons—and Tess and Phoebe were the only ones

41

there with no other family to celebrate with. She'd gotten used to it over the years with both of her sisters being gone and then her mother passing away, but it had been different when she had a family of her own, of course.

"When are we going to get a tree, Mommy?" Phoebe dropped a cherry into her mouth.

"Yeah, Mommy," Jeff quipped, making Phoebe giggle so hard that she had to spit out some of her drink. "When are you going to get a tree?"

Tess pulled in a breath. She *had* been planning on getting a tree. Of course, she had. She couldn't let Phoebe down like that. But the thought of putting it up and decorating it and being reminded, constantly, that it was Christmas and that Christmas was supposed to be a happy time, and that it wasn't...Well, it was too much.

Jeff's gaze softened. "How about we go together? This weekend? I've got my truck. I'll help you set it up."

Tess gave him a grateful smile. "Thank you."

"Any plans for the holiday?" he asked, looking from Tess to Phoebe. His expression was so hopeful that Tess almost wished she had better news to give him.

"Not sure about the holiday, but I had an interview to-day," she said.

Jeff looked surprised and then pleased. "Aw, Tess. That's great news!"

Tess made sure that Phoebe was engrossed in the coloring sheet on the back of the kid's menu. "Well, we'll see if I even get it." It wasn't anything exciting, an assistant at a bank, but she realized that she wanted it. That she *needed* it.

"Hey! Why wouldn't they hire you?"

Tess just shook her head. "I haven't been in the workforce in about nine years, and I forgot how to use any software other than the internet and basic word processing."

"I'm pretty sure that the internet isn't software," Jeff said, and Tess swatted him.

"See?" She sighed. "The woman who interviewed me seemed young enough to be my daughter."

He cocked an eyebrow. "You're forgetting that I knew you back in high school. Hate to break it to you, Tess, but you were always more of a wallflower type, not a...reproducing type." He darted a glance in Phoebe's direction, but she was singing carols under her breath as she carefully colored an illustration of a reindeer.

Tess laughed. It felt good, rare. Like a release of something that had been building inside her. "I certainly wasn't as sure of myself as some of the other crowd."

She waggled her eyebrows because she happened to have spotted a few of the people in question at the bar on her way in. No doubt Jeff had too. Heck, he'd dated half of them. Winter Lake was small that way. Some people stayed, like her and Jeff. And Andrew. And others left. Like her sisters.

"Anyway," Tess continued. "I'm not sure I'll get the job." She felt tense at the mere thought. She'd begun applying for jobs when school started in September, knowing that their savings and Andrew's life insurance policy wouldn't last forever. The mortgage was steep and little things added up. There was still Phoebe's college fund to think about. Besides, as Jeff had pointed out early on, it would be good for her to get out of the house while Phoebe was at school. It would be good to have a purpose.

"There will always be another one," Jeff said, but Tess felt her smile slip. Sure, she could maybe get a position in one of the boutiques here in town, but the thought of having to be cheerful all day and chitchat with customers was a stretch at the moment. A desk job was a much better fit. And distraction.

Except that she hadn't had a desk job since her twenties, and considering that she'd gotten pregnant and decided to be a stay-at-home mother, that left her with only four years of experience. It felt like half a lifetime ago. She was out of touch. The world had moved on.

"Well," she said, eager to change the subject. "We should probably let you get back to the bar."

Jeff gave a lazy smile, showing that he probably agreed with her but wished he didn't. He worked hard, running this place. And it was a busy night. "What'll it be? On the house."

Tess gave him a long look. It was always on the house, and the large tips she left didn't seem to be enough to make up for his kindness. Nothing was enough.

"Thank you," she said quietly.

He grinned and turned to Phoebe. "Let me guess. Mac and cheese. Spiral noodles. And for your mom…" He roamed his gaze back to Tess, and when their eyes met, Tess felt something in her stir. She swallowed hard. Felt the room still. Heard the crackle of the flames in the fireplace behind her.

She shook all that away. Quickly. "I'll have the spinach salad," she said.

He nodded. "One glazed salmon with mashed potatoes and broccoli, coming right up."

It was her favorite dish, not that she ever ordered it, not when he insisted on it being on the house, and she looked down at her hands as he walked away, back to the bar, leaving her alone with Phoebe once more.

Her rings caught the light behind her, the diamond flashing up at her, reminding her of her past, and her promise.

She stuffed her hands into her lap before she could think any more about that tonight.

She leaned back in her chair, sipped her drink, watched her daughter color, and tried not to let all the decorations bother her too much.

It was Christmas. It would be uneventful. And soon, it would be over.

Chapter Four

Carrie

Carrie hurried down Broadway to her favorite coffee shop, the very one that she and Lucas came to every Saturday morning to read before they decided how they wanted to spend the rest of the day. Only now, she realized, when its faded red awning came into view, she wasn't exactly sure who it belonged to anymore. Was Lucas in there at this very moment, with his boring nature books and even more boring black coffee?

They hadn't exactly agreed upon the terms of their split, after all. There were the givens, like she knew better than to still show up at his firm's holiday party last night. Instead, she'd binged on cookie dough and ice cream (yes, separately) and polished off a bottle of red wine while she tried to focus on a made-for-television Christmas movie but ended up fantasizing about Lucas having a change of heart, coming to his senses, realizing that he'd thrown away the best thing that had ever happened to him, and knocking on her door. He had a key, after all. He could get into her building. But he hadn't come knocking or calling, and now two sleepless nights had passed since he'd said he didn't want to be with her anymore.

Carrie turned at the next corner instead of crossing the street, deciding to duck into a Starbucks instead. She didn't want to see Lucas. Not unless he was begging. Like, on his knees. With a ring. A big one. And flowers. Lots of them.

She was proud of herself for not looking in the windows of the café, but she secretly hoped that he saw her walk by. That maybe he had looked up from his book, spotted her, and felt lonely. That maybe he was in there hoping she would walk through the door, that he'd been waiting for her, that they would reconcile. That he might come running after her. Or call, later.

Still, just in case, she made sure the volume on her phone was set to the highest level, her heart sinking only a little when she saw she had no new missed calls or messages since she'd checked before leaving her apartment.

The Starbucks was up ahead now, and she stopped at the next corner, perusing the magazines of a newsstand while she waited for the walk sign to light up, her eyes homing right in on the wedding magazines. Smiling, radiant brides in exquisite lace and satin gowns seemed to stare back at her. She was supposed to be one of them. You didn't invest four years into someone without the assumption that you were in it for the long haul. That you had found the one. That you were committed.

She looked away as tears filled her eyes and hurried across the street, the wind slapping her cheeks. The Starbucks was crowded but she eyed a table near the corner, one where she could be alone, left in peace to read before she figured out what else to do with the day. With winter break. With the rest of her life.

She kept her eye on the table as she stood in line, debating whether or not she should get a seasonal beverage. Normally, she'd love nothing more than to embrace the holidays, but celebrating alone was far from inspiring, even if Lucas had never really seen the appeal in eating cutout cookies dusted with glistening green and red sugar, or drinking hot chocolate or trudging a tree up the four flights to her apartment. Melody was away for the break; she'd left straight from the party at school. Carrie didn't feel like reaching out to any of her other friends and explaining that not only was she not wearing a ring, but that she also no longer had a boyfriend.

Melody had texted, of course. Right away. Thursday night. She wanted pictures. When Carrie eventually mustered up the energy to reply, in as few words as possible, Melody declared that she was happy that Lucas was done wasting Carrie's time.

At least one of them was happy. Sure, Melody had always been vocal in her opinion that he should have proposed years ago, but Carrie had faith in Lucas. Without a ring or a promise, she figured he would have ended it if he'd wanted to and didn't. And many men did end things. Her father was at the top of that list. He'd ended jobs. Then the marriage. Then their family. But Lucas was conservative and had a stable job and they had a routine—one he'd been faithful to. She could count on it. Just like she'd thought she could count on him. And he was probably back at the café right now. And she should be there with him.

"What can I get you?" The man behind the counter stared at her with naked impatience and Carrie had the uneasy feeling that he had been waiting for her to snap out of her funk for quite some time.

"Sorry." She licked her lower lip and tried to think of what they offered, what she even liked. She had grown so used to her routine with Lucas at the other coffee shop—a skim latte with chocolate shavings and the table near the window—that she didn't even know what to do with herself. "I'll have a...a...skim latte."

"Nonfat latte?" It wasn't a question, though. "Name for the order?"

"Carrie." Only she didn't feel like herself. She felt different. Worse. Like the person she had never wanted to be.

She paid and moved to the end of the line to collect her drink. She looked in the corner, sighing when she saw that someone else had taken her preferred table. A couple. A happy one, at that. The girl was pretty in a natural way, with blonde hair and flushed cheeks, and a plaid scarf that was exactly like the one that Carrie had given Lucas last Christmas. She remembered how selective she had been when choosing it, making sure that it wasn't too light or too dark, and that it would match his camel, navy, and black coats. And his eyes. He had such beautiful blue eyes.

The woman said something and the man laughed, and every nerve ending in Carrie's body went on high alert. She knew that laugh. She'd only been hearing it for the last four years. Except, come to think of it, she maybe hadn't heard it quite as much in recent weeks.

She swallowed hard as the holiday music and din of the

conversation seemed to melt around her, like she was under water, listening from below. Drowning.

Her heart was thudding and she inched to the right, for a better view, and that's when she saw him. Unmistakable. His navy-blue coat. His scarf on *another woman's neck*.

It was Lucas. Her Lucas. The same man who, up until thirty-six hours ago, had been the man she thought she would marry, have children with, and grow old with, preferably in a cozy house in Connecticut with a reasonable commute to the city. And now, while she had stayed home alone inside her shoebox of an apartment, drinking cheap wine and crying so loudly that she feared the neighbors in her building might call her landlord out of concern or, worse, tap on the door to check on her, he had been getting out and about. With another woman!

Her hand flew to her face when she realized she wasn't even wearing makeup. Of course, Lucas had seen her hundreds of times without makeup, because they had spent *four years* of their lives together. But now she felt vulnerable and exposed, and she couldn't have him see her. Not like this. Not when he was with *her*.

Whoever she was.

One thing for certain was that she was no good.

Carrie backed up, stepping on someone's foot.

"Ouch!" An older man looked at her with such scorn that she almost felt the need to defend herself. It had been an accident. She wasn't a bad person. She was actually a very good person.

And she'd been a good girlfriend, too. The best. She couldn't have been any better. Attending every function, laughing at all his lame jokes. Not mentioning kids or marriage—too much.

"Sorry," she muttered and pushed away. She was starting to sweat, and she felt dizzy, like she might faint at any moment. She needed air. She needed to get outside. She needed to get away from Lucas. That woman. And the scarf. It was shameless!

She moved quickly, slanting a glance at the table, even though he was unaware, his back to her. She was almost at the door when she heard the barista call out her order. "Carrie? Nonfat latte for Carrie!"

She froze. She looked at Lucas. Watched to see if he would turn at the sound of her name, if he would see her.

But he didn't move at all. Clearly, she was long forgotten. Already replaced.

She needed to get out of this city. If she didn't, she feared what would become of her in the two weeks that she was supposed to be planning her wedding. It wasn't even noon, and already, she had changed back into pajamas, taken a fitful nap (under the covers and everything), and then wept over all of Lucas's belongings that still lingered in her apartment: extra tee shirts, his green toothbrush, a book he never had finished reading. She toyed with the idea of using it all as an excuse to text him, to see if he would swing by, but she realized that he wouldn't care about any of these things, just like she didn't care about the pink toothbrush at his apartment or the extra pair of sweatpants she had there, maybe a few movies she'd brought over to watch on his oversized television.

The only thing she wanted was for Lucas to come to his senses and beg for her back.

And that scarf. She wanted the scarf back.

At this, she snorted, loudly, so loudly, that she was momentarily silenced, but not for long. She wailed, long and hard. And she wept. She wept until her pillowcase was wet and she became cold and she needed to crawl out of bed and walk to the closet and pull out a sweater.

The phone on her bedside table was flashing. Lucas? Her tears subsided as hope filled her. She picked up the device gingerly, willing it to be him.

She had three missed calls, and again, her heart raced with anticipation. Of course. Lucas had never been one for texting. He much preferred an old-fashioned phone call.

He'd seen her. There was an explanation!

Holding her breath, she tapped the button. Melody. Melody. Except for the call Thursday night from Jules.

Carrie never had called her back.

Now, she supposed that she could. She could tell her everything. Or she could say nothing at all. With five years between them in age, usually, it was Carrie giving the advice, but Jules was always eager to connect. More than Carrie had been, she realized, especially in recent years. But a voice. A human connection... It would be nice right about now, even if Jules did probably want to go in on a gift.

Carrie decided they could go in on Tess's gift, in that case. She was stumped on that one and Tess, being Tess, always bought everyone the perfect gift, unique to their personalities and tastes. Last year, Tess had sent Carrie a vintage jewelry box, decorated with hand-painted butterflies. She was somewhat of a butterfly expert; even at a young age, she could hold out her finger, very still, and they would come to her.

She smiled now, thinking of that. Life was so simple then. And even when it wasn't, it was certainly less complicated than it was now.

She went to the bathroom to wash her face, and, after eyeing Lucas's toothbrush for an unnaturally longer period of time than one would usually stare at a toothbrush, ran it all along the rim of the toilet and then dropped it into the trash. Then, she called her sister while she uncorked a bottle of wine.

Jules answered on the second ring, even though Carrie had half expected to be sent to voicemail. Jules was unpredictable. Her life wasn't settled.

Not that Carrie could talk.

"Hey!" Jules sounded breezy and out of breath, usually because she was always running late and scrambling to get to her destination on time. Also, she lived on the top floor of a brownstone, and lugged groceries and even her bike up those stairs countless times a day.

"Did you just get in?" Carrie asked.

"Nope, just getting ready to head out soon. The snow is really coming down, though."

Carrie frowned. "Says the girl who used to run out to the lake without a hat or gloves at the sight of the first flurry."

"What can I say?" Jules said. "I'm a city girl now. I suppose we both are."

Carrie took a sip of her wine. She glanced at the clock. She should pace herself, but then, what else did she have to do, other than think about the girl with the scarf? The scarf she had bought with the gift card all the class parents had pooled together to buy her.

She narrowed her eyes. Took another sip of wine. A longer one.

"It's funny how that ended up," she said, forcing herself back to the conversation. Distractions were needed, and all too soon she would be left alone again, in the silence of her minuscule apartment. "Given that we grew up in Winter Lake."

"Population four thousand and six," Jules laughed. It was an estimate, but a good one. "Actually, I don't think it's surprising at all. We wanted something different. Something..."

Better? Carrie considered that. From the day her father walked out when she was seven, everything had changed. "I miss it sometimes."

"Then go back!"

Carrie resisted the urge to roll her eyes. It was always like that with Jules. She couldn't understand structure or commitment or responsibility.

"I have a full-time job," Carrie replied.

There was silence on the other end of the line and Carrie held the phone away from her ear to make sure they were still connected.

Eventually, Jules said, "I thought teachers had, like, crazy time off."

True. Carrie hadn't even considered Winter Lake as an option for the holidays, though. It had been too long since she'd been back to even put it on her radar. And then there was the issue with Tess to consider...

"But you're probably busy with Lucas," Jules said.

Now it was Carrie's turn to go silent. She took another sip of her wine before asking, "And what are your plans for the holiday? I saw you called."

"Oh. That. I was just calling about Phoebe's gift. You know me. But our conversation has me thinking. Maybe I will go back to Winter Lake for Christmas. It's Tess's first Christmas since Andrew died."

Of course. How could Carrie forget? Guilt pulled at her stomach, twisting and turning it until it felt like a hard knot. She hadn't thought enough about Tess lately. Truth be told, she'd tried not to.

"Maybe I'll come too," she blurted before she'd had a chance to think things through. It was the wine talking. Surely. And her emotional state. A Christmas in Winter Lake meant skating and festivals and lights and carolers. It meant all the things that Carrie wasn't really up for anymore.

It meant seeing Tess.

But it also meant getting out of the city. Away from Lucas. And the scarf girl.

"Really? You mean you don't have plans with Lucas?" Jules sounded stunned.

Why did she have to keep bringing up Lucas? Carrie opened her mouth to say that, actually, she was no longer with Lucas, and that for all she knew, Lucas was spending Christmas with his new girlfriend, but then she would have to explain it, and listen to Jules's surprised reaction, and that wasn't the point of this call.

"Lucas has other commitments this Christmas," she said blandly.

"Oh, this will be great! All of us together again!"

She wasn't so sure that Tess would see it that way, but then again, maybe she would be happy to have their company, and maybe it was the right thing to do, not just for her, but for Tess. And Phoebe. At the thought of her niece, Carrie warmed up to the idea.

Until she remembered Tess's last words to her, less than a year ago. *If you aren't coming back for Andrew's funeral, then don't ever come back at all.*

"I'll call Tess and let her know," Jules said.

"If she doesn't want me there—"

"Nonsense!" Jules said firmly. "We're sisters. Of course, she wants you there. It will be...a Christmas surprise! Take the morning train to Boston tomorrow. We can get the bus together from here."

Tomorrow. Carrie disconnected the call and stared out the window, which gave an ever-pleasing view of the brick side of an adjacent building. Growing up, the window of the bedroom she'd shared with Tess looked out onto snow-frocked trees, an entire winter wonderland that used to fill her with awe and hope, even when there wasn't any to be found in life's current circumstances.

Christmas in Winter Lake. It would certainly be better than her present situation. It definitely couldn't be worse. Really, how bad could it be?

Chapter Five

Jules

Jules hung up the phone and stared at it for a moment. That was...odd. Good, but odd. Normally, Carrie didn't go anywhere without Lucas. Her entire world had revolved around him from the moment they'd first met. She spent every holiday with Lucas, every vacation with Lucas. Except for her coworkers, Carrie had drifted away from her childhood and college friends and replaced them with Lucas's friends. Half the time, Jules even suspected that Carrie felt closer to Lucas's sisters than she did to her or Tess.

For Carrie to not spend Christmas with Lucas made no sense. Unless...

Jules shook that thought away. Impossible. Carrie and Lucas would never break up. They'd been together far too long, their lives were completely intertwined. In many ways, Carrie had no life without Lucas, other than her teaching job, of course. Lucas was her entire world.

Jules tried to imagine that for a moment. Spending day after day, night after night, meal after meal with the same person, knowing that you would never mix it up, never feel the spark and excitement that came with something or someone new.

It felt dull. And mildly depressing.

But that was what she'd been doing with Aaron, in a way. Only Aaron was just a friend. Her romantic life was separate. She still looked forward to the rush of a first date. Still relished in knowing that if it didn't work out, someone else would eventually come along and that she was no worse off for it. Change was good. Being adaptable was good. Pinning all your hopes and dreams on one person was asking for trouble and she'd seen that firsthand. Her mother had never recovered from their father leaving her. She'd barely lived, and now, she was gone. So no, there was no sense in relying on one person like that.

Still, she appreciated the stability of her friendship with Aaron. She did not, however, appreciate that weird little moment they'd had last night.

Hopefully, by the time she returned from Winter Lake, Aaron would see that really, he had misinterpreted his feelings. It was easy to do, of course. After all, there had even been times where she had felt a pang of jealousy if he dated a girl for more than a month (which albeit was rare, now that she thought about it). He was cute and scruffy and funny and kind. But as soon as she started to feel all squirmy and possessive, she realized that her feelings were not of the romantic sense. It was more a fear of losing what they had. Of being replaced.

Certainly, with a little space, Aaron would see that too. Really, it had probably been the beer talking. It was easy to start imagining how simple it would be to just stick together, forever. But it didn't work that way. Life wasn't that simple.

She pulled up Tess's number and let it ring. She'd be sent to voicemail, she knew. She always was anymore. It had started when Tess went to college, in state, but a couple of hours away. She'd made promises to call, and check in, and visit as often as she could. And she had, at first. Later, when Phoebe was born, Tess tried to explain to her that she had a baby now, she didn't have time to talk every day, or even once a week, and it only got worse from there as Phoebe grew. Tess had responsibilities, she liked to stress, in a tone that made Jules think that Tess didn't believe Jules had any responsibilities of her own. Tess had to run her child around, entertain her, and host playdates, and she had a husband.

Had a husband. Jules let that sink in for a moment. When Andrew died, Jules started trying to call more often, only once again, the phone just rang and rang, and eventually, she got the voicemail system. Sometimes, it was too full for her to leave a message.

She knew better than to take it personally, at least recently. Tess had a perfect life. And then, suddenly, she didn't. She was alone. It was Christmas.

And Jules was coming for a visit.

Tess's message clicked on. Jules thought fast. Should she mention Carrie specifically or keep it vague? She didn't want to upset Tess, but she also wasn't so sure that Tess knew what she needed anymore. Shutting out the world, not answering her phone, none of that was good.

But Carrie…Well, that was certainly a very tricky situation.

There was a beep. Her heart raced. She thought on her feet. Split second decision.

"Hey, Tess, it's Jules, your favorite sister." Shoot. Why had she said that? Carrie had always been closer to Tess, up until recent events, not just because of their similar interests but their birth order. Being only two years apart, they'd forged their friendship long before Jules had arrived in the world five years after Carrie. They were a pack, a team, two girls with blonde hair as opposed to Jules's dark curls. They liked to play boring games like house and teacher while Jules wanted to jump off the rocks into the cool, murky lake. Jules was the little sister, the tagalong, the one that Tess looked after, like a child not as a peer, especially when their mother couldn't be relied on half the time. Why draw attention to the fact that, thanks to Carrie's recent behavior, Jules had slid into the position by default?

She continued. "Anyway, just wanted to let you know that Carrie and I were thinking of coming to Winter Lake for the holiday. The bus gets in at two tomorrow. We can't wait to see you and Phoebe!"

She hung up and threw her head back against the sofa. Tess might be happy that Carrie was finally visiting, or maybe she'd call, insist that Carrie not come. Or that Jules not come.

Jules thought about that for a moment. Both scenarios were entirely possible, after all. Tess and Carrie hadn't spoken in nearly a year, and the majority of Jules's calls to Tess went unanswered. Neither of them had exactly been invited. But they were family. Winter Lake was their hometown. And it was Christmas.

If Tess called, Jules decided, she would just give her a taste of her own medicine. She'd let it go to voicemail.

If she was going to show up in Winter Lake for a week (or two?), then Jules supposed she had better not show up empty-handed.

The problem, of course, was that she didn't know what to buy her sister. Or even Phoebe, for that matter. Tess was always the quietest of the three sisters. Carrie was the most creative. Jules wondered where she fit into this equation, what single adjective her sisters might use to sum up her personality?

Irresponsible, she settled on. That's how they saw her back when they were kids, and that's how they still saw her. Even when Jules was in college, on a scholarship that she had earned from good grades and a killer essay, her chats with Tess often felt more like a trial by fire. Was she attending her classes? Had she thought about what jobs she might pursue? And later, when she started freelancing, she'd been lectured on the merits of a retirement plan.

All the more reason not to mention that she had just lost her latest gig, and that she'd been passed over for a full-time position.

One glance out the window told her that the snow hadn't let up and probably wouldn't. She bundled into her warmed coat and scarf and only realized that she had forgotten her gloves when she was already in the vestibule of her brownstone, next to the mailboxes. She paused and considered going back upstairs, but she already felt frustrated and overheated as it was. Besides, if she went back upstairs, she might change her mind; she might push off the whole present-buying thing until she was in Winter Lake, and tell Aaron to meet her at the pub instead. Christmas was a week from tomorrow, after all. She had time...

But it was this exact mentality that gave her a bad rap in the family. No, she would buy all the gifts today and wrap them, and then everyone would be surprised, and not just by her appearance in Winter Lake. She was twenty-eight years old. It was time to stop being treated like a kid once and for all.

Still without a clue as to what anyone might like for Christmas, she took the T to the Prudential Center and decided that inspiration would strike when she saw it. It usually worked that way in life, didn't it? You didn't know what you liked until you saw it, and it became so obvious, like it had been right there all along, just waiting for you.

It was that way with her jobs. Some gigs she thought she would love turned out to be major busts. Others that she was dreading except for the pay grade turned out to be pleasantly surprising.

And it was that way with love, too. Well, not that she'd ever been in love, per se, but she had been in her share of relationships. Sometimes it just clicked. Sometimes it didn't. It shouldn't have to be weighed and considered. When you knew, you knew!

And she knew that she and Aaron were only friends.

Happy for a seat, she scanned her phone while she waited to reach her destination. No response from Tess yet. She'd take that as a good sign today.

She texted Aaron to let him know she was, as usual, running five minutes late. Normally this would be met with a snarky response, but today, none came back.

She waited a beat, and then put the phone into her pocket. No need to over think things. She would focus on shopping. Gift-giving. Tis the season and all that.

Except, despite the snow and the decorations that seemed to wrap every lamppost and flank every front door, she couldn't drum up much Christmas spirit at the moment.

Her life felt uncertain, and not just because of her employment situation. But it would all be better when she saw Aaron and everything went back to normal again, she told herself.

Aaron was late.

Jules tried not to read into this too much. After all, it was snowing hard, the roads were bad, the sidewalks worse, and...Well, it was just a coincidence. Surely it had nothing to do with that weird little moment last night.

Jules had just polished off her second hot pretzel when she saw him, coming up the escalator, in his charcoal grey coat. His hair was again dusted in snow, and his eyes were scanning his surroundings. Her heart soared with relief.

He was here. Of course he was here. She could always count on him.

She tossed the buttery pretzel wrapper and grease-stained napkins in the nearest trash can and waved her arms over her head, trying to get his attention without calling out his name. It took a few moments, but finally, he caught her, his face breaking out into a smile as he hurried his pace to meet her.

"Hey, you!" She hesitated for a minute before leaning in to

give him their usual hug, not sure if she should, but thinking it would be worse if she didn't. *Just act normal,* she told herself. Then everything would be right again.

He held her a beat longer than usual, and she stiffened, alarmed, and pulled back more abruptly than she'd intended. His face seemed to drop into a frown but she quickly recovered the moment, linking his arm as she led him to the bookstore. Phoebe could read, and a child could never have too many books, in her opinion. And Tess would approve.

"You just missed out on the hot pretzels," she said. "But for you, I might be able to eat another."

He laughed, and then grinned over at her. "You have butter on your lips."

"Do I?" Butter stained. She remembered this from the time that her mother had brought all three girls out to celebrate Tess's birthday—a rare occurrence that Tess had lobbied for. They'd gone to a diner that had long since closed, wearing their best dresses and feeling special. It was one of those fleeting, spontaneous times that their mother had made a real effort, encouraging them to order whatever they wanted, and that was a baked potato with extra butter for Jules. Jules had been about six and didn't heed Tess's warnings about the melted butter that was dripping off her fork, insisting that she was fine, that she did not need to tuck her napkin into the neckline of the beautiful pink dress that *she* had lobbied for on her birthday one month earlier, and of course, minutes later managed to get three great big spots on the front of the skirt. She could still picture the dismay in her mother's eyes, and the accusation in Tess's stare. Even now, it hurt. It hurt a lot more than maybe it should.

64

She licked her lips quickly, not exactly liking the way that Aaron was watching her as she did, and said, "I decided to go back to Winter Lake for the holiday. I can't think of what to buy Tess, though."

"That's a tough one," Aaron agreed, but he seemed distant as they walked into the store. "How long are you gone for?"

"Oh, a week," she said. She picked up a book on the display table, even though it was for an adult, not a child, and actually, it was something that she'd been interested in reading for a while now.

She set it back. It was the time for giving, not treating herself.

"Maybe two." She moved over to a stack of toys, but they all seemed too young for an eight-year-old.

"Two weeks?" Aaron looked disappointed.

"Think you can survive without me?" Jules joked, but she sensed something amiss between them. Something that didn't sit right. "I'm glad you came," she said, looking at him guardedly. "I wasn't sure if—"

Aaron's brow pinched. "If what?"

She thought fast. No sense in bringing up the events of last night if he wasn't going to. "I wasn't sure if you were willing to brave the storm."

"A snowstorm couldn't stop me from seeing you. Besides, you and I always hang out together on the weekends. Where else would I be?" Aaron gave her a knowing grin.

Jules relaxed. All this could be forgotten. He was probably just as uncomfortable as she was. He might want to apologize. She seriously hoped he wouldn't. No, it would be better to never broach the topic again and to let things evolve naturally, until, by the end of today, everything would return to normal. In fact, they were already normal. She was just being...touchy.

"And we usually spend holidays together, too," he said.

Jules said nothing as she stared at a wall of books. True. All of this was true. And she had a bad feeling that Aaron was getting at something. For the past four years, she'd gone up to his parents' cabin in Maine for Christmas. They played cards at the big table near the picture window with a view of the fire and watched cheesy holiday movies, huddled under blankets. While they hadn't made any official plans yet, he might have assumed it was a given.

"It's Tess's first Christmas since..." She still couldn't bring herself to say it. Andrew had been special. One of a kind. More like a father figure than a brother-in-law, and someone that she could turn to, someone who knew how to fix things and make it all better, like the time that she'd maxed out her first credit card because she thought that the credit limit was monthly, not in total. Oh, how Andrew had laughed and laughed, but he'd sent her a check to get her through for a few weeks. She was fairly sure that to this day, Tess hadn't learned about that. And now, she never would.

"No, of course. I get it. Tess is your family. You should be with her." Aaron cut a hand through the air, but his smile was strained. "You'll be missed, that's all."

"And I'll miss your mother's mashed potatoes," Jules sighed, thinking of the woman who always greeted her with a warm smile and a tight hug. "And her."

"There's always next year," Aaron said, forcing a smile.

"You're welcome to come to Winter Lake with me," Jules

offered. It would be fun. A lot of fun. And it would help break up the dynamic with her sisters. With Aaron there, Tess couldn't exactly throttle Carrie, after all. She'd have to be polite, seeing as she'd only met him once, years back at Jules's college graduation. Phoebe had only been a toddler then, and Tess had spent most of the two-day visit doling out crackers and explaining the need to duck back to the hotel for nap time. "We can go skating. I can show you all around the town where I grew up."

"I don't think that's a good idea," he said. He stopped walking, and Jules had the uneasy feeling that he was waiting for her to turn and look at him.

Finally, reluctantly, she did.

"I meant what I said last night," he said, his voice low, his eyes earnest and searching. "Don't you ever think about it?"

She sighed. She couldn't deny that she hadn't.

"You know me, Aaron," Jules pleaded. "I don't...commit."

"You do," he said, an edge creeping into his tone. It was an edge of hurt, she realized with sadness. "When it's something you really want."

"But I want this. You. Me. Just like it's always been."

"And I want more." His words were firm. Clear. And mildly threatening.

She blinked at him, unsure what this could mean. "I don't know, Aaron. I haven't thought about this. You've taken me off guard."

He held up a hand, and for a moment her Aaron, her best friend, her closest companion, was back in full form. "I know, and I'm sorry. I just...I needed to say it. I love you, Jules. You know that."

She stared at him. Her heart was pounding so hard that she could feel the rise and fall of her chest. She knew he loved her, of course she knew that. But loving someone and being in love with them were two very different things.

"And it's just become too hard for me," he continued, shaking his head.

Wait. What?

"What do you mean?" she asked, her voice raising a notch.

"I mean I love you, Jules. But if you don't love me, then I...I need to move on. I need to...protect myself."

Protect himself? From her? But she was his best friend! This was crazy. It made no sense! She almost laughed out loud, until she saw the pain in his eyes and she knew he was serious. He meant it.

"I can't lose you," she said in an urgent whisper.

"You don't need to," he said. He reached out and held her hand, and even though it was a hand she had held casually a hundred times before, as recently as three nights ago when she slipped on a patch of ice coming out of a cab and he had reached for her, today it felt different. And she didn't know if that was a good thing or not.

"I'm afraid of losing what we have," she said, hoping to make a reasonable argument here.

"We don't have to."

Jules was aware that her heart was beating and that the store clerk who had clearly been watching the entire exchange now dashed away, pretending to straighten an already straight pile of books on a nearby table, but her face was tilted so that she could still overhear the end of the conversation.

Only Jules didn't know how the conversation would end. She didn't know where they went from here.

"Think it over while you're away," Aaron said. He gave her a long, heartbreaking look and then leaned in, pecked her cheek, and walked away, leaving her standing in the middle of the bookstore, feeling completely alone.

So much for Winter Lake being a place to clear her head, Jules thought miserably. It was now officially a place to hide.

Chapter Six

Tess

As promised, Jeff called on Saturday morning and suggested that they meet at the tree lot off Lake Street at two sharp. "And don't even think of coming up with a lame excuse," he warned, which, she had to admit, made her grin.

After all, she'd been tempted.

The tree lot he was referring to was the only lot in all of Winter Lake, family-owned for three generations and a tradition amongst long-time residents. Tess had grown up with a fake tree (at least for the years that her mother was willing to put it up, or until Tess was big and strong enough to do it herself), and every year she vowed to have a real tree in her house when she was old enough, like the one in her friend Natalie's living room, and when they were married, each year she and Andrew would come to this lot and pick out a tree, pay some kid to strap it to the top of their car, and then lug it into the house, sweating and laughing.

Tess smiled at the memory when she pulled into the small parking lot, next to Jeff's truck.

"Why are you smiling, Mommy?" Phoebe asked from the backseat.

"Oh." Tess hesitated, not sure if she should mention the reason. She didn't know how to handle the subject of Andrew, even now, after all these months, when she'd naively assumed she'd be used to it, maybe even recovered, when his absence wouldn't be so noticeable. But it was. Painfully so. How many times did Phoebe do something cute and she would want to pick up the phone, dial the number she still had stored in her phone? How many times did she still call the number anyway, just to hear his voice, sometimes even leaving a message? But he would never call back. And that...well, that was something she still couldn't quite believe.

She wanted Phoebe to remember her father. But she didn't want to upset her. "I was just thinking about Daddy. He'd be happy that we're carrying on the tradition of picking out our tree from this lot."

The truth was that she didn't want a tree this year. Didn't want to celebrate the holiday at all. All those traditions were from a different time, another life. Would she bother with a turkey and the cornbread stuffing and the homemade bread this year? It wouldn't be the same. Just like going to Jeff's parents' house for Thanksgiving hadn't been the same. Everything was different. And Christmas would be too. She would much prefer to just stay in bed, the curtains drawn, emerging on December 26 with a sense of relief.

But that was something her mother would have done, and had done, more than once. Other times, she went overboard, trying to make up for lost time with smiles and cheer that never lasted long and were gone all too soon. And Tess had made a promise to herself—and to Andrew, that horrible winter day when she said her final good-bye to him—that she would take care of their daughter. And she would.

"Daddy would be proud of us," Phoebe agreed. She released her seatbelt and reached for the door handle. "Now, come on, before all the good trees are gone!"

Tess climbed out of the car, bracing herself for slim pickings. It was the weekend before Christmas; most people had probably had their trees up since Thanksgiving like she used to do. Each year she and Andrew would step back and admire their handiwork, say they'd outdone themselves, each year declaring that this Christmas they had the most beautiful tree, and then each year after that, they'd say the same.

This Christmas, Tess wasn't betting on that. She'd settle for modest. She'd settle for bare. She'd settle for just having something with branches that might hold an ornament or two to keep Phoebe happy.

Jeff was waiting for them at the entrance to the lot with two steaming paper cups. "Cider," he said, extending his hand. Tess noticed a third cup resting on the windowsill of the little shed that served as the checkout stand.

"Thank you," she said, taking her cup. She took a sip. It was warm and spicy and it made her feel a little better. Or maybe she just felt better because Jeff was here. Another adult. Another person fighting through each day.

"Glad you came," he said, giving her a long, knowing look that might have made Tess feel ashamed with anyone else. But Jeff got it. They'd suffered together, from that first, awful, shocking night when Jeff called to tell her the news. A skiing accident. Of all things. A freak accident on the very mountain where Andrew had learned to ski as a child. Where he'd taught Phoebe to ski. He probably didn't even feel anything. He was gone on impact. There was nothing that Jeff could do. Nothing that anyone could have done.

Jeff had come over that night, wracked with guilt and apology and confusion and sadness and anger and every other emotion a human being could process. And they'd cried long and hard, and they'd figured out what to do, what to tell Phoebe, and she'd talked to Phoebe, herself, because that's what a mother should do, and she had to be strong. But she was only able to get through it because she knew that Jeff was downstairs. That he was waiting. That he, too, felt the enormity of Andrew's loss.

And then came the feelings. So many feelings. The wake and the funeral and the casseroles. And then the casseroles stopped. Everyone moved on. Maybe they expected her to as well.

But not Jeff. Because Jeff knew her. And he knew Andrew. And they were all each other had now.

"I'm glad I came too," she said, giving him a small smile. The sparkle in Phoebe's eyes was worth it. "But I can't admit that this is easy."

"This is going to be a nice Christmas," Jeff said quietly.

She eyed him ruefully. "It's going to be the worst Christmas ever, Jeff. Don't try to convince me otherwise."

He gave her a sad smile but didn't argue, at least. They began to move through the rows of trees, Phoebe running up ahead, pointing to each one she saw, liking each one better than the last.

"You know, this is my first time doing this," Jeff surprised her by saying, and Tess gave him a funny look.

"You mean you don't put up a Christmas tree?"

He shrugged. "When I was a kid, but we had one of those fake, plastic things."

"Something in common, then." She took another sip of her cider. No sense in thinking of those days. She had her own life. The one she'd built herself. Except it had all come crashing down around her.

"We have a lot in common," he said, giving her a knowing look.

She gave him a sad smile and then decided to shift away from upsetting topics. "You decorate the restaurant, though."

"Professional requirement. But I don't see much point in decorating a tree just for me," Jeff said. "So this is a new adventure."

A new adventure. That was certainly an optimistic spin on things, not that she was arguing.

"I found one!" Phoebe ran up to them excitedly, her smile so wide that she was showing off the gap where she'd lost a tooth just last week. Tess had needed to steel herself from the reminder that it was Andrew's turn to play tooth fairy this time.

"Already?" Jeff frowned. "But we haven't even walked the lot." He sounded almost disappointed.

"That's because you and Mommy walk too slowly. I found the best tree, so hurry up!" She stared at them, her dark eyes wide. "Hurry up!"

"I guess we'd better hurry up," Tess whispered to Jeff, laughing.

They increased their pace, but not by much; the crowds made that impossible. Phoebe's bright pink coat was easy to spot through the evergreens and white snow and sea of dark, dreary shades of blue and black winter coats.

They came to a stop, and Tess felt her heart sink. Phoebe was standing next to the biggest tree in the lot. Of course she was. A huge smile extended up to her shining eyes as she held a branch with propriety.

Tess would have to let her down. Again. And more and more, she hated letting Phoebe down. Oh, why couldn't she have chosen a simple tree? Something small but pretty? Something that wasn't towering up to the sky and probably cost a small fortune to boot.

Because she was eight years old. And it was Christmas.

"I don't think that will fit in our house, honey," she said, but Phoebe's smile didn't fade.

"Sure it will. We have high ceilings in the front living room."

Tess tried another tactic. "Yes, but the doors, honey." She walked to the tree and glanced at the price tag, her eyes bulging. "And it's a lot of money for something we're only going to keep up for a week or so."

Phoebe nodded but she was blinking rapidly and her lips were pinched to hold back her emotions. Tess swallowed a sigh, wishing just now that they had never come. That she'd grabbed something small from outside the grocery store instead. This was a proper tree lot. Where they used to get their tree. When things were different.

Of course, if Andrew were here he would have taken control of the situation, told her that was far too big and led her over to an aisle of more reasonably sized options. He was always so good with Phoebe.

And right now, even though this was something as silly as a tree that would be gone in a week if she had any say in the matter, she wished he was here to help her out.

A flash of anger, sudden and sharp, pierced her. It happened every once in a while when she opened the mortgage bill or Phoebe came home from school crying because someone had said something to upset her, something about a father-daughter event that made her feel left out. *Why'd you have to go night skiing? Why'd you have to go so fast? Why'd you have to take the steepest path?*

He was always a daredevil when it came to skiing, and she'd loved that side of him, the side that wasn't the straight-laced accountant—the mountain was the one place he let loose. She loved the mischievous gleam he would get in his eye when he talked about hitting the slopes, loved the boyish side it brought out, even when he was a grown man. But he wasn't just a man. He was a husband. A father. *Why'd you have to be so irresponsible? Why'd you have to leave us?*

Jeff was watching her, and without a word, he stepped forward, gave the tree a silent, but rather dramatic inspection, and declared, "The needles are all falling off."

Phoebe's eyes popped in alarm. "They *are?*"

"Yep." Jeff tossed up his hands. "Good thing we spotted this. Don't think you want all the ornaments falling off it while you're sleeping." He pointed to a row of fat spruces, all about six feet high. "Now those over there are good, strong trees. Why don't you pick your favorite?"

Tess gave Jeff a long look. "Thank you," she said, fighting off the impatience that had built up inside her.

"Not a problem. It's not easy, I know. Well, I don't know, since I don't have kids, but…"

"But nothing. Thank you. For…everything."

He reached out and squeezed her elbow, a simple, easy gesture, but one that couldn't have happened at a worse time.

Trudy Flannigan, Andrew's mother's oldest friend, was watching them with a look of alarm.

"Hello, Mrs. Flannigan," Tess said, smiling at the older woman. She hadn't seen Trudy in quite some time, not since Trudy had dropped off two pot pies that she promised would freeze well. They were still in Tess's freezer. Her appetite just wasn't what it used to be. Besides, they seemed far too large for just herself and Phoebe.

Trudy looked from Jeff to Tess and blinked. "Tess. And Jeff. So nice to see you both." But her voice was pert, and her tone, Tess thought, was judgmental.

"Nice to see you too," Jeff said good-naturedly. He took a swig of his cider and grinned.

Tess glanced at him. He appeared not to feel any of the awkwardness that she did, and maybe she should take her cue from him. After all, they were just two old friends at a tree lot. It was Christmas. It wasn't scandalous.

Only, from the look on Trudy's face, it appeared that it was.

Guilt reared its ugly head, and Tess thought of Andrew, walking through the lot just a year ago, with Phoebe's hand in his, Tess snapping pictures as she did every year, and then framing the best one to place on their mantle, beside a plate of cookies they would leave out for Santa, but which Andrew would eat before Phoebe was even asleep, because he never could resist sweets.

"Phoebe's just over there," Tess said, motioning to the row of trees where Phoebe had wandered. "She's selecting our tree. Jeff here was happy enough to help us set it up."

"They have a service for that," Trudy said, narrowing her eyes slightly.

"Do they? I wasn't aware." A white lie, but she felt she deserved it under the circumstances. "Andrew—" She stopped herself. She'd almost said that Andrew always took care of it for her.

Jeff cleared his throat. She felt him glance over at her, even though her eyes were now firmly on the snow-covered ground beneath her feet.

"Well, we should probably let you get back to finding your tree before they're all gone. Have a merry Christmas, Trudy," Jeff said.

"You too," Trudy replied in a steely voice.

Tess turned toward the row of trees where her daughter was waiting and felt the sudden need to leave. Immediately.

"I guess we'll take the tree then," she said, not even feigning enthusiasm.

"We can decorate it together," Jeff said, giving her a little nudge. "It'll be fun."

Only something in his eyes told her that he was forcing his feelings just as much as she did with Phoebe these days. There was no fun in decorating this Christmas.

Except for Phoebe.

Jeff carried the tree into the house and set it up in the center of the big, front bay window where it had always gone, since Tess and Andrew had first moved into the house, more than ten years ago.

Tess and Phoebe stood back and gave him instructions. A little to the left. An inch to the right. Now it needed to go left again.

By the end, they were all laughing, and the tree…the tree looked perfect. Even Tess had been forced to admit it.

"Let's decorate it!" Phoebe said excitedly.

Jeff lifted an eyebrow in question, taking Tess's lead rather than pushing the matter. She had hoped to just put up a string of lights. Maybe a few of the paper ornaments that Phoebe had made in school. But seeing her daughter's expectant face confirmed that none of that was really an option.

"I'll get the ornaments out of the attic," she said wearily, sparking a peal of delight from Phoebe.

"I can get them," Jeff offered.

Tess gave him a look of gratitude. "I'll make hot chocolate," she offered. She may as well, she figured. If they were going to do it, they may as well do it right. Marshmallows and all. "The boxes are clearly labeled," she told Jeff, who was already heading down the hall to the stairs.

He tossed her a grin over his shoulder. "I never doubted it."

Tess shook her head as she walked into the kitchen and started the preparations for the hot chocolate. It was a grey, winter day, and it was already growing dark, even though it wasn't late, and from the window in the kitchen, she could see the backs of neighbors' houses. The trees lighting up their living rooms. The glow coming from outdoor lights that were covered in a thick blanket of snow.

She set a pot on the stove and filled it with milk, setting the burner on low so she wouldn't have to hover too closely.

In the living room, Jeff had already returned with one box, and from his lack of presence, she could only assume that he'd gone off in search of more.

"We start with the lights," Tess reminded Phoebe when she began hanging her favorite ornaments, on the lowest branches of course. Several branches already contained more than one ornament, which would be spread out later, when Phoebe didn't notice.

Or maybe Tess would leave them this year. After all, what did it matter? She'd had the perfect house. Perfect tree. Perfect family. And now…

"And why is that?" Jeff interrupted her dark thoughts as he came to the bottom of the stairs, carrying two large plastic containers stacked on top of each other. "Why start with the lights?"

Tess reached for the top one and set it on the area rug. "You really haven't decorated a tree in a long time."

"Nope. And I'm out of practice. Besides, most of the time, my sisters took over decorating the tree. I was usually more interested in what was left under it." He winked at Phoebe.

"I can show you how to do it," Phoebe sighed, giving her mother a look that said, *Do you believe this?*

Tess and Jeff exchanged a secret smile and Tess left to check on the milk, hoping it hadn't already started to boil, listening to Phoebe expertly advise Jeff where to start with the lights and to first be sure that none had burned out. She'd been paying attention, all those years, Tess realized. Building up knowledge. Memories. Memories of Andrew.

The milk had just started to simmer, so Tess added the chocolate and stirred it until it melted. It smelled rich and sweet, and the house was warm with the faintest scent of pine. And for a moment, everything felt right in the world.

Except when she thought of the look on Trudy Flannigan's face at the tree lot.

Guilt twisted in her stomach and she pushed it aside, flicked off the burner, and called out, "Who wants hot chocolate?"

"Me!" came two voices, one small and high-pitched, the other deep and strong.

It could have just as easily been Andrew's voice, calling out from the other room, but it wasn't, it was someone else's. And how would Andrew feel about that?

Happy, she decided. He'd want to know that his wife and his best friend were taking some comfort in each other. That she wasn't alone. That there was a reprieve, something to look forward to every now and again.

He'd have wanted Jeff to be there for them. Expected it, really. Jeff was more than a friend, after all. He was family.

Closer to her than her own family in many ways, she thought, as she carried a tray with three mugs and a bowl of marshmallows into the living room and set it on the coffee table. The lights were already up on the tree. They definitely weren't distributed as evenly as she might have preferred, and in years past she would have spent another hour perfecting them before the ornaments went up. Today, though, she found that it didn't matter to her anymore. Phoebe was smiling, her eyes alive and bright, and they had a tree. And it didn't crush her to see it there, the way she had feared.

Tonight, when Jeff was gone and Phoebe was asleep and all that remained was the big empty house, then maybe it might. She decided to turn off its lights right after Phoebe went to bed.

It was all about management. One day at a time. And Christmas Day…that was a big hurdle.

"Your phone's blinking," Jeff told her.

Tess leaned forward with curiosity, her heart picking up speed when she considered it could be news from the job interview. But then she remembered that it was Saturday, and a week before Christmas, and that she'd only interviewed yesterday. The world didn't operate that quickly, even though so much could change so suddenly.

"My sister called," she said, frowning at the screen. She hadn't even heard it ring. She'd learned to turn off the ringer when Phoebe was with her. To shut out the rest of the world.

Jeff gave her a knowing look as he readjusted the string of lights. "The one…"

She shook her head. She knew exactly how he was going to finish that question. The one who didn't come to Andrew's funeral?

No. That one knew better than to call Tess. And she hadn't. Not since Tess had told her that if she didn't come to the funeral, she shouldn't come back to Winter Lake, ever. She'd spoken in the heat of emotion, of course, when her nerves were raw and she wasn't sleeping or eating and the slightest thing, good or bad, felt like something enormous. Only her sister not coming to her husband's funeral *was* enormous. And unforgivable.

But as the months passed, sometimes Tess didn't know where the hurt rested anymore. Was she angry at her sister for not coming, sad that they had reached this place in their relationship, or disappointed that there hadn't been reconciliation in all this time?

She sipped her hot chocolate. She didn't need to think about any of this now. It wouldn't make a difference. Carrie had made her choices. And now they were both living with the consequences.

"Jules calls all the time," Tess said. "I'll call her later."

Another round of guilt brewed to the surface. Jules did call, it was true, but Tess rarely returned the calls—she didn't always have the patience for it. Jules was young, reckless, and painfully irresponsible. She didn't understand the meaning of responsibility. She'd never held a full-time job from what Tess knew. No pets. No kids. No husband. And she certainly wasn't moving in the direction of having any of those things. Her apartment was small, it was rented, and she didn't own a car. She had nothing to her name. And she was fine with that.

And this...well, this had always been the gap between them. Jules couldn't understand why Tess couldn't talk at dinnertime, or after dinnertime. And Tess couldn't imagine having so much free time that to be busy would actually be incomprehensible! For so many years, their relationship had been more like mother and child than sisters, but then Tess had her own child, and Jules...well, it was high time for Jules to grow up!

Jules meant well, Tess knew that. But she also had the creeping sensation that she was letting Jules down, and she was already worried enough about letting her own daughter down, and then she felt more worried and more guilty and more fed up with Jules for needing her and more fed up with herself for not being able to protect her or to fix Jules's life.

She couldn't worry about everyone, Andrew used to tell her, even though she felt like somehow, she was supposed to.

"I'll listen to the message," she said, holding the phone to her ear. She expected the usual, Jules being breezy and chatty and giving her a rundown of her week, asking Tess to please call when she could. But this call was different. And this message was much worse.

She stood up, nearly tripping on a box of ornaments, knowing that Jeff and Phoebe were both looking at her with concern.

"Is everything okay?" Jeff stepped forward, but she held up a hand.

"It's fine. It's fine." But actually, it wasn't. It wasn't fine at all. Jules was coming to Winter Lake for Christmas.

And by the sound of it, so was Carrie.

Chapter Seven

Carrie

Like Jules, Carrie didn't own a car. On a preschool teacher's salary, she couldn't exactly afford one. And in Manhattan, it would be a headache, a frustration.

But lugging a huge suitcase, a tote, an overstuffed back-pack, and several shopping bags filled with presents down the stairs of her apartment building and into the back of a waiting cab was an even bigger frustration. And getting them out of the cab and through Grand Central Terminal had proven to be downright impossible.

Carrie stood just inside the doors of the train station, sweating through her wool coat, wishing she hadn't worn a thick turtleneck sweater that now felt as if it were choking her. She stared at the pile of her belongings, wondering just what Tess would say when she saw it all. She'd been presump-tuous, really, assuming that Tess would let her even stay for one night, let alone until Christmas. And just in case things worked out and she was granted access across the threshold, she'd packed enough to get through New Year's because the thought of spending it alone, in her empty and dark apartment, while Lucas was kissing the girl with the scarf was too horrifying to even think about right now.

Luckily, she *couldn't* think about it right now. Her train was scheduled to depart in seventeen minutes and she still had to buy a ticket, and find a seat. And haul her load.

She took a deep breath and decided that she had no other choice but to problem solve. What would she tell her students when they dumped a box of toys and didn't even know where to begin with picking them up? One thing at a time. Small bites. She started with the backpack. Then she loped the shopping bags over the handle of her suitcase. She deposited her tote into her other carry-on and there. Her back and shoulders and neck were cramping but she had done it.

She was an independent woman. She did not need Lucas!

But oh, how she wanted him. Wanted the comfort of her routine. Sundays were usually spent at their favorite brunch spot in Greenwich Village, followed by a walk in the park or a movie, and then they'd browse a bookstore before heading to a lazy dinner near one of their apartments.

That was their life. That was her life. Only now, another woman was living it.

In her scarf! Because she'd bought it!

Fighting back tears, she hauled herself toward the ticket counter and purchased a ticket.

"Return date?" the teller asked in a bored tone.

"One way," Carrie replied because honestly, she couldn't pinpoint a return date, just like she couldn't predict Tess's reaction upon seeing her. For all she knew, she'd be back in town by tonight. In her cozy, empty bed, in the bedroom that was so small that she could close the closet door without leaving her bed.

It wouldn't be so bad. She could order takeout from her favorite Thai restaurant and binge-watch past seasons of the reality shows she'd missed when she was busy watching those boring history documentaries that Lucas preferred. She'd keep her phone off so that Lucas couldn't even reach her if he tried, but she'd be close enough to the door to answer if he stopped by.

That thought came to a screeching halt. No. Lucas was not going to be stopping by, at least not until he got bored of his new girl toy. And until then, she was better off out of town, where she couldn't be tempted to do something really crazy like hover outside his apartment building, staring up into the windows from three flights below, or climb up his fire escape for a better look. (Yes, she had thought of all three, last night, when the misery of replaying the image of him sitting with that other woman had reached a breaking point.)

The train was surprisingly full, but then it was the week before Christmas, and people were heading home for the holidays, not that Winter Lake had been her home in a very long time. In a few hours, they would stop in Boston, where Jules would be waiting. They would arrive in Vermont together as a united force. Just knowing that made her feel better.

Still, when the drinks cart came around twenty minutes into their journey, Carrie shelled out some cash for a glass of red wine even if it was morning, and sipped it while she attempted to read a new paperback, one she had been looking particularly forward to enjoying on her break—a simple pleasure that she refused to let Lucas steal from her.

Once they were well outside of the city limits, the countryside opened up and the route became scenic, like a winter wonderland outside her window. With each passing mile, she felt her spirits lift. The physical distance between her and Lucas was a good thing, and she was doing the leaving this time, even if he wasn't aware of it. Even if he might not care.

At some point in time, she dozed off, thanks to the aid of the wine, and she didn't wake until they were only half an hour from Boston. Carrie smoothed down her hair and checked her reflection in her pocket mirror, not that she had to worry about impressing Jules. It was Tess that required some primping. But Jules was carefree and nonjudgmental. She barely wore makeup herself, not that she really needed it with her rosy cheeks and naturally long lashes, and she didn't really give much care to the appearance of those around her.

Tess said it was because Jules didn't notice much of anything around her, that she was like their mother in that way, a free spirit, who took the day in stride and didn't bother with little details or practicalities, that even when she was the last of the sisters in their childhood home, it had been Tess who still dropped off groceries for their mother and sometimes a meal or two.

Still, right now Jules was Carrie's favorite sister. In many ways, she felt like her only sister. Tess…well, that was rocky territory.

She pulled out her phone and texted Jules, excited at the prospect of seeing her again. The last time they'd seen each other had been more than a year and a half ago, on a brief stop in Boston on Carrie and Lucas's way to the Cape, back when she had been convinced for a short time that that was when Lucas was going to pop the question. Would she ever learn?

Her phone pinged seconds after her message was sent. From Jules, of course.

She blinked at the screen, not wanting to believe the words on the screen. Jules was running late! Of course she was!

Carrie felt her chest heave as she stared at the screen and tapped, I'll wait. There was no way she was arriving in Winter Lake without Jules at her side. But Jules replied: Sorry, but I snagged the last ticket for the later bus. Good thing you already bought your ticket for the early one! See you at six!

Six! But Carrie was arriving at two!

Was Tess aware that Jules was not going to be on that bus? Or aware that Carrie was even coming? And now—oh God—coming alone?

She should text Jules and ask. Or better yet Tess.

But she just couldn't deal. She had dealt with enough for one week. And as she'd learned the hard way, some things in life couldn't be controlled or planned or even counted on.

Sometimes you just had to sit back and see what happened. And say a silent prayer that it would all turn out okay.

Winter Lake never changed. Carrie stared out the window as the bus made its final push into the station on the edge of town, but close enough to give her a view of the snow-covered orchard where she and her sisters would pick apples each fall and berries each summer, of the old mill where their father had once worked before he'd ditched town, and them, when Carrie was seven, and the long, country road that led right to the house she had lived in until she was eighteen, ready to leave, and go out into the world.

Jules and Carrie had done just that. But Tess... Well, Tess had always felt a need to take care of the nest, not flee it. And of course, she had Andrew—her high school sweetheart.

The nostalgia was quickly replaced by something else, a creeping sense of anxiety as the bus door opened and she and her fellow passengers (make that passenger, singular, since the rest had all left, one by one, or two by two, at the stops along the way) stood and gathered up their belongings.

Knowing Jules, she had failed to inform Tess what time they were expected to arrive. She probably wouldn't have thought that far ahead. Probably had assumed they would wing it, or call a cab, even though Carrie had begun to worry if there even were cabs in their quaint small hometown. She'd never had to think about that on her visits before. Not that there had been many. There had been Tess's wedding, a visit a few weeks after Phoebe was born, and then Christmas five years ago. And then, of course, her mother's funeral, three and a half years ago.

Her stomach squeezed like it always did when she thought of those visits, and she quickly pushed the thoughts aside. What was done was done. She couldn't go back and change anything. She was here now. Back in Winter Lake. And she was bound to see a face she recognized. Meaning, time to put on a good front. Chin up. Pleasant smile. It was going to be a very happy holiday indeed.

The wind was fierce, worse than in New York, and she'd forgotten how unforgiving the winters could be here in

Vermont. She pulled her belongings down onto the snow-covered pavement and into the station, which was empty and only a few degrees warmer than the temperature outside.

This was it. Her stomach heaved as she walked to the front doors and peered through the glass, hoping against hope that there was nothing but a nice long line of taxis, or better yet, nothing. She could just sit here all afternoon and wait for the next bus to arrive. Head over to Tess's house with Jules at her side for moral support. After all, this whole plan had been her sister's idea, hadn't it?

But there was only one car outside the window, its engine running. Inside was the unmistakable profile of Tess with the shoulder-length cut she'd worn since college, straight nose, strong chin. And in the backseat a child who seemed far too big to be Phoebe, even though it was.

Carrie closed her eyes, said the serenity prayer she used at the preschool when Zachary was really trying her nerves, and pushed outside into the cold, nearly slamming one of the shopping bags in the doorway in the effort. So much for a smooth, breezy entrance.

Phoebe's face was now pressed to the car window, her eyes as wide as saucers, which certainly didn't bode well. Carrie gave a weak smile and tried to wave but the package on top of the shopping bag she was holding began to topple from that effort, so she dropped her hand quickly, but a few gifts still fell.

She leaned down to pick them up, almost grateful to have something else to do, anything but look Tess in the eye or climb inside that car with her. But as she reached for the last gift, another hand pulled it from the ground.

The time had come. Carrie pulled in a breath, stood up, and looked right into the face of her older sister, who didn't seem remotely pleased to see her.

"Where's Jules?" Tess finally said, her eyes flat.

Carrie tossed up her hands. "She's arriving at six. She missed the bus."

Once, they might have shared a look over this, even an eye roll. It was just so typical of Jules. But today Tess only pinched her lips and said, "Of course she did. And she didn't even bother telling me."

Carrie didn't have to ponder why that was. Jules knew the strain that existed between her two older sisters. She probably worried what drama would ensue if she told Tess that Carrie was arriving on her own. If there was one thing that Jules hated, it was getting in the middle of things. She was much more comfortable on the outskirts, keeping a safe distance, not getting too close or attached.

"Do you think Jules did this on purpose?" Carrie dared to ask.

Tess thought about it for half a second and then said, "No. Jules isn't that cruel."

The only thing saving Carrie from getting out of Tess's car at the very first red light and dragging her luggage back to the station was Phoebe. Children were wonderfully cheerful and eager to please, whether they were oblivious to the tension around them or just hoping to fix it.

Carrie had the impression that Phoebe was unaware of the strain between her mother and aunt. A good thing, all considered. Maybe that meant that Tess wasn't as mad as she had feared.

She dared to slant a glance to her left. Tess's jaw was set and both hands gripped the steering wheel. She still wore her rings: a perfect solitaire diamond and a matching set of bands. And even though Carrie knew it was wrong of her, like, really, really wrong, she couldn't resist the pang of jealousy she felt when she saw those rings. It wasn't because they were beautiful (and they were). It was because someone had given them to Tess. Someone had chosen her. Someone loved her.

Had loved her, Carrie reminded herself. Like Carrie, Tess had lost love. Only in Tess's case, it was much worse. All the more reason not to mention her own troubles right now.

Tess hadn't spoken since she'd offered to help load Carrie's bags into the trunk and then slammed it hard enough to make Carrie jump. But then, maybe Carrie was just being jumpy. Expecting the worst. After all, Tess could have driven off and left her standing in the cold.

"We have a tree now!" Phoebe was saying excitedly. "And there are only six more nights until Christmas Eve!"

Carrie turned around and smiled at Phoebe, her heart tugging when she thought of how much she resembled Andrew. Whereas she and Tess were both fair in complexion, with blonde hair and blue eyes, Phoebe had inherited nut brown hair and big, dark eyes. She'd grown so much since Carrie had last seen her, reminding her just how long it had been. Three and a half years. Sometimes it was hard to believe their mother had been gone that long. In many ways, she had been gone so much sooner, but the permanency of it was something different.

Something that Tess must be struggling with on even a deeper level, Carrie thought, as guilt encroached.

"You know, when your mom and I were little, we used to stare at the clock all day on Christmas Eve just waiting until we could finally go to bed!" Carrie glanced at Tess, but this memory didn't spark even a hint of a smile.

Carrie pursed her lips and blew out a sigh. This was going to be just as tense as she'd feared. She'd talk to Tess. Clear the air once Phoebe was in bed. It was something she should have done before coming here, only then there was of course the chance of being told she couldn't come at all. Now there was just the chance of being kicked out of Tess's home. But that would be a more difficult scenario. Tess had always prided herself on being an excellent hostess.

"Tell me all about what you've been up to in school, Phoebe," Carrie said. "I'm a teacher, you know."

"I know. Mommy told me." Phoebe grinned, and Carrie had to wonder what else Tess had told her daughter. That Carrie was selfish and didn't have her priorities straight? Things that she'd accused Carrie of on the phone when Carrie had given the difficult news that she would not be able to make it to town for Andrew's funeral? She'd sent flowers. And a card. But she'd never heard if Tess had received them. Never heard from her again, not that she'd tried reaching out. Tess had been hurtful. She'd been unfair. But it wasn't the time to point any of that out. Now, though...

Phoebe filled the silence, talking all about her school pageant, the ornaments they had made in art class, and the class party they'd had last week. Carrie looked out the window as they approached the center of town. It was magical; there was no other word for it. But then, it always was at this time of year. No matter how bad things got in their house as kids, they always had Christmas, and Winter Lake was never shy when it came to the holiday.

Carrie took in the garland-wrapped lampposts, the store windows that boasted seasonal displays and lights, and greenery in pots and wreaths on doors. The town square tree was tall and fat with sparkling white lights that lit up the entire space and made the snow at its base seem to glow. Even on this grey, winter day, the town felt sparkly and alive and golden and bright.

Up ahead was the lake, where they'd skate in the winter and swim in the summer, and fish in the spring, even if they never caught anything. Well, Jules might have, once. With her hands.

Carrie smiled and turned to remind Tess of that story, but Tess's gaze was still fixed on the road, her expression hard.

Carrie hadn't been to Tess's house in years, but she would have been able to describe it easily, because it was, quite simply, beautiful. A tall Victorian with a wraparound porch within walking distance to the lake and a slightly longer walk to town. The last time she'd been to Winter Lake for Christmas, Phoebe had only been three, and Carrie had stayed at her childhood home, rundown by then, tucked away on a country lane, about a mile from the lake—but not far enough to keep the girls away from it. Had she known that it would be the last time she ever stayed there, would she have made the trip longer, or come back again? The house had been sold, another family lived there now, or so Jules said.

It was only at the insistence of Tess that she'd come back at all. Phoebe was at that age where she was fully aware, embracing all the magic, and how could Carrie miss out on that?

Their mother had never been much for the holiday, but Tess...Tess made up for that. Her front door was flanked by not one but three wreaths, and she'd put a smaller wreath on each window, with an electric candle at each sill. The front porch had been wrapped in garland and lights and secured with red ribbons and the entire house had smelled of cinnamon and nutmeg and cranberries.

She sat back, waiting to take it all in, but as they turned off Main Street and the house came into view, Carrie frowned. There was no wreath. No garland. No lights. She thought she saw some shadow of a tree in the front window, but it was not lit.

She looked at Tess, realizing how tired her sister looked, and how thin she, and Carrie knew then that even though Tess might not want her here, this was where she was needed.

This Christmas was going to be special. One way or another. That would be her silent promise to Tess. That would be her apology. And that would make everything better. For both of them.

It had to.

Chapter Eight

Tess

Tess could sense that Carrie was giving her a funny look as they finished depositing her rather alarming number of bags in the front hall. Was it the hair? The lack of makeup? The fact that she had aged about five years in the ten months since Andrew had left this world?

"Phoebe," she said as she closed the door, securing the house from the cold wind. "Why don't you show Aunt Carrie to one of the spare rooms?"

One of the spare rooms. A reminder that this house was empty, not full. It was meant for a family. Meant for more than one child, really. It had four bedrooms and a third floor that wasn't yet finished. She'd mentally assigned the small room at the back of the house as the next child's room. The baby's room. Only there never was another baby and now there never would be. Instead, it served as a makeshift study, with a desk and pull-out couch. A spare room. But to Tess, it served as a reminder of a dream that wouldn't come true, and a future that no longer felt certain.

She watched as Phoebe and Carrie disappeared up the stairs, Phoebe carrying some of the shopping bags containing the wrapped presents, chattering on about what might be inside while Carrie maneuvered her luggage. It was too much for one person, really, and it should have required two trips. But Carrie seemed to have a system. Or maybe she just knew better than to ask for Tess's help. And Tess didn't offer any. Instead, she remained at the bottom of the stairs, wishing that for once, things had gone as planned and that Jules had arrived when she said she would.

Now, she had hours to wait until her youngest sister arrived, leaving her in the house with Carrie, their unspoken words, and the memory of the last conversation they'd had. Even with Carrie upstairs, her chest still tightened with anger that wouldn't fade with a conversation or an apology, not that she was yet to receive one. Nope, her sister seemed determined to pretend that nothing was wrong.

Tess's jaw hurt from clenching it so tightly. There was only one thing she could do when she got like this.

She walked into the kitchen and pulled out her baking gear. Cupcake tins. Mixing bowl. Flour. Sugar. Unsalted butter that she preferred at room temperature. She didn't need her recipe box—not anymore, at least. The base of her cupcake recipe was simple, passed down and tweaked, and then tweaked some more as she experimented with different flavors. Today she decided to make a simple red velvet base, something festive for Phoebe's sake. Something she could offer up to her sisters, because other than casseroles in the freezer, there was little else she could give them right now—not emotionally, not even physically, she thought, her stomach tightening as her mind wandered to her account balance. She'd bought everything on Phoebe's list for Santa. How couldn't she? But now she thought of what she might return, what Phoebe might not notice was missing. There was enough, for now, but soon…

She washed her hands, letting the warm water run for longer than usual. Until she heard back from the job, hope sprung. Until she heard back, she wouldn't panic. Except that it was hard not to panic when she thought of how long she had waited for that one interview to come along. If it took just as long to get another call, then the school year would be nearly over, and summer break would be upon them, and…

And her heart was beating so fast now that she had to take a calming breath and remind herself to wait. Wait to hear back from the interview.

The standing mixer had been a wedding gift—over a decade old, but she'd taken such care of it that it could have been new. She added her wet ingredients to the bowl and turned it on. The whirr of the machine instantly calmed her, just like it always did, even when she was just a kid not that much older than Phoebe, using her mother's handheld beaters. When, like Phoebe, her entire world felt uncertain.

Only she didn't want Phoebe to feel the way she had as a child. She wanted more for her daughter. Better for her daughter. She always had. Always would.

It was the only thing that got her out of bed most days, even though she wondered how life could ever be much better for Phoebe. She'd tried. And somehow, events had turned against her. Like her, Phoebe had lost her father. Only Andrew hadn't chosen to leave them.

"Are you making cupcakes?" Phoebe bounded into the room, her braids flying. "Can I help fill the tins?"

"Filling the tins" was Phoebe's code for licking the remaining batter from the bowl when she was finished.

Tess gave her a knowing smile. "Only if you promise to actually fill them this time and not leave a cupcake worth of batter in the bottom in the hopes of eating it. You know you'll get a tummy ache from that. I'd be a bad mommy if I let you eat raw eggs." Bacteria. Salmonella. Visions of Phoebe spending the holidays in the hospital filled her mind. She was being ridiculous, she knew, but she couldn't help it. You could never be too careful.

"Did your mommy let you eat raw eggs?" Phoebe asked as she climbed up onto a stool at the large island that had been one of the greatest appeals of this home, along with the carved wood banister and the stained-glass window at the second-floor landing. She and Andrew had made an offer the very day they'd seen the house and moved in six weeks later, armed with paint cans and rollers and smiles and dreams.

Her heart ached when she thought of how much they'd loved this house. She couldn't leave it. And she couldn't lose it.

And until she heard back on the job, she would not panic.

Tess measured out the flour and began sifting it. She realized that Phoebe was still waiting for an answer to her question.

"Yes. Grandma let me eat raw eggs." Her mother had let her do many things she'd never in a million years let Phoebe do, like ride her bike to town without adult supervision on the main roads, and, of course, without a helmet. Like try a few sips of beer from the cans she kept on hand for Tess's father, back when he was still at least sometimes coming home at night. Like letting Tess disappear without saying where she was going when she was Phoebe's age or younger, giving only a promise of returning by dinner, eventually not even demanding that much. By then, dinner was the last thing on her mind, forgotten about when she was in her bedroom in one of her dark moods, or immersed in the custom furniture pieces she made on commission: end tables, bassinettes, and dining tables with turned legs. There was always cereal, she'd made sure of that. Whether it was eaten or not went unnoticed, as many things did.

Her mother never knew about the time that Tess, about twelve then, got dared into trying to swim across the lake, how she'd gotten a cramp halfway out, and didn't think she would make it back to shore. How it was Carrie, always the more athletic of the sisters, who swam out and got her.

Tess pinched her lips.

"You ate raw eggs? Disgusting!" Phoebe wrinkled her nose and stuck out her tongue.

Tess laughed. A fleeting moment of complete distraction. She'd take it. "Not an actual raw egg, silly. But in batter, yes. I certainly ate my share."

And yet she was still here.

And Andrew wasn't.

She focused on the cupcakes before her mind ran into dark corners and stayed there. Baking was the one thing she and her mother had in common. One peaceful activity that kept her mother grounded, where, outside of her craft, she seemed to shine. Whenever Tess saw the darkness encroaching, when she would knock on her mother's door and get no answer, or see the mound shape of her body still in bed, under the covers when she came home from school, she would take it upon herself to bake all on her own, pretending that her mother was at her side, rifling through her recipe box, scooping out sugar, tasting their homemade creations. She'd share them with her sisters, and leave one outside of her mother's bedroom door.

"Where is Carrie?" Tess asked Phoebe in a low voice as she inspected the batter for any lumps.

"In the spare room," Phoebe said.

Good, Tess thought. With any luck, she'd stay there.

Still, as she added the remaining ingredients and watched the batter evolve, she felt a twinge of something she couldn't place. Nostalgia? Regret? Sadness? Maybe all of the above. Her sister was upstairs in her house. It was Christmas. It shouldn't be this way.

It should be very different. For many reasons.

Carrie eventually came downstairs. Tess supposed they both knew this moment had to happen eventually. The cupcakes were baked and cooling on the rack. Phoebe had gone off to her room to make some paper ornaments to decorate her room. Tess was finishing up a peppermint butter cream that she thought would complement the red velvet cupcakes. She'd crush some candy canes on the top when she was finished. Phoebe would love it.

"Baking?" Carrie hovered in the opening to the kitchen as

if she wasn't exactly sure she was welcome over the threshold. Technically, she wasn't. Tess hadn't invited her here. In fact, the last time they'd spoken, Tess had made it clear that Carrie was never again welcome here.

And yet here she was.

In fairness, she looked just as uncomfortable as Tess felt. Pale, with her hair pulled back and her eyes wide. Her fingers played with the edges of her sleeves. A nervous habit she'd had since...Well, since their dad left, Tess supposed.

For a moment, her heart softened. Just a little.

Tess shrugged. "It's what I do."

It was something she shared with her mother all on her own. Carrie wasn't interested and Jules was too young. It felt special, to stand out, to have something in common, and to know that no matter what else happened, they always had their cakes and pies and cookie baking days. Their good days.

Slowly, Carrie walked closer to the island where Tess stood. She eyed the unfrosted cupcakes eagerly. When they were younger, Carrie would always be the first to taste one, even before Jules—even before Tess. Tess didn't mind this; she'd actually appreciated it. Carrie was her number one taste tester, her trusted source for feedback when Tess experimented with new flavor combinations. Some were wins (like the lemon meringue cupcake that she always took to summer barbeques) and others were flops (really, zucchini had no business being in a cupcake).

All three Campbell sisters were creative in their own ways. Their mother had made sure of that, always keeping the house stocked with books, fabric, markers and colored pencils, plain paper and printed paper, yarn and thread, and for Tess, butter and sugar. Maybe it was just a way to keep them busy, or maybe it was a glimmer of their mother's true spirit.

When a recipe didn't turn out exactly as she'd wanted, Carrie would offer up suggestions—something to cut the sweetness, or a dash of more vanilla. Tess always heeded Carrie's advice. She relied on her. Always did. Always could.

Until last February.

She set her jaw as she transferred the butter cream to a piping bag and began swirling the frosting onto each cupcake.

"You make that look so easy," Carrie observed.

"I've had a lot of practice," Tess said tightly. Lately, more practice than ever. When Phoebe slept in, Tess baked. She dropped off her cupcakes at class parties and bake sales, at nursing homes and neighbors' houses. Her friend Natalie had a freezer full and admitted once that in a pinch, she'd offered some up for a class party at the twins' preschool. Tess didn't mind. She'd been flattered.

She glanced up to see her sister staring longingly at the tray. "Go on and have one," she said, somewhat halfheartedly. After all, it wasn't a peace offering. If anyone needed to extend an olive branch, it was Carrie.

"Thanks," Carrie said and helped herself to the cupcake on the end of the wire tray, careful not to upset any of the others.

Tess waited until Carrie had taken a bite, closing her eyes while she chewed, just like she did when she was a little girl. Back then, she'd get frosting on her nose and lips and laugh at the mess.

Tess felt her chest pull at the memory. At so many memories. It seemed all she had left anymore were those memories.

Right. No thinking about any of that. Things had changed. Carrie had changed.

Tess had changed, too. She'd been forced to. She adjusted the piping bag in her hands and finished topping the remaining cupcakes.

"I've missed these cupcakes," Carrie said, licking her fingers.

A filthy habit, Tess thought. Something she never allowed Phoebe to do but something their mother had never instilled in them. She resisted the urge to pluck a sheet of paper towel from the roll and hand it to her sister. Carrie was a grown woman. She knew what she was doing.

Which was exactly why Tess couldn't forgive her for not coming to Andrew's funeral.

It had been a choice. A conscious, deliberate choice. And all choices had consequences.

Her mind flashed to the last time she'd seen Andrew, the quick kiss he'd planted on her cheek as he headed out the door to his car, into the night. It was a cold night. Too cold for snow. A front had moved through after the warm-up the day before.

The slopes would be icy, Tess remembered warning him, but he'd just shrugged her concerns away. He wanted to go.

She closed her eyes for a moment and then, because she saw no alternative other than to go upstairs into her bedroom and crawl under the covers and never come out, she walked to the pantry and pulled out the candy canes that Phoebe had dropped into her cart the last time they'd been to the grocery store.

"I missed these cupcakes," Carrie said again, her voice quieter this time. "But…I've missed you too."

Tess stared into the contents of the pantry for a moment

and then slammed the cabinet doors closed. She averted her gaze from Carrie as she walked back to the counter. Her rolling pin was in the drawer under the oven. She grabbed it now and turned to her sister. Carrie eyed the wooden rolling pin warily.

Tess nearly smiled at that.

"I don't know what you expect me to say, Carrie," she said heavily. She felt weary. Exhausted. Sad. She wished in many ways that Carrie had said nothing at all, that they had gone on talking about cupcakes and frosting. The weather. Anything but something real. Anything but something painful.

"I'm...I'm sorry, Tess."

Tess started shelling candy canes from their wrappers and tossing them into a storage bag. Carrie's voice was soft and pleading and filled with regret. She couldn't look at her sister. She was afraid if she did that she might cry, that all the hurt and pain that had been tied up inside her would come spilling out.

But most of all, Tess was afraid that she would forgive Carrie. And as much as she needed her sister right now, just as much as she'd needed her that awful day last winter, she couldn't forgive her. She just couldn't.

"Sorry that you didn't come to the funeral? Or sorry that you weren't there for me the one time I needed you the most? Or sorry that we aren't close anymore?"

"All of it!" Carrie cried. "I'm sorry for all of it!" Carrie's face crumpled and Tess felt herself waver.

Tess shook her head. She didn't want to hear it. It wouldn't change anything. She moved the bag of candy canes to a cutting board and picked up the rolling pin. She gave the candies a good hard whack. And then another. She was aware that she probably looked half-deranged, that maybe Carrie was even a little scared of her. Well, good!

"Where is Lucas, anyway?" Tess paused for a moment to ask. She looked Carrie straight in the eye, communicating what they both knew. Carrie hadn't been there for Tess because she wasn't willing to leave Lucas. Not for a funeral. Not for the aftermath. Not even for a weekend.

Carrie's gaze shifted. "He had to work. A big case."

"That's never been a reason for you to leave New York before," Tess pointed out.

Carrie's cheeks were blotchy now. She set down the remainder of her cupcake. "Well, I wanted to spend this Christmas with my family. With my sisters. I…I wanted to be here for your first Christmas since…"

Carrie trailed off, and Tess didn't finish that sentence for her. Instead, she sprinkled the cupcakes with the crushed candy canes, stood back, and admired them.

"Well," she said, glancing at the clock. "It's almost time to pick up Jules."

Never in a million years did she think that her youngest sister could be the answer to her problems, but life had a funny way of readjusting your expectations, she'd learned.

Chapter Nine

Jules

Jules wasn't sure if it was a good thing or a bad thing that neither of her sisters had texted or called since Carrie was
scheduled to arrive at the Winter Lake station. At first, she
thought this was a bad thing. Perhaps they'd been fighting the
entire time. Perhaps they would still be fighting; perhaps they
would not even take a break to pick her up from the station.

But then she thought that maybe the silence was a good
thing. She resisted the urge to reach out to them, to check in
and make sure that everything was okay. This wasn't her con-
flict and she didn't want to make it her problem. She wanted
to be the neutral party, and she was fairly certain that Tess
would not be ready to hear this, but she could see both sides
of the argument. Tess had experienced a family tragedy. And
Carrie, much as she wanted to be there, couldn't just cancel all
her plans at the last minute.

It was messy. It was life. And it was hard.

Life was hard. In many ways, it always had been. She'd expected it to get easier the older she got, but she was finding it was just the opposite. Bigger problems. Bigger decisions.

Jules put her phone into her bag and sighed. Nothing but silence from Aaron as well, not that she'd reached out to him either. She couldn't tell him what he wanted to hear, and until she could, well, he didn't want to hear from her, did he?

It seemed impossible. Downright cruel. But it would be crueler of her to tease him, to mess with his feelings, to not consider his heart.

He *loved* her.

She pulled in a sharp breath. She couldn't think about this now. The bus was approaching the Winter Lake station. The entire point of coming here was to take a break from thinking about her problems, and Aaron (of all people!) was now one of them.

Well, and of course she'd come to be here for Tess. Tess had taken care of her nearly her entire life. But Tess didn't see her as a sister, not like she saw Carrie. And Jules was determined to change that. She wanted to be friends, not a responsibility. She wanted to be close, not a burden. But lately, Tess had been determined to shut her out.

She stood up as the bus slowed, and grabbed her duffel bag and tote. She traveled light. She didn't require many beauty products and she didn't see a reason to impress with clothes, especially here in Winter Lake of all places, where sweaters and jeans and solid cold weather gear would do. Besides, anything she'd forgotten she could borrow from one of her sisters. Tess would share, even though growing up it had mostly been Tess and Carrie who swapped clothes or makeup, who sat behind the closed door of the bedroom they shared, discussing things that they said Jules wouldn't understand.

Well, it was different now, or at least, it should be. She was an adult, one of the gang, just like them. Something they'd have to accept eventually.

Tess was waiting outside her car when Jules walked out of the station. Snowflakes swirled in the air and she was reminded of all the times she would stick her head back and let one drop onto her tongue. She was tempted to do it again, here and now, but she suspected that would only be met with a frown of deep disapproval from Tess, who seemed to think of Jules as an eternal child.

Tess was thinner than the last time she'd seen her, Jules noted with concern. Her hair was pulled back in a low ponytail and her face looked lined and tired. Tess had always been the prettiest of the three sisters, in Jules's opinion. She had fine, classic features, unlike Jules's upturned nose and a dusting of freckles. Jules knew she looked more like their father. It was the only connection she had to him. But Tess, Tess looked the most like their mother, always had. That hadn't changed. But the sparkle of her smile and the light in her eyes had dimmed.

Jules felt her heart pull. Reminded herself that it was her turn to step up now. She'd rise to the occasion. Tess needed her for once. And terrible circumstances aside, that felt good. She'd perk her sister up, suggest some fun activities, and by the end of the trip, Tess would not only be back to her old self, but she would also see Jules in a whole new light. Last winter, Jules had pulled her weight by tending to Phoebe on her visit, but even then, Tess hadn't fallen apart. She'd been pragmatic, worried about storing the casseroles that were dropped off on the hour, it seemed. She'd been focused on what needed to be done. What was within her control. Like always.

"Tess!" Jules gave her an understanding smile and leaned forward to hug her, but Tess's embrace was chilly.

"So you weren't going to tell me that you were springing Carrie on me alone?"

Uh-oh. Jules stared into her sister's eyes, trying to read them. But instead of the annoyance she was used to, she saw weariness.

"It's time that you and Carrie worked out your problems," she said firmly. "Besides, I missed the bus." Was that really so difficult to believe? The roads in Boston were a mess. It wasn't like she lived next door to the station.

Tess gave her a long, suffering look, one that Jules knew all too well. One that was given when Jules broke their mother's favorite vase when she was practicing cartwheels in the living room, or when she came home from school talking too loudly when their mother had another one of her headaches and was in bed, the curtains pulled, even though it was only three o'clock and it was a warm, sunny spring day.

"What? You try getting a cab in Boston in a snowstorm!" Jules jutted her chin, determined not to nurse Tess the way Carrie may be inclined to do, because as much as Tess was the mother hen, Carrie was the one who clucked about, fussing over everyone and offering smiles and wanting everyone to just be happy. Especially Lucas. Jules narrowed her eyes at the memory of a time she'd visited Manhattan for a long weekend, when she was, once again, between contracts. She had seen Carrie actually pour the milk in Lucas's coffee for him as if he were a child in her classroom! No, what Tess needed was a good hard shaking. Some tough love.

And maybe some blush to make up for the lack of color in her cheeks.

Tess opened the trunk of her car and Jules dropped her bags into it. It was only then that she noticed that Phoebe and Carrie were in the backseat. She hadn't seen her niece in ten months, and Carrie in even longer than that, and even though they talked on the phone every few weeks, it wasn't the same.

She flung open the door and Carrie stepped out, looking so relieved at the sight of her that Jules could only wonder what had transpired in the hours since her sister had arrived.

Phoebe was next, shivering in the cold and excitedly telling Jules all about the tooth she had lost last week, proudly pointing to the gap in her mouth.

"That calls for a celebration!" Jules said, grinning at the little girl. She was happy to see her in such good spirits, all things considered.

Tess started to shake her head in protest, but Jules decided to pretend she hadn't seen it. "Let's head into town. Dinner's on me. You pick the place, Phoebe."

She didn't meet Tess's eye as they all climbed back into the car. Sitting through a dinner with both of her sisters may be more difficult than she'd feared, but it was probably better than each of them disappearing into their own corner of the house.

What Carrie and Tess needed was to confront their feelings once and for all.

And given that Jules was yet to see Tess shed a tear since Andrew's death, she suspected that Tess needed it the most.

Phoebe picked Preston's. An excellent choice, and easily Jules's favorite spot in town. It had been around since before they were kids, changing ownership only when Jeff Preston took over the business from his father and revamped the menu, making it the heart of the town since around the time Jules was a teenager and went there with her friends for burgers and wood-fired pizzas with the money she earned from her part-time job at the newspaper, working as a fact checker.

"I'm going to get the mac and cheese and a kiddie cocktail," Phoebe said. "They have the best kiddie cocktails, Auntie Jules."

Jules blinked out the window of the car. What exactly had Tess been telling her? That Jules was just one of the kids?

"It sounds like you come here often," she said, deciding not to feed into that last comment. She was being overly sensitive; something that happened every time she got around Tess. She couldn't help it. Tess was bossy with her. Always had been. She knew it was because Tess cared, because she felt it was her role and all that, but lately, it had gotten old.

"It's our favorite place," Phoebe said. "It's our only place, really."

Tess gave a tight smile. "Jeff owns it."

Of course. Jeff had been Andrew's best friend. He'd been with him that awful night. He'd been the one to call Jules— Tess wasn't able to say it out loud. And Jules had been the one to call Carrie. And then. Well.

They drove in silence, and Jules glanced over at her sister, wondering if she would turn on the radio at least, and hoping that she would. Normally Tess was the hostess, asking questions, and putting everyone at ease. Now she seemed oblivious to the tension in the air. Didn't see the need to cut it.

But Jules did. She flicked on the radio without asking for permission. Slanted a glance at Tess to see the purse of her lips.

She scanned through the channels until she found a station playing Christmas carols, but Tess's finger jabbed at the button, turning the music off.

"I need to concentrate on driving," she said tersely.

In the backseat, Carrie was quiet. Jules said nothing for the rest of the ride. She was starting to worry that it might be a little more difficult to get through to Tess than she had hoped.

Fortunately, Preston's was not far from the station, and within a few minutes, they were parked one block away, beside a lamppost wrapped with garland and twinkling lights. It was beautiful, like something out of the storybooks that Jules used to read in her room, where she spent a fair amount of time alone, sometimes by choice, sometimes because she had no other choice.

"Here we all are!" Jules said cheerfully, linking her arms through both of her sisters. Phoebe giggled, wanting in on the fun, and held onto her mother's other side as they walked toward the big wooden doors of the restaurant. "Together again. See? It's all going to be okay."

She flicked a warning glance first to Carrie and then to Tess as she dropped their arms and reached for the door. Carrie looked downright miserable and Tess, well, Tess had always been difficult to read. She was stoic; she had been as far back as when they were kids when their mother hadn't gotten out of bed all day and there was no dinner and Carrie was crying and Jules was scared. Tess would sit silently on the armchair, her brow knitted pensively, and then, she would stand, walk to the kitchen, and pull out bread or cheese, or whatever she could find.

When their mother died, Tess handled all the arrangements in a brisk, efficient manner. She was stoic at Andrew's funeral too, standing in her black coat and hat, holding Phoebe's hand. Her eyes covered by dark sunglasses. Afterward, Jules had tried to get her to open up, to say how she felt, to let it out. But Tess had just looked at her sharply and said, "I'm a mother. I can't fall apart. I won't do that to my child."

And Jules had said nothing more. Because she understood best of all.

Only now, she understood even more. Tess had always been the caregiver. But she needed someone to take care of her, too, even if she resisted at first. Jules just had to keep trying.

Inside the restaurant, the music was loud and the lights were festive. Jeff waved to Tess from behind the bar and then, when his eyes drifted to Jules and Carrie, he froze for a moment before waving again. Jules had always liked Jeff, not that she knew him well. He was the same age as Tess and Andrew, landing him squarely in the "big brother" category and not the "romantic suitor" category, but now, looking at his solid frame and warm grin, she was starting to see the appeal and understand why he'd always had a reputation for being a bit of a flirt.

All rugged good looks and strong forearms aside, though, Jeff was a good man. Jules had seen the way he'd handled Andrew's service, watching Tess carefully, keeping things light for Phoebe's sake, handling most of the arrangements, and doing most of the talking when Tess couldn't find her voice.

Andrew would have been grateful.

And of Tess, she thought, looking down at the grinning Phoebe, he would have been proud.

She pushed back the lump that formed in her throat every time she thought of Andrew and widened her smile as Jeff approached, in a navy sweater that brought out the deep blue of his eyes.

"Tess told me you were coming back," he said, leaning in to give her a bear hug. Jules allowed herself to fall into it, to even enjoy it, but even though Jeff was strong and solid, there wasn't the same comfort in hugging him as there was in hugging Aaron.

Her heart pulled a little as she stepped back. She missed Aaron already. She couldn't imagine her life without him in it. Didn't want to live that life. How could he do this to her?

"Carrie. It's nice to see you again."

Jules couldn't help but observe that Jeff, while still polite, was considerably less welcoming to Carrie. If Carrie caught on, Jules couldn't be sure. Carrie seemed to be in her own world tonight. Quiet. Pensive.

She'd get the dirty truth out of her before she turned down the duvet tonight.

"I have to go to the bathroom," Phoebe announced.

"I'll take her!" Jules volunteered, and Tess darted her eyes at Carrie.

"I don't mind," Carrie blurted, taking Phoebe's hand. She made no show of releasing it, and Jules knew how to take a hint.

"We'll both go," Jules said, smiling at Tess, whose shoulders seemed to sink in relief. Happy to get rid of them, was she? Jules supposed that they hadn't exactly been invited.

Tess turned back to Jeff, smiling the first genuine smile that Jules had seen since...well, since Andrew was still alive, she thought. Jules and Carrie both followed Phoebe to the back of the restaurant, weaving between tables, trying not to bump into a waiter carrying a row of plates up his arm.

"How's it going?" Jules whispered, once Phoebe had pushed into the bathroom, leaving Carrie and Jules to wait outside the door.

Carrie rolled her eyes. "I wish you had told me you had missed the bus sooner—"

Oh, this again!

"I couldn't get a cab!" Jules cried, but Carrie just gave her a long look. "And yes, I'll admit that I was hoping you and Tess might make some progress before I showed up."

Carrie sighed heavily. "I probably shouldn't have come. It would have been better to stay home alone—"

Jules frowned. "Alone? What about Lucas?"

Carrie blinked. "Right. I mean. Well, I meant stay home. Instead of coming here." Her cheeks flamed and Jules studied her carefully. It wasn't like Carrie to leave Lucas's side. Usually, she was attached to his hip, and when she wasn't, she was waiting for his next move. Her entire world revolved around Lucas. The last time Jules had been in New York, she was horrified to see that Carrie let Lucas order their food, and she didn't even protest when he ordered an appetizer that included mushrooms, and Carrie had always hated mushrooms. She didn't even like the smell of them.

"Well, I for one think it's a good thing we came. Tess doesn't look well." She lowered her voice to be sure that Phoebe wouldn't overhear.

"No, she doesn't," Carrie agreed. "But I'm not sure that my presence is what she needs right now." Her shoulders slumped as she leaned back against the wall. It was the saddest that Jules had seen her middle sister since their mother's funeral. And they'd all been sad then. All suffered the loss together, shell-shocked by its suddenness, relieved that their mother had not felt any pain, but Jules suspected that they were all thinking the same thing. Their mother had been in pain. A lot of it. For far too long.

"You're her sister," Jules said firmly. "You're exactly what she needs." Whether Tess was willing to admit it or not.

"All finished!" Phoebe said, bounding out of the door.

Carrie gave Jules a look that showed how impossible it was for her to match their niece's enthusiasm, and they walked back into the dining room, where Tess was now seated at a table, laughing up at Jeff, who hovered at its edge.

Jules narrowed her eyes, noticing the way that Jeff's gaze seemed to linger on her sister, the way the tension in Tess's face had relaxed and that a grin had replaced the pinched look she'd worn all the way from the station.

They both fell quiet when Jules and Carrie reached the table and Phoebe started inquiring about the status of her kiddie cocktail, which Jules gathered was something cherry-flavored and not something that the old Tess would have easily approved of.

But the old Tess was gone, Jules was beginning to think, glancing from Jeff to her sister and down to her menu. And she wasn't exactly sure what to make of that.

She waited until their orders were placed and their drinks had arrived to do what she had come here to do. Phoebe was busy coloring the back of the menu, and Carrie, ever one to dodge the tough stuff, was engrossed with her.

"I'm so glad we're here," Jules smiled broadly as she looked around the room and planted her gaze on Tess. She hoped her smile made up for the fact that she had sort of sprung this on Tess, especially the part about Carrie.

"You were able to take time off work then?"

My, Tess sure didn't waste any time, did she?

Jules pulled in a breath and took a long sip of her wine, crafting her response. "I just wrapped up a gig."

She couldn't help but notice the look that passed between Tess and Carrie, who was quick to look back down at the table before she'd been caught. Even now, when they were more enemies than sisters, they were a united force. And she...well, she was the odd man out.

She sniffed, lifting her chin. "No one has anything going Christmas week."

Tess frowned a little at this. Finally, she said, "True. I've been waiting to hear back on a job, actually. Maybe I should be more patient."

Well, this was a surprise! And, secretly, a wonderful shift away from her own troubles.

"That's great, Tess!" Carrie offered with a smile.

Tess pursed her lips and flicked her eyes back to Jules. "We'll see."

"It's a step in the right direction," Jules said. "I'm sure it will be good for you to get out of the house. Get your mind off things. Stay busy." Tess loved to be busy.

"Well, obviously we need an income," Tess said, managing a tight laugh. She straightened the napkin in her lap. "But that's all."

Now it was Jules's turn to frown. She didn't buy it. She couldn't buy it. Tess had adored Andrew. They'd dated since high school, and known each other long before that. Even Jules struggled to think of him without tearing up.

"Tess," she said flatly. "It's okay. It's us. Your sisters."

Tess blinked at her, but for one telling moment, she thought she saw Tess's lips quiver. Just as quickly, Tess cleared her throat and said, "I appreciate it, Jules, but Phoebe and I are just fine. We're keeping busy."

Jules nodded. Of course.

"Almost too busy. The holidays are an overwhelming time for parents."

Even more so for single parents, Jules wanted to say. They'd known it firsthand.

Instead, she sighed and took another sip of her wine. If things continued like this, it was going to be a very long week, indeed.

Chapter Ten

Carrie

The house was quiet when Carrie woke the next morning. She'd slept well considering that she had been given a pull-out couch with a lumpy mattress and what she was fairly certain were not Tess's best sheets, while Jules slept in the proper guest room, complete with a queen-size bed that Carrie would have been happy to share.

Still, she was just as happy to have her own space. Her own corner of the house where she could let her guard down, let her smile fade, and think about Lucas and what he could be doing right now. It was Monday, and even though it was Christmas week, she was almost certain he was at work. The only reason she couldn't be completely certain was that she was starting to wonder if she didn't know Lucas as well as she had thought she did. The Lucas she knew lived in a world where the scarf girl didn't exist. The Lucas she knew did not go to Starbucks. And the Lucas she knew would be at the office Christmas week. But the real Lucas had shared a Saturday morning coffee with another woman, mere hours after dumping her. The real Lucas had somehow met her, long before that fateful dinner. Had possibly spent Friday night with her. And could easily be on a vacation with her this very week. The real Lucas may even have decorated a Christmas tree with this other woman yesterday!

Still, the Lucas she knew couldn't have just been replaced! It was highly likely that he was at work. Right now, at his desk, with his second cup of coffee and his computer powered up. He'd be wearing a blue tie because he always wore blue ties. Surely he couldn't have changed that much?

She could call him, see for herself, without the risk of scarf girl being around, and make up an excuse like she needed back something from his apartment. Or she could just call and then hang up, just to be sure that he wasn't off to Bali or Fiji or Paris with her replacement.

But what if he was in a meeting? How could she be sure?

She could call the main line and ask the receptionist for him. Pretend to be a prospective client. Yes, that was a good one!

But that was lame. And it would defeat the entire purpose of coming here to Winter Lake. She needed to put Manhattan behind her, both physically and mentally.

The aroma of freshly brewed coffee greeted her when she opened her door. She pulled a sweatshirt over the tee shirt she'd worn to bed and padded down the stairs, her hand gripping the rail. Afraid of her own sister. She was afraid of her own sister! If it wasn't enough to make her want to cry, she'd almost feel the need to laugh. Growing up, she and Tess were as close as two sisters could be, sharing every secret, every fear, every dream. They knew each other's first crush, first kiss. They'd spent hours in the room they shared behind a closed door, safe and secure, knowing that inside those four walls, they were in control and that their world could be happy.

Now, Carrie frowned when she reached the hall and saw the sad excuse for a Christmas tree in the window. The lights were off (again) and the ornaments were clustered on the bottom branches. Phoebe's doing, most likely, but still odd. And the rest of the house was bare. There was no Christmas spirit. No laughter. No joy.

She had the uneasy memory of Christmases past, the ones spent in this very town, at their childhood home. "When I grow up, my Christmases will be magical," Tess used to say. "Every room will be decorated. Every Christmas will be the best Christmas ever."

And she'd stuck to that promise, hadn't she?

Until this year.

Carrie wanted to give Tess that feeling of comfort that Tess had offered her all those years ago, when their dad was gone and their mom was quiet and sullen, and Tess jutted her chin instead of breaking down in tears. She wanted to make things right, not just between them. But for Tess. And for Phoebe.

Jules was sitting alone at the kitchen table when Carrie walked into the kitchen, bracing herself. She darted her eyes and, sensing that no one else was home, released a pent-up breath.

"Where's Tess?" she asked as she opened a cabinet in

search of a mug. She didn't know her way around the house, hadn't spent enough time in it. That didn't sit well.

"She took Phoebe to the grocery store," Jules replied. "You just missed them."

Was it terrible to admit that she was relieved?

"That's good she's getting out." Carrie found the mugs and closed the cabinet. "Last time we were here for Christmas, she went all out. Did you see the tree?"

Jules pulled a face. "I know. It's small, and the decorations aren't what they used to be. She rarely returns my calls anymore, too. At least before she would tell me she was too busy to talk. Now she just doesn't talk. She's completely withdrawn."

Carrie nodded. It was true. Tess was in survival mode, the way she used to get when they were little and their mother would forget to pay the power bill and the lights would go out, and Tess would sit in silence until she traced her way to the dining room cabinet, grabbed a few candles and matches, and lit them. She was always tense until a resolution was found. Always unwilling to show her emotions.

"Maybe she's mad that we came," Jules continued.

"More like she's mad that I came," Carrie said. Really, what was she doing here? Did she think they'd go back to the way things were before? Andrew had died, and nothing was the same. And the Campbells knew all too well how permanent it was when a family member was lost.

Still... "She seemed to warm up a bit last night at dinner. She's gotten close to Jeff." She filled her mug and added a heavy splash of milk and a generous amount of sugar. She eyed the cupcakes on the counter, resting under a covered dome. Normally, she would have helped herself to one. Now, she felt stiff and formal. She walked over to the table and took a seat opposite Jules. Jules was wearing an old college tee shirt and had her curls pulled back in a messy bun. She wore her glasses, but even with them on, her blue eyes were striking.

Jules seemed to consider this for a moment. "Makes sense. He was Andrew's best friend. He probably feels responsible. He was there that night, after all."

Carrie sipped her coffee, saying nothing. "Well," she finally spoke. "I think it's a good thing. At least there's one person that seems to bring out her old self."

"Maybe we can too," Jules said with more confidence than seemed realistic.

Still, Carrie appreciated her optimism. Someone had to hold this family together, after all.

Carrie gave her sister a little smile. "I was hoping you would say that. I was thinking that maybe we could get her into the spirit of Christmas. Give her a really nice holiday."

"I know where the decorations are," Jules said, pushing back her chair.

Carrie glanced at the clock as they hurried into the hallway, factoring in that the grocery store was small and only about a mile away. "We don't have much time."

It took only a few minutes to locate the clearly labeled boxes in the attic. There were three of them, and one appeared to have been opened recently.

Carrie hesitated before lifting the largest container. "Maybe we shouldn't. What if Tess doesn't want her house decorated?"

"Tess doesn't know what she wants," Jules replied as she scooped up a box in her arms. "That's why we're here. To show her what she wants and needs. To let her see that she can find it in us."

Carrie nodded, hating the fact that she wasn't only here for that reason, and that her other motive, possibly her main purpose, was purely selfish. That maybe she was the person Tess thought her to be. The kind of person who didn't come back to town when her sister needed her the most.

But then she thought of Lucas. He'd needed her that weekend too.

"You're right," Carrie said, reaching for a box. It was heavier than she'd anticipated, but she would manage. She'd have to manage. She was a single girl again, on her own. No one to open doors or help carry luggage or boxes down from attics, not that she would ever have a house with an attic at the rate she was going. She was much more likely to end up living out her final days in the same rent-controlled apartment, childless, alone...

She didn't even realize she was showing the horror of this thought on her face until she caught Jules staring at her.

"Is everything okay?" Jules asked, frowning.

"What? Oh. Fine. Just...this is heavier than I expected."

"Here. This one's light." Jules set down her own box, strode over to Carrie, and pulled the box from her arms. Her annoyance was evident in the pinch of her lips and Carrie didn't know whether to feel amused or insulted. Jules was an independent woman. Didn't "do" relationships, and seemed to silently judge Carrie's decision to commit to Lucas and prioritize their relationship.

Now Carrie wondered if Jules had been right all along. She'd made Lucas her top priority. And he'd gone and replaced her.

"Let's at least get the mantle decorated and wrap the garland around the banister," Jules said as they walked single file down the stairs, Jules balancing two boxes while Carrie managed just the one.

"Let's leave some little things for Phoebe to set out, though," Carrie advised when she popped open her box and saw the nutcrackers inside. "Kids love feeling included."

"Finally figured that out, huh?" Jules gave her a wry look, and it took a moment for Carrie to catch on that Jules was referring to herself.

"Jules," she said gently. "We included you. You were just so much younger." Five years was a big difference back then. In many ways, it still was. When they were younger, Carrie and Tess were riding bikes into town before Jules was out of diapers. And now, she and Tess were saddled with responsibilities while Jules didn't even have a steady job. But she'd always made time for Jules, still talked to her on the phone on a pretty regular basis. Told her pretty much everything.

Well, except for one thing.

"And Tess adored you. You were like her first child," Carrie pointed out.

Jules gave her a pointed look and opened her box. Carrie let her comment drop and they worked silently, quietly, as if they were afraid that Tess might walk in at any moment, and secretly, Carrie was afraid of just that. It would be much easier for Tess to protest if they were in the middle of the project rather than finished. Besides, she wanted the joy of surprising her, of doing something nice for her, of trying, however small, to make things right between them, and to show that she cared.

"So," Jules said as she quickly wound the garland around the banister. "How's Lucas?"

It was bound to happen, Carrie knew. Still, she felt rattled and her heart was starting to race. How was Lucas? She'd like to know the answer to that herself. Was he happy, laughing, and going about his day without a care in the world? Was he relieved to be free of her? Did she even cross his mind at all?

Her mind wandered to the image of him in the café, and she swallowed back the lump in her throat.

"Lucas is great," Carrie said, happy that her back was to her sister. She narrowed her eyes on the ornament she held— a delicate porcelain snowflake—and set it on a high branch where Phoebe wouldn't be able to reach it. Breakables and all that. "He's just great."

There was a long silence before Jules said, "Still think he's going to propose soon?"

Oh no. Carrie couldn't be vague with that question, could she? It wasn't like Jules to be so direct either, not when it came to Lucas or anything with relationships. She usually seemed disinterested or put out when Carrie started talking about her boyfriend.

Ex-boyfriend.

"You never know," Carrie said in what she hoped passed for a breezy tone, but her voice felt pitched and tight. She tried to think of a way to turn the conversation back on Jules, but Jules didn't have relationships, or if she did they were casual, usually lasting a few weeks, or, at best, a few months.

"I'm just thinking," Jules continued, and Carrie felt her eyes flutter. "Andrew was definitely the one for Tess. It was so obvious. Not just to her but to us, to everyone."

True. So true. And could the same be true for Lucas, Carrie wondered. What did Jules think of Lucas? She'd never made that opinion known.

Not that it mattered now.

"How do you know when you've found the one?" Jules suddenly asked.

Carrie looked at her for a moment, and noticed, rather surprised, that Jules was being serious. She thought for a moment, realizing that she had no insight, no words of wisdom to share. Her boyfriend of four years had left her. She'd thought he was the one and he thought she was replaceable. "I guess you just know."

Or you don't. Or you get blindsided.

Jules pushed her lips to the side, as if she was thinking about this answer, and went back to adding thick red ribbon to the garland on the banister.

"It's just…"

Carrie's hands froze mid-branch and she had to bite back a curse word. Couldn't they just do this in silence? Distract themselves with half an hour of decorating?

"I wonder if there's more than one person for us out there," Jules finished, and Carrie, much as she hated to admit it, turned and gave her sister a small smile.

"I sure hope so, Jules," she said.

For all of their sakes.

*

Tess's car pulled into the driveway just as they were setting the nutcrackers on either side of the fireplace. Carrie was sure to leave a few in the box for Phoebe to set out, along with some of the less fragile parts of the porcelain village that Tess had collected over the years.

"Hurry up and hide the boxes!" Carrie cried, and she and Jules scrambled to close the containers and run them upstairs to the attic. By the time they began their descent, they could hear Tess's voice in the kitchen, instructing Phoebe to set her wet mittens on the radiator in the mudroom to dry.

"Do we tell her?" Jules whispered.

"Let her discover it herself," Carrie decided. She pulled Jules back against the wall. "We'll wait here."

The wait was longer than she expected. Tess not only had to set all of Phoebe's things out to dry (apparently Phoebe had decided to make a snow angel while Tess unloaded the groceries) but then put all the groceries back in their proper place, and with a kitchen as large as hers, this seemed to take much more time than it took Carrie to cram all the processed food into the only cabinet that wasn't being used to house dishes and glassware.

She was just about to toss up her hands when she heard Phoebe scamper into the living room, and then heard the gasp emerge from her mouth. Carrie rested a hand on her heart and gave Jules a look. They'd brought their niece a moment of joy. They'd done the right thing.

Carrie waited expectantly for Tess to come into the room.

"Mommy, Mommy, come look!" Phoebe cried.

"What? What is it?" Tess's voice sounded alarmed,

strangled and tight, and almost...*fearful* if Carrie didn't know better.

She and Jules hurried down the rest of the stairs just as Tess walked into the room. "Surprise!"

Tess's eyes were wide, her mouth slightly open, but she wasn't smiling, and the tears that seemed to be building were definitely not tears of happiness.

"Isn't it beautiful?" Phoebe was saying as she ran around the room.

"How could you do this?" Tess's jaw set as she turned on her sisters. Her eyes were stony and demanding.

Carrie blinked, at a loss for words. "We wanted to give you some Christmas cheer," she explained, only, saying it like this, now, she realized that she had messed up.

"Cheer?" Tess looked at her with disgust. "When did you become so insensitive, Carrie?"

"It was my idea too," Jules cut in. She tried to set a hand on Tess's elbow, but Tess pulled back quickly, muttering under her breath as she ran up the stairs.

"I shouldn't have come," Carrie said, looking at Jules, waiting, she realized, for her sister to disagree with her, to say that she needed her. Wanted her.

But Jules just gave her an injured look and then let Phoebe take her by the hand to wind up a music box.

Carrie looked up the stairs, her heart fighting with her head, wanting to run up to Tess's bedroom more than anything and knowing that she couldn't.

She grabbed her coat and slipped on her boots and walked out the door instead.

Chapter Eleven

Tess

Tess heard the door slam and a moment later she saw Carrie walking down the street toward town, her head bent against the wind and snow that had started early this morning and that showed no sign of letting up anytime soon.

She stepped back from the window and let her eyes drift to the bed, knowing how easy it would be to succumb to it and knowing that this was exactly what she didn't want to do. It would be selfish, and weak, and she wasn't in a position to be either of those.

She was a mother. She had her child to think about. And right now Phoebe was delighted by the decorations that were now splayed all over her home, thanks to her sisters.

The regret that filled her was nearly as strong as the anger. It wasn't the decorations. It was the liberty. The fact that Carrie thought she could come back to town, waltz into Tess's house (and Andrew's house!), and do as she pleased.

That somehow some tinsel and garland could make everything right between them. Ha!

Tess took a deep breath and walked to the mirror. Her hair was a mess—windblown and unkempt from trudging groceries in from the detached garage—and her cheeks were still flushed. From the cold? Or from anger? But she wasn't even sure that anger was what she felt. More than anything it was a deep sense of loneliness. A nagging, dead weight in her chest that lingered day after day.

And there was one way to cure that.

Jules was in Phoebe's room when Tess emerged from her bedroom a few minutes later, her hair smoothed into a ponytail, some lipstick on her mouth. An effort that felt overwhelming these days but had once been part of her daily routine, without requiring any thought.

"I'm running an errand," she told her sister. "Mind watching Phoebe?"

Jules's eyes widened and she seemed pleased at the request. "Not at all! And no need to rush back. I've got everything covered."

Tess held back her thoughts to that remark. After all, Jules had no experience with children, and she was practically one herself, still living in a post-college apartment, still not committed to a job. But Phoebe was a responsible girl, and, probably because of the way Tess had raised her, a rule-monger. No doubt she'd keep Jules in line, Tess thought with a little smile.

She put back on her coat and boots, but the cold still clung to them and they didn't bring much warmth. She pulled the covered tray of cupcakes she'd made yesterday from the

133

counter, deciding that she could always make more later, and probably would, given all the pent-up energy she had with her sisters being here. Besides, it was something to do, something other than sit around with Carrie and Jules and talk about feelings, or the past, which was what they seemed determined to do.

Preston's wasn't technically open until lunchtime, but Tess knew that Jeff would be there. He was always there. His apartment was just upstairs from it, accessible from a separate entrance, not that she'd ever been inside. He'd lived there since he took over the place, right after college. More recently, right after Phoebe was born, he had closed the place for a two-month renovation and revamped the menu while he was at it. She and Andrew had hired a babysitter for the night of the restaurant's grand reopening. Tess could still remember feeling nervous and anxious about leaving her baby home, kept checking her phone, fighting the urge to call and check in. She'd left her with a sitter, an honor roll student that Natalie swore by, even though her mother had offered to take Phoebe for the night. It was a gesture of goodwill, and Phoebe did tend to bring out the better side of Barb Campbell, but Tess also knew that the dark moods could creep up just as quickly, and then her mother couldn't even be counted on to show up on time. Tess had fretted all night, hoping that the girl she'd handed over her precious baby to wouldn't do something like slip down the stairs or drop Phoebe on her head. Really, wasn't she being selfish to even leave her at such a young age? Andrew had told her to relax, that she was in good hands, and Tess had envied him for his calm demeanor, his belief that everything was going to be okay.

Now she longed to hear him reassure her, just one more time. Would Phoebe be okay? Would *she* be okay? Half the time, she didn't know the answer to that. Each day brought new emotions, and just when she thought she was turning a corner...

Christmas came along.

Tess hoped the walk to town would clear her head. When she approached Main Street, she looked up, took in the shops and the people, the lights that seemed to frame every window, and the windows that were full of seasonal displays— snowmen and snowflakes and presents and angels. She idly wondered where Carrie had gone, thought about seeking her out in the coffee shop or bakery down the street, but decided against it. She had a lot to say to Carrie, but she couldn't pinpoint where to start. Until then, it was better to say nothing at all.

The door to the restaurant was locked, as she expected, but one glance in the window showed Jeff behind the bar, straightening glasses. Tess tapped on it lightly, catching his attention, and then smiled when his expression lifted into one of surprise.

He held up a hand, his grin wide, and he disappeared out of view before reappearing at the now open door.

"To what do I owe the honor?"

She felt instantly better as she followed him into the warm restaurant. It was different here at this time of day. Quiet. Still. Lacking the usual bustle that she'd come to know. The fire in the hearth had not been lit and the Christmas lights hadn't been plugged in. There was no music spilling from the speakers, reminding her what time of year it was. It was calm and subdued and exactly what she needed right now.

"I brought you these," she said, handing over the tray. "As a thank you, for helping with the tree."

Jeff's eyes gleamed as he looked down at the cupcakes. "I would say you shouldn't have, but these are just too good to resist." He grinned at her. His deep eyes were crinkled at the corners and his smile was familiar and warm, and she smiled back, a smile that relaxed all the tension in her chest and filled her with something else. Something better. Something happier.

He offered her one but she held up a hand. "I've eaten enough cupcakes to last a lifetime."

"Coffee then?"

She nodded and waited as he poured them each a mug and then came around the bar to sit beside her. She was immediately aware of his presence, his size, and the smell of his freshly washed hair. And his warmth. She felt at ease, but there was something else, something that she wasn't quite sure should be there—a stir in her stomach. A flick of her pulse.

She reached for the cream and sugar. Slid him the container of cupcakes. She watched as he picked up the one closest and took a large bite.

"You could sell these, you know," he remarked, when he was done chewing.

"Ha." Tess brushed away the compliment, taking it for what it was. "Maybe at a school bake sale. Come to think of it, they do tend to sell better than the gluten-free, sugar-free, dairy-free, carb-free cookies that Phoebe's friend Lulu's mother makes." She grinned.

"I'm serious," Jeff said. "These are really good."

"It's just a family recipe I've tweaked over the years. One of the only good things I took with me from my childhood." She glanced at him, chastising herself for bringing it up and darkening her mood. She was here for some cheering up, not to think about things that bothered her. "Sorry. I promise I didn't come here to bog you down with my problems."

"That's what I'm here for," Jeff said, pushing the tray of cupcakes to the side, and turning to face her head-on. He was so close that she could smell the musk of his cologne, and see the fine lines around his eyes that only gave him character. Her heart raced.

"Please," she said, looking away. "You're a single guy. Surely you have better things to do Christmas week than listen to a widow's problems."

"Not really," he said, and they both laughed. He leaned back in his chair. "You know me. This is where I'm happy. And for what it's worth, I don't pity you. I care about you."

She slanted a glance at him. "Thanks. Wish you'd tell my sisters that. All they do is pity me."

He lifted an eyebrow. "Visit isn't going well, I take it?"

Tess wrapped her hands around the mug, feeling the heat from the coffee warm her palms. "Let's say it's bordering on disastrous but not yet catastrophic."

Jeff laughed again. "And here you thought this would be the worst Christmas ever. Sounds like you've managed to outdo yourself."

"I feel guilty," she said, admitting the horrible, honest truth that she didn't even want to admit to herself. "I know that Andrew would have wanted Phoebe to have a nice Christmas, but it doesn't seem right to be celebrating when he isn't here."

137

"Andrew would want Phoebe to have a nice Christmas," Jeff agreed. He gave her a sad smile. "But he'd want you to have a nice holiday, too."

"You sound so sure," Tess said, searching his face.

"Because I *am* sure," Jeff said. "You may have been married to him, but I knew him long before you. He loved you and Phoebe and he would only want what was best for you."

"It seems that everyone thinks what's best for me is to have a house full of lights and music," Tess grumbled.

"Maybe they don't know what else to do," Jeff pointed out.

Tess thought about this for a minute. It was childish, really, not different than the cards that Phoebe made her at school and joyfully presented to her at the end of the day, all in an obvious effort to see Tess smile.

No different than the cupcakes Tess used to make for her mother, right up until the moment that she was gone.

They were trying. But it was too little too late for Carrie.

"You only get one Christmas a year," Jeff said. "May as well make the most of it."

"Says the man with no tree," Tess reminded him.

"What can I say?" Jeff grinned. "Andrew always said I was in dire need of a woman's touch."

"Probably because he appreciated my cooking so much," Tess laughed. "Fortunately, you've got that area covered."

"I do." Jeff smiled into the distance. "I remember the night that Andrew told me he was going to ask you to marry him. Did I ever tell you this story?" His eyes hooked on hers, and she couldn't look away, even though she wanted to.

Tess felt a chill run down her skin, even though she was

still bundled in her coat and scarf. She hadn't even removed her gloves.

"No." Her voice came out strangled, like she wasn't sure if she was ready to hear it, or savor it. A piece of Andrew's life—of their life—that she hadn't yet heard. A new story, not just an old memory. It made him feel alive again. And it made her miss him. Terribly.

"You'd only been dating for oh…six, seven years?" Jeff cocked an eyebrow. "He had the ring all picked out, sure that you would like it, and he took me to see it, to get my approval."

Tess ran her thumb over the back of the rings she still wore, under her glove. Each time her finger brushed the metal, she felt assured, and relieved. That a part of what they had was still with her.

"It's a beautiful ring," Tess said. She adored it. A brilliant-cut stone on a thin band covered with more tiny diamonds. Carrie admired it every time she saw it, and the last time she'd seen her she'd said she hoped Lucas would give her one just like it.

"It is," Jeff said slowly, "only it's not the one that Andrew originally chose."

Tess's heart began to pound, and for some reason, she felt anxious, not pleased. This wasn't the memory she'd stowed away. This wasn't their history as she knew it. "What do you mean?"

"He had picked out something old-fashioned. Something that resembled what his mother wore." Jeff leaned forward in his chair and whispered, "Ugly."

Tess merely blinked at him. If the ring on her finger was not the one that Andrew had chosen, then who had?

She swallowed hard. Jeff. Jeff had chosen her ring.

"I didn't know what to say, honestly. I mean, I could have said nothing, let him go through with the purchase, but...I wanted that engagement to be special. I wanted it to be a success."

"I would have loved whatever he gave me." Tess felt her defenses rise.

"Oh I know!" Jeff gave her a knowing smile. "But I had to help the guy out. When he finally proposed, he took me out for a beer to thank me. Said he'd never seen you so happy. The truth was that I'd never seen him so happy."

Tess didn't know what to think about any of this. She'd always assumed that Andrew knew her so well, right down to buying the exact style of ring she would have picked for herself, and she hadn't even needed to drop any hints! But now...now she wondered what else she didn't know, what other stories hadn't been shared.

"I suppose I owe you another batch of cupcakes then," Tess said, trying to keep her tone light. "For guiding Andrew in the right direction."

"He would have figured it out on his own eventually," Jeff said. "He knew what he was doing. He chose you, didn't he?"

They locked eyes for a minute and Tess finally broke away. When he put it like that, she didn't need to worry that there was a part of her husband she hadn't known or that he didn't understand her as much as she'd thought. He was a good man. And he'd surrounded himself with good people.

"I'm lucky to have you in my life, Jeff," she said. Cupcakes hardly communicated the gratitude that she felt.

"I feel the same way," Jeff said, reaching out to swipe another cupcake.

"Not everyone seems to share that sentiment," Tess said, raising an eyebrow. "You saw how Trudy was at the tree lot over the weekend. It was like she was judging us or something."

Jeff waved a hand through the air. "Oh, ignore her. She's reading into things."

Tess nodded, but she wasn't so sure that was the case at all. Was Trudy Flannigan just reading into things, or was there more going on between her and Jeff than either of them had dared to voice?

She shook away that thought as quickly as it had formed. Jeff was right. Andrew would want to know that she was happy. That Phoebe was happy. And that his oldest friend was happy.

She wasn't happy. How could she be? But for now, for this reprieve in a closed restaurant in the center of town with the snow falling outside and the radiator warm and steady inside, she was hopeful that someday she would be.

"I miss him," she said softly. She couldn't look at Jeff for fear that the tears might start to flow and never stop.

Instead, she took a sip of her coffee. Her throat was tight. She blinked rapidly.

After a long silence, Jeff said gruffly, "Me too, Tess. Every damn day."

They sat like that for a moment. No need to say anything.

"You coming to the Ice Fest?" Jeff asked when Tess finally stood up. He pushed back his own chair, so he was standing right in front of her. He was taller than Andrew, and more solid, too. Of course, being a confirmed bachelor meant that he devoted himself in equal measure to his career and working out, she knew.

141

Still, she took a step back, creating some healthy distance.

"I hadn't thought of it..." If anything, she'd purposefully tried to forget about the Ice Fest and hoped that those around her would too. Growing up, it had been one of her favorite days of the year, and she'd been sure to carry on the tradition with Phoebe. She and Andrew would bundle her up, set her on the sled, and walk to the lakefront where the festivities were held: a skating show put on by the local children, followed by skating races, a hockey game that tended to get a little too competitive, and of course, the ever-popular ice-sculpting contest. Phoebe had even had her first taste of hot cocoa at the Ice Fest. Tess had a photo to prove it.

To remember it by.

"Phoebe would like it," Jeff pointed out, and she knew he wasn't trying to guilt trip her, just...encourage her.

She nodded, decision made. "I'll come." One more night to push through. What was one more night? Besides, it would beat sitting around the house with her sisters.

He looked surprised, as if he hadn't expected that answer at all. "That's great. So, I'll see you tomorrow night then."

"You don't have to work?" she asked, looking at him quizzically.

"I do get some time off, you know." He laughed. "I have some perks to owning the place."

Yes, she supposed he did, she thought as she pushed back out into the chilly air. The lights glowed from inside storefronts and she thought about walking into some of the shops, looking for gifts for Carrie and Jules. She'd been secretly planning to mail Jules a gift card this year. Out of character and a bit lazy, but probably what Jules would have preferred to the more thoughtful gifts that Tess used to labor over in previous years.

Her phone pinged and she stopped walking, her heart speeding up when she remembered the job interview, the news she had been waiting for.

Carefully she pulled her phone out of her pocket and looked at the screen. An email. From the twenty-four-year-old who had popped gum all through their interview and had blue painted nail polish.

An email from the girl who Tess now desperately hoped would be her new boss. She could do it. Be an assistant to a woman who only seemed to rival Jules when it came to maturity.

But just as much as she had wanted the job, now she feared it. A job meant more change. It meant less time off, and aftercare hours for Phoebe. But it meant financial security, too. And structure. A purpose to her day.

She pulled in a breath and tapped on the screen. The email filled her screen before she was fully prepared and her eyes scanned the words, barely digesting a single, full sentence.

Still, the message couldn't have been clearer.

Another candidate had been chosen. A more qualified candidate, specifically.

Tess felt her cheeks grow hot despite the fact that she was standing outside on a cold, winter day. She thrust the phone back into her pocket and turned in the direction of home.

A more qualified candidate. She didn't even know why she should be surprised. After all, she wasn't an office worker. She was a mother. And, up until recently, a wife.

And the only other thing she was any good at was baking cupcakes.

And worrying, she thought, as she began the slow walk back to her house. All around her, shoppers bustled, and people brushed past in a hurry, their shopping bags bursting with last-minute gifts. Some she recognized and managed a cheerful sounding, "Happy Holidays" even if there was nothing happy about it.

From inside stores she passed, she could hear the sound of music. The squeals of children playing in the snow in the town square. There was an electricity to the air that usually thrilled her, and lifted her spirits. A sense of hope.

But she didn't know what to hope for anymore. She only knew that this Christmas couldn't be over soon enough.

Chapter Twelve

Jules

If there was one thing that Jules had no interest in, now, or ever, it was cooking. She'd never been taught, either by her mother or Tess, who took on the brunt of that responsibility once she was around twelve, maybe even younger. Jules remembered looking forward to those meals her sister made, finding Tess a much more competent cook than their mother, who sometimes didn't cook the pasta all the way, or cooked it for too long. Tess was different. She planned things out. Put thought into each meal, even pride. When Jules or Carrie said they liked something, Tess would beam. And when they didn't like something, they both still said they did, because they didn't want to hurt her feelings.

Just as often as Tess cooked, she was too busy with homework or the after-school jobs she took on as soon she was able to work, and then they got used to microwaved dinners or cold cereal for dinner—something that Jules still ate most nights because it was strangely comforting. But something told her that cold cereal wasn't an option in Tess's house, and she wasn't sure that she should sit around and wait for Tess to cook for them, either.

Every other time she had come to town, Tess had cooked big meals, including a dessert course. But that was before…and the fact that Tess wasn't popping a pot roast in the oven told Jules that despite her stiff upper lip, Tess was not herself and that Jules was right to have come here.

She glanced at the clock in the hallway. She'd been reading a magazine and trying not to think about Aaron ever since Phoebe had run upstairs to see her mother, who had spent the better part of the afternoon upstairs since returning this morning.

Carrie had arrived shortly thereafter and also shut herself in her room.

Jules refused to do the same, even though it was tempting. About as tempting as texting Aaron, or calling him. Because that's what she would have done, any other time. And that's what she wanted to do. Desperately.

He always added levity to a situation, even one as tense as this. And he always made her feel better.

Well, she'd just have to find another reason to feel better. She stood, walked up the stairs, and went to Tess's bedroom door.

Memories of turning the knob to a room darkened by drawn curtains and a lump in the bed in the shape of her mother made her uneasy.

She knocked first, bracing herself, but Tess opened the door fully clothed, her bedroom lit warmly by lamps, with

Phoebe on the bed watching a television that was housed in an armoire in the corner near the window. The only sign that things were amiss was the pale complexion of Tess's cheeks. On the desk near the window, a laptop was open, bills shed of their envelopes.

"Just wondering if you were up for dinner in town again?" Jules ventured. Her stomach rumbled. She wondered if Tess even had cereal. It seemed that Phoebe ate oatmeal for breakfast. Jules hated oatmeal. It reminded her of the mushy, overcooked pasta of her youth.

"I have some work to do tonight," Tess said, by way of apology. "Bills and paperwork."

She gave Jules a look that seemed to imply that Jules wouldn't understand such responsibilities. And maybe she didn't. She'd never been married. Never had a child. But she'd never ruled it out, either. After all, she'd never thought she'd try for a permanent position either. Only that had been the ultimate lesson, the one she'd already known, deep down. Be careful what you want, because it might not turn out the way you had hoped. And then, all that's left is disappointment, and sometimes, worse.

"Okay, well, mind if I go?" Jules asked. "I have a little cabin fever."

That was an understatement. She'd spent the afternoon reading, but she couldn't focus on the book and her eyes kept drifting. She'd reread the same page for a solid hour before she gave up and tried another, only to be stuck with the same problem.

No word from Aaron. And Aaron was all she could think about. And she didn't know how she felt about that. She only knew one thing, and that was that she didn't feel good. Didn't feel good missing him, didn't like the way her stomach felt all funny at the thought of not talking to him. Didn't like that she'd gotten to this place at all.

"Of course," Tess said, seeming relieved. "Sorry I haven't been up for much today. I've been preoccupied."

"Anything you want to talk about?" Jules asked hopefully, but Tess just shook her head, shutting down any chance of sisterly bonding. Jules sighed in defeat. "Okay, well, I'll leave you to it. Don't wait up for me."

Neither of them mentioned Carrie, but somehow, Jules knew that they were both thinking of her. She could ask Carrie, get her out of the house. That would probably be the best thing to do, and she could use the company. It might take her mind off Aaron. Might make her heart feel a little less empty, which made no sense because usually, that was his role.

She walked down the hallway to the back bedroom. The door was shut and no sound came from the other side, but she could see light filtering through the gap near the floorboards. Jules hesitated. Something had seemed off with Carrie when they'd been decorating, and she hadn't spoken since returning hours ago, either.

Still, she knocked anyway. She owed it to Tess to get Carrie out of the house, even if some time together was exactly what her two older sisters needed. Carrie came to the door with wide eyes but seemed to relax when she saw that Jules wasn't Tess.

Jules pursed her lips. By the end of this week, she was determined to make her sisters close again.

And closer to her, too.

"I'm heading into town for dinner. Just me," she added, lest there be any confusion. "Want to come along?"

Carrie nodded eagerly. "Just give me five minutes."

Good, Jules thought as she walked down the stairs. By the end of the night, she hoped to get to the bottom of what seemed to be bothering Carrie, because she suspected it was more than her strained relationship with Tess.

And it was much easier to focus on Carrie's problems than on her own.

Preston's was just as busy tonight as it had been last night, and Jules and Carrie had to push their way past the crowd of waiting customers near the door to grab two spots at the bar just as a couple was leaving.

Jeff's face lit up when he saw them and then flitted to the empty space behind them, his disappointment noticeable.

"Tess is home with Phoebe," Jules clarified and then did her best to hide her smile. She leaned into Carrie when Jeff's attention was pulled away by a customer asking for another round. "I'm beginning to think there might be something brewing between those two."

Carrie looked at her in shock. "Between Jeff and Tess?" She shook her head. "They're just friends. They've been friends forever." She shrugged off her coat, shaking her head as if determined to show her disagreement.

True, Tess had been friends with Jeff since childhood, and mostly through Andrew, but Jules had noticed a shift in their dynamic last night and Jeff couldn't seem to hide the fact that he was let down by Tess not being here with them tonight.

He came over to them with a slightly resigned smile. "What'll it be?"

Since they'd walked over, Jules ordered a holiday special cocktail and Carrie did the same. They sipped their drinks while they studied the menu. Carrie was quiet, more quiet than usual, and she was still yet to mention Lucas when usually, that was all she could talk about.

Still, her phone was on the table, as it often was the rare times she was ever without him—the one time Jules could recall being their mother's funeral, right around the time that Carrie became serious about Lucas.

Maybe she felt guilty mentioning Lucas, Jules thought. After all, there was no confusion that he had played a role in Carrie not coming to town last winter. But Tess wasn't here right now. It was just the two of them. And Carrie knew she could tell Jules anything. Didn't she?

Jules fought the urge to pull out her own phone, but knew it was pointless. Normally she and Aaron texted throughout the day or made quick calls to share the latest news. But since Saturday, there had been nothing but silence. For the first time since she'd met him, she had no idea what he was doing tonight. He was probably packing for the upcoming weekend, getting ready to spend a cozy Christmas at his parents' cabin in Maine as he did every year. Jules pictured the tree in the corner and the stockings hanging from the mantle and the fire blazing in the fireplace. There would be bowls of popcorn and endless holiday movies and puzzles and games and joy and laughter. Jules couldn't help herself; she was starting to wish that she was there for Christmas instead of here, with two sisters who seemed determined to shut her out.

She supposed she could leave early. Say she had gotten a freelance gig (that would please Tess more than upset her) and take the bus up with Aaron like they always did, sitting side by side, their bags packed with snacks for the long ride that didn't feel long at all when they were together.

Only Aaron wouldn't want her there. Not unless…

She flipped to the back of the menu, trying not to think about it.

Carrie tapped her arm and leaned in. "Isn't that Cole?"

Jules felt her pulse skip a beat. Cole Dempsey had been her high school boyfriend. The longest relationship she'd ever had at four months. They'd gone to senior prom together, signed each other's yearbooks, and spent one last wonderful summer here in Winter Lake, back when Jules was the last remaining sister in the house and Tess had already married and tucked into a house of her own, even if she did invite Jules to Sunday dinner each week and send her home with containers full of leftovers.

Cole had loved her, and though she'd never said it to him in return, a part of her had loved him, too. For getting her out of the house. For caring. For being there when she needed someone the most. For being fun, because she needed a little fun to look forward to each day. By then, their childhood home was quiet, too quiet, and while her mother spent more time turning the wood in her studio into something functional and beautiful than lying in bed, she was still distant and distracted.

She scanned the room, looking for a hint of dark hair and brooding eyes. Back in high school, he'd ridden a motorcycle, something that had thrilled her to no end. He used to take her for rides, all along the back roads of town where there weren't any cars, and she'd hold onto his waist, feel the wind in her face, and the sense of adventure and excitement that could only come from living in the moment and not worrying about the past or the future.

Her gaze landed on a guy at the back of the room. She hadn't seen him in at least five years—hadn't bumped into him on her last two visits to town, which wasn't surprising, given the somber nature of her visits. His hair was shorter, but he was otherwise unchanged.

And the little flutter in her stomach hadn't changed much either.

He caught her eye and she stiffened. She could look away, quickly, or she could do something bolder. She waved. After all, he was an old friend. It would be rude to ignore him.

She waited to see how he would respond. Did he hate her for breaking up with him? Or was it old news, forgotten history?

He waved back. She felt inexplicably relieved, forgiven. Like she wasn't the worst person in the world like she hadn't gone around hurting men to the point of never being forgiven. Maybe if Cole could move on, and still be on good terms with her, then Aaron could too.

"He's coming over here," Carrie hissed, her eyes lighting up with excitement. Before Jules could process what was happening, her sister had hopped off her barstool, grabbed her cell phone, and was striding to the back of the room. Probably to call Lucas. How convenient.

Jules looked to the door and then to the bar, hoping that Jeff might use this time to come over and chat about Tess, but he was busy with some women at the end of the bar. Tourists, Jules assessed, in town for a ski week.

Cole grinned as he approached and then shook his head as he slid into Carrie's spot. "Julie Campbell," he said, looking straight into her eyes. She'd forgotten about those eyes. How intense they were. How you felt like the center of the world when Cole looked at you like that.

"Cole Dempsey," she said. She reached for her drink. God knew she needed it.

"I thought that was you," he said. He wasn't shy in looking her up and down. "What brings you to town?"

"My sisters and I are celebrating Christmas here," she said. *Celebrating* was a bit of a stretch. More like going through the motions. Avoiding topics. Avoiding each other.

"I hear you're still in Boston," he said, and Jules couldn't help but feel flattered. He'd followed up on her.

She nodded. "Still in Boston." She omitted the part about still being in her post-college apartment and her current unemployment status. "And what are you up to?"

"Still working at the resort," he said, referring to his job as a ski instructor that he'd had since graduation. "You ever write that book you talked about?"

She blinked at him for a moment. "I can't believe that you remember that." She'd practically forgotten it herself. That last summer here in town, she'd been full of big dreams. They were her escape from the daily routine, much as the stories she immersed herself in had served in her childhood. Once she'd gone to Boston, she didn't need to think about a fictional life, far from Winter Lake. By the time she arrived in Boston, she had a new reality, a new life, and she didn't have to worry about the past catching up with her.

"I remember a lot of things about you, Jules. I remember that you broke my heart." He raised his eyebrows at her as if challenging her to respond to that, even though he was grinning.

She narrowed her eyes at him and then, after a beat, gave him a swat on the arm. "Oh, please. You had me replaced before I crossed the state line." Cole had never been single for long. It was part of his appeal. Part of what made it easy to stay with him a little longer than the others. He was looking for fun. Nothing too serious. She didn't have to worry about hurting him or getting hurt.

Her chest tugged for a moment when she thought of how different it was with Aaron. The way his eyes had drooped with sadness the last time she'd seen him.

"You going to the Christmas Festival?" he asked. The Christmas Festival was one of the biggest events of the year, held the day before Christmas Eve, every year. The entire town joined in the event, with shops offering specials and businesses closing to partake in the festivities.

She grinned. It was a tradition in their family to attend these local events—magical moments of her childhood that were all too uncommon and that she liked to hold onto. "I'll probably be at the Ice Fest too."

"Maybe I'll see you there, then," he said, his eyes twinkling.

"Maybe you will." She did a poor job of hiding her smile as he hopped off the barstool and skimmed her cheek with a kiss. He smelled musky and woody and felt warm and solid and she could feel her heart racing from the proximity.

Butterflies. It was what you were supposed to feel, wasn't

it? Not just the comfort of routine and companionship and all of that. You needed chemistry. Attraction. Excitement. That was the difference between friends and…something more.

And Aaron would soon discover that. Only she couldn't let him discover that the hard way, once they'd tried and failed to be more to each other than they really were. Because then their friendship would never be saved, and he'd really be out of her life forever.

And that was something that she couldn't let happen. No matter what.

Chapter Thirteen

Carrie

Carrie wasn't sure how she expected this Christmas to go exactly, but it certainly wasn't turning out in her favor. Tess still hadn't spoken to her since their argument yesterday morning, and Jules had spent half the evening flirting with Cole Dempsey and then talking about him, leaving Carrie to order one too many candy cane cocktails that now made her stomach roil at the mere thought of anything flavored with mint.

She held her toothbrush in her hand and the tube of toothpaste in the other, trying to summon up the courage to get this daily routine over with. Maybe Phoebe had some kid-flavored option, something in the bubblegum family? Anything but mint would do.

She decided to find out. She wandered into her niece's pink and white bedroom, her heart hurting just a little when she saw all the careful details that Tess had overseen: the billowing curtains that framed the bay window, the array of mix-matched yet color-coordinated pillows along its seat. A bookshelf was stacked with classics for little girls, and a hand-painted tea set was set up on a play table in the corner. On Phoebe's bedside table was a jewelry box, and, tempted, Carrie walked over to it and lifted the lid, just to see the ballerina turning inside.

She closed the lid as soon as the music started, feeling like a voyeur in her own sister's house. A fresh wave of self-pity reared before she could stop it.

She would never have a child of her own at this rate. She was thirty-three years old and single. She was starting over. It could take years before she ended up married, much less engaged, and how many men would she have to date before she found an actual relationship? How many of them would be first date disasters? How many of them would let her down a week, a month, a year into things?

Before Lucas, she'd rarely had more than a two-month relationship, and not for lack of trying. The guys before him weren't committed. But then, she supposed, blinking back tears, neither was Lucas. Her dreams had all seemed within her reach, and now the girl with her scarf would be living the life she was supposed to have.

It wasn't fair.

Although, she thought, thinking of Tess and Phoebe and Andrew, who'd had the rock-solid family she'd always pined for, life wasn't fair at all.

She walked into Phoebe's en suite bathroom, made up in a theme of mermaids. She smeared sparkly pink toothpaste on her toothbrush and tried not to think of how different her shared room with Tess was growing up from this airy, happy space. There had been no white furniture or custom-made curtains with matching throw pillows in their bedroom. There were two beds. Some mismatched quilts for function. A heap of toys and books and markers and paper and anything else the girls collected along the way. They had free rein to make it their own, whereas clearly, Tess had full authority on how Phoebe's room was decorated. Carrie had cut out pictures from catalogs and magazines and made a collage on the wall above their beds, she remembered. And Tess had strung Christmas lights from the windows that remained there all year long. She said it made everything more beautiful. More magical.

Tess had always loved Christmas.

Carrie frowned and went back to her room. Things changed, she told herself. And not always for the better.

With her teeth brushed, she pulled her hair back, managed the faintest bit of lipstick, and, knowing she looked as hungover as she felt, decided to go into town for coffee rather than risk a conversation about why she was drinking so much the night before—she'd easily had two for each of Jules's rounds. Drowning her troubles, that's what she had been doing. And it had worked—at first. By the third candy cane cocktail, she had stopped looking at her phone, and by the fourth, she had stopped thinking of scarf girl. And by the fifth, she had done the unthinkable and removed her relationship status on Facebook—something that had to be done and that she couldn't bring herself to do sober.

And there it was. Status: single. Age: thirty-three. Future: bleak.

Maybe she'd slap that on a dating profile, she thought,

managing a wry grin as she made her way down the stairs on shaky legs, trying to hold onto the banister without messing up the garland. See, there was humor to be found in her pathetic turn of events. She'd get back to New York and downplay the entire thing, or build it up in a truly self-deprecating way, right down to the detail about her fresh manicure and the girl that Lucas was spotted with only days later.

Only something told her that no one else would be laughing.

And really, neither was she. In fact, she realized with horror, she was crying.

She brushed a hand to her cheek and quickly pulled her sunglasses from her bag. The room darkened around her, even though it hadn't been lit at all, even though Tess hadn't turned on the lights on the tree or the banister or on the garland on the mantle.

It made Carrie sad. It made her think of their mother, and her childhood, and she didn't like to think about those days anymore. When she'd left Winter Lake, she'd vowed not to think about any of it again, to move forward, and to have a different life.

So much for keeping that promise.

From outside, Carrie heard a squeal, and she walked to the kitchen window to see Jules and Phoebe playing in the backyard, having a snowball fight. Her eyes scanned the rest of the snow-covered space, nervously looking for Tess, but there was no sign of her. The door to her room had been open, the bed made and the space empty, when Carrie had passed by it just a few moments ago.

Errands, Carrie supposed, deciding to stay clear of the grocery store when she was in town, not that she had any appetite at the moment.

Carrie went back to the front of the house where her coat was hanging on a hook. She pulled it on and stuffed her hat and gloves into her bag. She didn't even bother to button up—she needed fresh air before she did something really unforgivable and vomited into Tess's neatly trimmed boxwoods.

She gulped in the cold air, which was so much fresher than the air in the city, walking slowly, wondering if the café had outdoor tables this time of year or if she might find a bench that wasn't piled in three feet of snow.

The Juniper Café was at the edge of downtown, an old institution where she used to hang out after school with Tess, but which lately seemed to appeal to the young mom crowd. She had noticed this last time she was in town, when she still held the hope of someday being one of them. She briefly considered avoiding it today, but her brain felt fuzzy and she couldn't think of another option, not unless she wanted to try the diner, which was known for its watery coffee, especially when Bernie Adams was working—his vision had been bad even when she was in high school.

She walked slowly, past the shops, until she finally saw the dark green awning. She pushed inside, only after a quick self-evaluation that she was not going to be sick all over the wood floor, her eyes sweeping over the rustic room with the wrought-iron tables and chairs and big, paned windows looking out on the snow-covered town. She kept her sunglasses on to cover her bloodshot eyes and scanned the offerings in the bakery case. Normally she would have loved an oversized cranberry muffin or a chocolate croissant, even if she probably wouldn't have eaten the entire thing (women in New York were so thin, and she didn't need Lucas to get a wandering eye) but today she had no appetite. Still, something was probably needed. She opted for a plain bagel.

"And a large coffee," she managed, her voice barely a whisper. She cleared her throat. This was why she didn't drink, at least, not excessively. That and because she and Lucas liked to go to movies or restaurants on their weekends, where they might share a bottle of wine at most. Now, she supposed she'd have to increase her tolerance level and prepare for the bar scene again. Unless she wanted to try online dating.

She closed her eyes against the tears that prickled the back of her eyes, happy again that she was wearing her sunglasses. She may as well just wear a sign around her neck: Dumped. Desperate. Rapidly approaching forty.

"Cream and sugar are near the door," the girl behind the counter said.

Carrie nodded and took her coffee and the bag containing her bagel, no butter, no cream cheese. Just a bag of carbs that she saw no reason in avoiding at the moment. She walked to the stand and considered her options as her stomach heaved in the most unsettling way. Skim. Cream. She reached for the cream. Her hand shook. Now was not the time to worry about putting on a few pounds. No one was going to see her in that dress she'd bought for Lucas's holiday party. At best, she'd find a reason to wear it next season.

She tried to picture her life a year from now and came up blank.

And by the way things were going, chances were low she'd be invited back to Winter Lake next year either. She sighed as she splashed too much cream into her paper cup, and then spilled some onto the counter.

Maybe she'd get a pet for her classroom. Take it home with her for weekends and breaks. A hamster. She would be the lonely lady with a hamster. She grabbed a few napkins and wiped up her mess. She had just popped the lid back onto the cup when she thought she heard someone saying her name.

"Carrie? Carrie Campbell?"

Oh dear God. Carrie turned with dread at the sound of her name, trying in vain to summon up the enthusiasm needed to greet an old high school friend. Melissa Smythe. Under any other circumstances, she would have reached out to Melissa, told her she was coming back to town, and arranged to meet for drinks so they could catch up. But she hadn't had time to think about any of that. And the last thing she wanted to do was share her disappointment.

"Melissa!" Her eyes dropped to the stroller in front of Melissa, where a baby was drooling all over a plastic toy. She felt her forced smile slip, and she quickly pulled it back into place. Her head was starting to pound, and she now assumed it was from more than the vodka in those drinks. "Who is this?"

Surely, it couldn't be hers. She would have heard. Tess would have told her. Except that she and Tess weren't very close anymore.

Still. She didn't even know that Melissa was married. She'd been dating Stephen Manning since high school, but when Carrie was back in town for her mother's funeral, they'd already broken up. That was only three and a half years ago. Surely she couldn't already have moved on, married, *and* had a child in less time than Carrie and Lucas had only dated?

Melissa had an older sister. Janie. Carrie felt better remembering that. Surely this was Janie's baby. Considering that Janie was already coming up on forty, she couldn't really feel too jealous of that.

"This is William," Melissa said, beaming. "My son."

Again, Carrie was grateful for the oversized sunglasses which hid the pop of her eyes. Her mouth felt dry as she stared at the baby, who sure enough had the same big blue eyes as Melissa.

"And another this summer," Melissa continued, patting her stomach, which sure enough boasted a hint of a baby bump.

Two children? Melissa had remained in Winter Lake, population next to zero, male offerings slim to none, and she had managed to have more to show for it than Carrie.

"I didn't realize you and Stephen—"

"Oh. Not Stephen." Melissa started to laugh, as if the mere idea that someone she had dated for years could have been the father of her children. "No, my husband is named Mike. He works in real estate like me. We met at a work thing a few years ago and he popped the question six months later. And the rest as they say is history!"

Carrie nodded slowly, trying to wrap her head around this. Six months. He had proposed after six months. And now she was going to have two children. And Carrie didn't even have one.

How did she not know this? She and Melissa were con-

163

nected on social media, but she supposed she'd never thought to check in on her. She'd been too busy with Lucas. Planning their weekends. Planning their future. Too wrapped up to think about her old friends back here in town.

Or her family, she thought, shame replacing nausea when she considered Tess's words last year.

"I'm sorry," she said. "I'm rarely on social media, and I haven't been back in so long."

"Not since your mom," Melissa said, giving her a look of pity that Carrie didn't quite know how to react to. She and her mother had never been close. They couldn't be under the circumstances. Her mother was too distant, too unavailable to be the caregiver that Carrie was looking for. But she was still her mother. The only mother she'd ever had and ever would. And now she was gone.

And she didn't like thinking about that.

"You didn't come back to town for Andrew's funeral, did you? Or did I miss you?"

Carrie felt her defenses heighten, but she could see no malice in Melissa's eyes as she reached down to pick up a toy that her son (her son!) had tossed on the floor.

"I wasn't able to make it back," Carrie said regretfully.

"Life gets busy!" Melissa opened her eyes knowingly. The baby started to fuss, reaching for his toy, and she jostled the stroller, nearly hitting Carrie in the knee. Carrie eyed the toy, wondering if Melissa was the kind of mom who would hand it back or disinfect it first. "And what's new with you?" Melissa asked cheerfully. She tucked the toy into the front pocket of her oversized shoulder bag. The baby howled. "How's your fabulous New York life?"

Carrie felt her lids droop but she forced a wider smile. The last time she and Melissa had met up had been just six months after meeting Lucas. She was in love. She hadn't been shy about it. Moving to New York had never felt more right. Staying there felt permanent.

"Just...fabulous." Here, she, too, laughed, even though it wasn't funny, and even though her life was far from fabulous at the moment. She was single, she was hungover, and she wasn't on speaking terms with her sister.

And she'd never have a baby. And she wanted one. Even one like William, who was now crying so hard that Carrie could feel the pulse of her headache in her eyeballs.

Melissa checked her watch and pulled a face. "Shoot. I'm late for story time at the library. But let's catch up. You're in town all week?"

Carrie nodded. "Yep." At least, that was the plan. Tess may have a different one.

"Great. We'll get coffee. Decaf for me, of course." Melissa grinned happily. The baby gurgled as the stroller began moving. "Just message me a time that works for you."

Carrie managed to nod, but her mind was spinning. She took a long sip of her coffee, thinking that right now, she'd rather have coffee with Tess than with Melissa. At least with Tess, she didn't have to talk about herself. And she certainly wouldn't have to talk about Lucas. They could just sit in silence. But Melissa was perky. Too perky. Perky enough to make Carrie suspect that she was still drinking caffeine after all.

As she watched Melissa bounce away, Carrie instantly regretted changing her relationship status on Facebook last night. It made her feel vulnerable and alone. And she hated both those feelings. Did her best to avoid them at all costs.

But then, she supposed it was better to change the status before Lucas did. After all, she had some pride.

Carrie walked outside and scanned the sidewalk, careful to avoid anyone she knew, anyone who wanted to stop and chat and catch up. She didn't want to catch up. She didn't want to talk about how "fabulous" her life in New York was any more than she wanted to be reminded of her mother. She'd died at the age of fifty-five, of a heart attack. High blood pressure. It might have been the stress. Or it might have been a broken heart.

Secretly, Carrie had blamed herself, for leaving town, for staying away, for not calling or visiting often enough. But Jules had just shaken her head firmly.

"Blame Dad, if you can even call him that," she'd said angrily. "Blame our father."

Their mother had never gotten over Carrie's father leaving them. None of them had, Carrie supposed. They'd all just learned to survive, in their own strange ways.

Only now Carrie couldn't help but wonder if running to New York had been the best choice. And if life might have been better for her right here in Winter Lake, after all.

Chapter Fourteen

Tess

Tess finished wrapping the last of Phoebe's Christmas gifts and carried them to her bedroom closet. She flicked on the light, the rush of seeing Andrew's clothes hanging neatly still surprised her, as if they were waiting for him to come home and wear them again.

She knew what her sisters would say if they saw the clothes. That he wasn't coming back. That there was no need to hold onto these things, just like there was no need to hold onto Andrew's toothbrush or shaving kit or anything else mundane and unsentimental. But they didn't understand. How could they? It was all sentimental because it was all a part of the life they'd shared.

The life she'd loved.

Her life with Andrew was so different from the one she'd had growing up that at times it had felt like a fairytale. Like a dream. And now, that's exactly what it had been. And she was back to living in reality. With loneliness. And fear.

And bills. And so much uncertainty.

She pulled her phone from her pocket and scrolled through her contacts list until she came to Andrew's name. She pressed the button at the bottom of the screen and held the device to her ear, closing her eyes as it went straight to voicemail, and his voice came on, strong and clear, warm and reassuring. Leave a message. He'd call back.

Oh, how she wished that he would.

She hung up the phone without leaving a message. What was there to say? I didn't get the job, Andrew. I'm scared, Andrew. I don't know what to do, Andrew. I'm trying to be strong, Andrew.

Come back, Andrew. That's what she wanted to say.

She stood in the closet for several minutes, feeling the weight of the phone in her hand, before slipping it back into her pocket. The moment had passed. She could still hear his voice if she closed her eyes. It was all that was left to hold onto anymore. The last piece of him that still felt alive in this world.

She tossed a blanket over the stack of presents and went downstairs, where her sisters and daughter were waiting for her in their warmest winter gear, one of the pot pies from Trudy Flannigan half-eaten and still resting on the stovetop, finally put to good use, that she couldn't take credit for. There would be heat lamps and bonfires at the lake tonight, and the wind had died down, but still, Tess rolled up Phoebe's sweater sleeve to make sure she was wearing her long underwear.

"Mo-om," Phoebe protested.

"Yeah, Mo-om," Jules chimed in, grinning in that mischievous way of hers.

"That's my name," Tess simply replied, giving Phoebe a wink. She glanced at Jules, shaking her head, resisting the urge to roll her eyes, to fight back the exasperation that was building in her chest. The irritability she felt that Jules was still a kid in so many ways, still not grown or mature, still not an adult. In many ways, she felt like Jules's mom. Still felt the need to set her straight, and make sure her life was on track. But how could she do that when her own life was crumbling around her? She'd been responsible for Jules from a young age, making sure that she had her breakfast and something for lunch, that her hair was brushed and that the sheets on her bed were fresh. Tess didn't mind it too much. Jules was cute and fun, whereas Carrie had been more serious, like her. And whereas Carrie was sensitive, Jules didn't let things bother her. She could fight her own battles, and stick up for herself when kids on the playground got mean, and eventually, as Tess started to build her own life, she assumed that Jules would be just fine on her own.

Now, she pushed back the guilty feeling she often had that she hadn't been there enough for Jules over the years. That she hadn't guided her enough, hadn't encouraged her enough, that she was too busy with her new family, spending time with Andrew, raising Phoebe. How many phone calls had gone unanswered because Phoebe needed to be rocked to sleep or taken to the park, how many conversations were cut short because Phoebe needed to be taken somewhere or Tess was trying to get dinner on the table?

Jules had only been in her mid-twenties when their mother

169

had died. And unlike Tess and Carrie, she didn't even remember their father. Sometimes Tess thought she was better
off that way. Carrie had cried herself to sleep for nearly six
months after he'd left, after all, while Jules was oblivious. And
Tess…Well, Tess hadn't cried. Tess had only tightened her
resolve that someday her life would be different. And better.

She gave Jules a grin as she put on her coat and zippered it
to the top, and Jules's eyes lit the way they did when she was a
little girl and Tess handed her one of the beaters from her
cupcake batter.

Tess felt a tightening in her chest. Jules loved her. And she
loved Jules. She didn't say it often enough, but she should.
Life was too short to not say what you meant.

She spared a glance in Carrie's direction. Carrie had been
particularly quiet on this visit, not even mentioning Lucas,
and usually, that was all she could talk about. Did she love her
sister anymore? She didn't answer that question. It would require too much thought. Too much stirring up of the past,
and she had made a promise to herself a long time ago to put
the past behind her.

"I can't wait to go skating in the dark!" Phoebe said excitedly as they began the walk to the lakefront where the festival
was held.

"Well, it's not completely in the dark," Tess assured her,
and herself. "Each year they fill a portion of the pond with
lanterns, and they hang lights from all the trees." She and Andrew took Phoebe to this event every year, but Phoebe still
treated it as something new, details of the prior years forgotten.

Would she forget Andrew too? How he used to put her on

his shoulders when they walked home? He'd been the one to teach her to skate because Tess was still a little wary of the ice ever since she'd split her chin open attempting a spiral in the third grade.

She wanted to keep those memories alive. But doing so meant talking about Andrew. And right now, it hurt too much to do that.

"Your Aunt Jules won the sprint three years in a row when she was younger," Tess recalled.

"That's right!" Carrie cried out, smiling. She seemed to sense her misstep and sobered herself. Tess frowned, hating that it had to be this way. That maybe it was her fault, for holding a grudge. But how could she not, on behalf of Andrew, her child, and the bond she and Carrie once had?

"The only reason I started losing was because my skates stopped fitting and my toes went numb on me," Jules said.

"I should have gotten you new skates," Tess said, giving her youngest sister a look of apology, but Jules just looked at her in surprise.

"That wasn't your responsibility," she said. "Besides, where would you have gotten the money? You were saving everything you earned toward college."

Tess blinked, thinking about that, but still feeling like somehow, it was her responsibility. That maybe, if Tess had given a little more of herself, Jules's life wouldn't be the mess it was today—that maybe instead she'd be settled.

They turned at the next corner onto Lake Street, and even from a few blocks away, they could hear the music and smell the hot chocolate that was sold at the wooden stands set up for the event. It seemed half the town was already there, standing around the bonfire, warming their hands and toasting marshmallows, drinking mulled wine and hot cider, and laughing and smiling.

Tess was struck at how little things could change; it was the same setup, the same tradition. The same crowd. Except for one. It was all the same and yet oh so different.

Phoebe ran ahead, Tess calling after her not to slip.

"She'll be fine," Carrie encouraged gently.

Tess turned to her sharply, but she saw the softness in her sister's eyes, pleading with her, and she closed her mouth. She was overprotective of Phoebe. But there were some things that she couldn't shield her from.

Phoebe was already lacing up her skates by the time the three women reached the edge of the lake.

"I want to get into the next race," she said excitedly.

Jules looked at the schedule of events, which was posted on a blackboard and lit by lanterns. "Looks like that's a team event, Phoebe." Her face fell, and she turned to Tess, frowning.

Curious, Tess leaned forward, her heart sinking at what she saw. It was the Daddy Daughter race. She firmed her mouth, wishing that they hadn't come, that she had put on a Christmas movie and made a big bowl of popcorn instead. At least at home they were warm and safe, protected from any chance of additional pain.

"Why do they do this?" Carrie ground out angrily.

Tess turned to her, seeing the hurt in her eyes that she knew had more to do with their own father and less to do with Andrew. Still, she saw the way Carrie went over and sat down next to Phoebe, trying to brighten her spirits with the offer of hot cocoa with extra marshmallows. This is what she had needed ten months ago. Six months ago. She needed understanding and unspoken support that only a sister could give. But it hadn't come. And now, she couldn't help but feel that it was too late.

"It's not right," Jules added. "Not every girl has a father."

"But most do," Tess said softly, meeting Jules's gaze. It was the one thing they had in common, the one, horrible bond that united them all, shaped them, and made them who they were today. Tess could still remember how hard Carrie had cried when she was about ten and learned that all her friends were going to a Father-Daughter Valentine's dance and that she was ineligible. Tess had tried to cheer her up, offering a night under a tent made from sheets, just the three of them. After all, she'd pointed out, Carrie's friends might have fathers, but they didn't all have sisters.

She sighed as she looked at Carrie consoling her daughter the way that she had once consoled Carrie. The past had a way of repeating itself. The good and the bad. But some of it was still in her control.

"Why don't we go look at the ice sculptures?" she said, hoping her tone was brighter than she felt.

"You don't want to do the races?" a voice said from behind her.

She turned to see Jeff grinning, a pair of hockey skates slung over his shoulder, gripped by the laces.

"It's a partner event," she said quietly.

Jeff frowned, glanced from the schedule to the disappointed Phoebe and back to her. "I could do it with her. I mean, if you...don't mind?"

"Mind?" She blinked, trying to process what it meant. That

Phoebe could do the event. That Jeff cared enough to make her child smile.

That it wasn't a father, but a stand-in.

That Andrew would probably be grateful. As was she. That she shouldn't be darting her eyes in case that busybody Trudy was here. That she should accept kindness for what it was, and not read further into it. That this was okay. Maybe, more than okay.

"You'll have to ask Phoebe," she said, but she was smiling, and the heavy weight in her chest had been lifted.

Jeff walked over to where Phoebe was slouched on the bench beside Carrie. "Hey, Phoebe. I was wondering if you could do me a favor."

Phoebe's brows knitted. Usually, a "favor" meant helping with the dishes or carrying in the grocery bags.

"What kind of favor?" she asked warily.

"Well," Jeff said, coming to sit on the other edge of the bench. "I really wanted to get into the next race, but I don't have any kids."

"Daddy said you didn't have kids because you like to play in the field," Phoebe said with a shrug.

Jeff's eyes burst open, and Tess stifled a laugh at the same time she hissed at Phoebe to be quiet. But then Jeff started laughing, and so did everyone else, aside from Phoebe, who looked completely confused.

"It's *playing the field*," Jules corrected.

"I suppose I do," Jeff said good-naturedly. "And since I don't have a family of my own, do you think you'd be willing to be my partner for this one?"

Phoebe's expression lit up in surprise and she glanced at

Tess for approval. Tess nodded, holding back tears at the joy on Phoebe's face as she flashed a smile and swung her arms around Jeff's neck.

"We'd better hurry then!" Carrie crouched to help Phoebe tie her skates before Tess could beat her to it.

Tess didn't mind. She stood back, beside Jules, watching as Jeff laced up his skates and Carrie got Phoebe situated, even making sure that her mittens were pulled up all the way.

"He's a good man," Jules said quietly, as she watched Jeff take Phoebe's hand and lead her off to the starting line.

"He was Andrew's best friend," Tess replied. Of course he was a good man.

"Are you sure that's all he is?" Jules asked.

Tess looked at her sharply. "Jules!"

Jules just shrugged. "I'm just saying…He's a good man. And you're still young, Tess. You have your whole future in front of you."

Tess grew quiet. She knew that Jules was right, that technically she did have her entire future in front of her. But every time she thought of that future without Andrew in it she felt paralyzed, locked in the past. Broken.

"It doesn't feel right to move forward when Andrew isn't here," she said.

"But it's like you just said, Tess. Andrew isn't here. But you are. And Phoebe is. And you deserve to be happy." Jules's tone was gentle, but her message was clear. Unlike Trudy Flannigan, Jules was giving Tess her blessing.

Tess shook her head. Jules didn't know what she was talking about. Sure, she could have fleeting moments of happiness, but happy in general? Those days were over. She'd had her happiness. And it had ended, without warning, ripped out from under her.

Besides, Phoebe made a very good point. Jeff played the field. He was thirty-five and a confirmed bachelor. He'd never even had a Christmas tree before.

"Let's go watch the race," she said, walking across the path to where Carrie stood along the shore of the frozen lake. She wanted to reach out and touch it with her toe, to make sure the ice was frozen through, that nothing bad would happen, and that Phoebe wouldn't be suddenly taken from her too.

But then she remembered that Jeff had her. That she was safe with him. She just wasn't so sure that her heart was safe with him for the long-term, or if she should even want it to be.

Jeff and Phoebe took second place in the race, something that Jeff blamed on a false start.

Jeff collected hot chocolates from Juniper Café's stand and distributed them to all the women, except for Jules, who had gone off with Cole Dempsey once the race was finished. Tess looked around the crowd in search of her now, seeing her standing near the roaring bonfire, laughing at something he was whispering in her ear. A pang went up in her. Concern? Worry? Or maybe...envy. For the first time, she dared to think how much easier her life might have been if she'd never loved at all. If she'd never given her heart away, the way Jules never had. If she'd just had fun. Nothing else.

She shook that thought away quickly. Nonsense. She had loved Andrew for half her life; she never could have made those feelings something less than what they were. She still couldn't.

"I want a rematch," Jeff said, loudly enough to catch her attention and pull her back to the present.

"Me too!" Phoebe cried, wrinkling her nose.

"Competitive!" Carrie commented, looking amused at Phoebe's frustration.

"She got it from her dad," Jeff said, giving Tess a secret smile. His gaze held hers for a moment longer than usual, and at that moment, she knew that she didn't need to think about Jeff replacing Andrew. That in Jeff, Andrew could still live on.

"Thank you," Tess said to him, once Carrie and Phoebe had run ahead to look at some of the ice sculptures. "Phoebe would have been crushed to miss that race or feel excluded."

"I should be thanking you for letting me borrow your daughter," he said with a grin.

Tess smiled to herself. "You never show me any pity," she said.

"That's because I don't pity you. You're a strong woman in a difficult situation, Tess. If anything, I'd say that I admire you."

Tess laughed in surprise. "Wow, that's quite a compliment."

He shrugged. "You don't give yourself enough credit sometimes."

She considered this. "It's hard not to feel like I'm letting Phoebe down. I'm only one person." She glanced at him sideways wondering if she wanted to ruin the good mood by bringing up her latest setback. "I didn't get the job."

Jeff stopped walking and looked at her properly. "Aw, Tess." His face was etched in regret. Compassion. But not pity, she thought. And she was grateful for it.

"It's okay," she said, even though it wasn't. Her voice

177

hitched and she caught the emotion in her tone, wishing that she didn't care so much. Or worry so much. Their savings would only stretch so far, and her confidence was shaken. She was a mother. A wife. What employable skills did she even possess?

"I know you wanted that job," he said, looking at her squarely.

She nodded slowly. "I did. But only for security. I guess it's not the fact that I didn't get the job that bothers me. It's more the fear of not finding anything else. I haven't even had another job interview and I've been applying for months."

"You know you can always come work at the restaurant," he said, and Tess gave him a wry look.

"You do know that my waitressing skills are limited to a summer job at the Boat House," she said, and they both burst out laughing at that. The Boat House was a popular seasonal lakefront restaurant that was packed with tourists on the outside deck from spring through fall. Tess had spent a disastrous summer after high school graduation working there, being demoted from waitress to busboy after she'd spilled not one, but two rounds of drinks on a table of customers, and eventually landed at the hostess stand solely on account of her long blonde hair.

"I'd hire you," Jeff said, winking at her.

"Thanks, but if you hire me to waitress, then I *will* know you pity me." Tess sighed. "I know there will be more to apply to once the holidays are over."

"Absolutely," Jeff said. He nodded firmly, enough to almost make her believe that it was true.

All the more reason to look forward to the holidays being over, she thought.

Chapter Fifteen

Jules

Tess was already positioned at the kitchen island when Jules came down the stairs the next morning. Her standing mixer was on full speed and the room smelled of milk chocolate and sugar. Maybe if Jules had a kitchen like her sister did, she'd be tempted to do more than order takeout, she thought.

But then again, cooking and baking meant clean up, and dishes, and she was more of a paper plates type of girl. Even with a house this big, with an island the size of the entire footprint of her kitchenette back in Boston, she was still the same person.

People didn't change. She was who she was. Her sisters were who they were. Her mother had always been their mother, her moods shifting with the tides. And her father, she had been told over the years, had always been who he was. Couldn't commit to a job. And later, couldn't commit to a family.

Jules felt uneasy when she thought about the job part. But then she remembered that she had committed to a job, or at least tried to.

But had she changed? Or was that side always in her, waiting to get out?

She didn't know. She didn't know if she could commit, even if she wanted to. And that, well, that was a very big problem.

"You got an early start this morning," Jules remarked. She helped herself to a cup of coffee. There was a time not so long ago when Tess would have insisted on serving it herself, playing hostess to her guests, cooking elaborate meals instead of defrosting the casseroles that had been in the freezer since last winter. Jules fought off the worry that Tess was burdened by her presence more than pleased by it.

Tess glanced at the clock on the oven. "It's after nine. I've been up for almost four hours."

Jules silently filled her mug and walked to the refrigerator for some milk. She refused to feed into this remark. Really, Tess needed to find her humor. Especially if she was ever going to move on with her life.

That being said, she seemed lighter in Jeff's company. Like her old self. Relaxed and confident and assured and…happy. Like the way she used to be with Andrew.

"Well, I slept wonderfully," Jules said, taking a sip of the coffee. It was partially true. She had slept well, no doubt thanks to the late night and the fresh air. But she'd woken up reaching for her phone again, wanting to call Aaron, tell him what she'd been up to, and hear his news.

Hear his voice.

She'd always loved the sound of his voice. But she couldn't tell him everything, could she? Not anymore. Once she would have had no trouble telling him about running into Cole. How he'd bought her a mulled wine last night and they'd reminisced about that last summer before college. Before everything changed.

She didn't like to look back on those days when she was still waiting for her life to begin. But being here, with Tess and Carrie, being a part of this town and all its traditions again made her remember that maybe it wasn't so bad after all. That there had been some highlights.

"What are these for?" she asked, coming to take a seat at the kitchen island. Carrie's and Phoebe's voices could be heard from the back family room. Jules could hear the faint sounds of the television in the distance, interrupted every few seconds by the sound of Phoebe's laughter.

She smiled. Phoebe was still the same happy little girl she'd always been. And that said a lot about how Tess was managing the situation. Maybe Jules had underestimated her. Maybe Tess was fine. Maybe she was only unhappy that Jules was here.

Maybe Tess really didn't need her at all. But she...she needed Tess. She always had. And she still did.

"These are for the Holiday Bake Sale tomorrow," Tess said with a sigh. "It's a good cause and Phoebe looks forward to it every year."

Something in her tone told Jules that Tess wasn't as enthusiastic about going as her daughter was.

"And it gets you out of the house," Jules pointed out. And it gave Tess something to do. A purpose. The very thing that

Tess had always been lecturing Jules about that she needed to find.

The thought of her lack of employment status loomed heavily, like a hard rock in the pit of her stomach. She'd never been much of a saver. She didn't have aspirations to buy a house or have a mortgage or save for a car. So long as she was able to cover her rent and bills and have enough left over for weekend activities, then she'd been set.

Only now she was starting to think that she needed to re-adjust that plan, stow some funds away, for times like this. Or for when she was old. And alone.

She'd never thought of her future before. Not that far out, at least. But if she was choosing not to marry or have children, or at least not prioritizing it, then the reality was that she'd have no one to fall back on but herself. Other people had family, but she and her sisters were far from close if she was being honest with herself. And Tess had a daughter. And Carrie had Lucas. Her mind went to Aaron again.

From the other room, Phoebe released another peal of laughter. Jules frowned into her coffee mug.

"You and Carrie seemed to be getting along last night at the Ice Fest," Jules ventured to say. Already she felt better shifting the topic onto her sisters' problems instead of thinking about her own.

Tess pursed her lips as she scraped the batter into cupcake tins. "It's all relative. It's not like I've forgiven her. How can I?"

Jules decided that she had tiptoed around the subject long enough. It was time to end this standoff once and for all. "Is it the fact that she couldn't come to the funeral or the reason behind it that has you so upset?"

Tess set the tin of cupcakes into the oven and set the timer. She tossed Jules a look of irritation over her shoulder. "*Couldn't* come? Come on, Jules. We both know she wouldn't come."

"Carrie hates funerals."

"Who doesn't?" Tess's eyes were wide.

"And after Mom...Well, she never came back here."

"She barely visited before that," Tess said.

"I think she feels guilty about that," Jules said. Before Tess could protest, she said, "Carrie wasn't as tough as us, Tess, and you know that. Being around Mom stirred up hard feelings, and then, when she died, well, it's easy to think about what might have been."

Tess sighed. "We all know that our mother was who she was. There was nothing we could have done to make things any different."

"But you were there. You stuck around. You supported her." Jules thought about that for a moment. Tess had never thrown that in their faces. Never expected help, even then. But that didn't mean she wouldn't have welcomed it.

"I should have come back more often too," Jules said. "I'm sorry."

"You were alone with Mom the longest," Tess said. "Besides, you were in college most of those final years."

"I was still capable of helping," Jules said, hearing the pitch in her tone.

"You know what I'm saying," Tess said, looking at her squarely. Jules felt her shoulders soften. She was getting defensive again. Maybe all Tess meant was that she supported her staying in Boston. "Besides, I was happy here." Tess looked down at her hands and the room fell silent.

There was so much that Jules wanted to do at that moment. Walk over and pull her sister in for a hug, tell her that she was going to be okay, that she wasn't alone. But Tess didn't like being on the receiving end of that kind of thing.

"Carrie took Mom's death hard. She was gone the longest and...coming back here hasn't been easy for her."

Tess was shaking her head. "It's not a good enough reason. And you and I both know that the reason she wasn't here was because of Lucas."

The sisters shared a look. Now it was Jules's turn to purse her lips.

"Do you think they'll end up together?" They'd been dating forever but there hadn't been any actual talk of marriage that Jules was aware of, and she was pretty certain that Carrie wanted to get married and have about half a dozen kids.

She wanted the storybook life. Just like Tess.

And Jules...Well, Jules didn't know what she wanted. She just knew, like both of her sisters, that she wanted something different than what she'd had before.

"What are you guys talking about?"

Jules turned to see Carrie standing in the doorway. She opened her mouth to say something, a polite excuse, but Tess surprised her by saying, "We were just talking about you, actually."

Carrie and Jules exchanged a look and Jules let out a long sigh. *Here it goes*, she thought. She wondered if it would be too obvious if she grabbed her coffee and headed into the family room to watch a Christmas movie with Phoebe. It was tempting.

But if her presence might help repair the relationship

between Tess and Carrie once and for all, then she supposed it was worth sticking around. Because more than anything this Christmas, she just wanted something in her life to be certain.

"Carrie," she said, feeling more like a therapist than the kid sister. "Maybe it would help if you could explain why you weren't able to make it to town last winter. Because I do know that you wanted to be here." She gave a meaningful look at Tess, who didn't seem to soften at all in her stance.

Carrie nodded and then looked at Tess. If Jules didn't know better, she might say that Carrie had gulped.

"I did want to be here," Carrie said pleadingly. "But you knew that Lucas was making partner at his firm. There was a big dinner. People flew in from the West Coast office and everything. It wouldn't have looked right if I wasn't there."

"And it looked okay that you weren't there for me?" Tess stared at her. "You loved Andrew, Carrie."

Jules sipped her coffee. There was really nothing to say to this. Carrie had chosen Lucas over her sister. She'd made her choice.

"I did love Andrew. And I love you. But you...you never needed me, Tess. Even when Mom died, it was me needing you. You taking care of Jules. I thought that Lucas needed me more."

Tess's face was tight with anger, but she said nothing.

"You understand, don't you, Jules?" Carrie turned to her. "I mean, you're not mad at me."

Jules did understand, even if she didn't agree. "I'm not mad at you, but I guess it isn't the choice that I would have made."

Carrie narrowed her eyes. "Well, that's easy for you to say

because your longest relationship with a man was Cole Dempsey and you were eighteen."

Jules stared at Carrie in shock, but she knew that there was nothing to say to that. Still, this sudden flash of anger wasn't like Carrie, even when it came to Lucas, who seemed to trigger a defensive side of Carrie. A nervous side.

"Nothing other than illness or airport closures and roadblocks would have stopped me from being here for Tess," Jules said firmly. Even, she thought a little sadly, if her presence wasn't wanted.

"Lucas's job is important to him. He worked hard for that promotion. Another thing I can't expect you to understand," Carrie said, rolling her eyes.

Jules stepped back as if she'd been slapped. The hurt of losing her job was fresh, and all she could think was that she was right not to have mentioned it—to expect them to understand.

"Jules understands that a family event trumps jobs and boyfriends, Carrie," Tess said, and Jules felt her chest warm at Tess rising to her defense.

"Well, you won't have to worry about Lucas anymore," Carrie said with a huff. And then, inexplicably, shockingly, she burst into tears. Long, heaving tears that left her gulping for air and her hands trembling as they came to her face.

Tess and Jules exchanged mutual looks of horror, the argument they were having, the hurtful words and accusations, all but forgotten.

"He dumped me!" Carrie wailed. "I thought he was going to *propose* and he *dumped* me! And then I saw him with another girl and she was...she was..."

Jules wasn't sure when she had last blinked. She leaned forward in her chair. Her heart was racing.

"She was?" She was *what?* Pregnant? Her mind raced with possibilities.

"She was wearing the scarf I bought him for Christmas last year!" Carrie sobbed, and her shoulders began to shake as she cried louder.

"Oh, jeez." Jules stood up and took Carrie into her arms while Tess walked to the bathroom for a box of tissue. It took a few minutes, but eventually, they had Carrie seated at the island, a balled-up tissue in one hand, her sobbing subsided to a few sniffles.

"I thought he was going to propose. He wanted to have a special dinner. It was…" Cue another round of choked sobbing sounds. When she had finally calmed down enough to speak, she said in a whisper of complete disbelief, "It was our four-year anniversary."

"What a jerk," Jules said, narrowing her eyes. Her heart began to race with newfound resolve. "See, this is *exactly* why I don't get involved with anyone seriously. You never know when they're going to up and leave you. Just like…" She saw Tess flash her a warning glance and she stopped talking, but it was too late.

"Like Dad?" Carrie shook her head miserably and brought a soggy wad of tissue to her eyes. "I thought Lucas was different. I thought he loved me," she said miserably.

Tess pulled in a breath and walked around the island to sit on the third stool. "Carrie, the man strung you along for four *years*. At your age, no offense. That's not love. That's…Well, it's a lot of things, and none of them are good."

187

"We never liked Lucas anyway," Jules said. Damn, it felt good to finally say it aloud. To not have to pretend to be anything other than completely annoyed every time Carrie spoke his name, which she did, incessantly, and only in the most positive reference. Lucas was training for the Boston Marathon. Lucas was on track to make partner at his firm. Lucas had surprised her with flowers, again.

But what she didn't say was what was so deeply obvious— like how Lucas had only given her flowers because he'd let her down again by not inviting her on his annual spring vacation to Cancun. Nope, that was a "guys only" trip. Or that Lucas was only focused on his career and had once referred to Carrie's job as "babysitting" or that Lucas went quiet every time Carrie so much as mentioned a love for children or a desire to have any. Or that training for a marathon meant more time away from Carrie, but that he expected her to be available any time he called or texted and would become strangely offended if she didn't pick up or respond right away.

"You didn't like Lucas?" Carrie looked completely affronted, and for a moment Jules almost regretted saying anything, until she saw the red brim of Carrie's eyes and the blotchy spots on her cheeks. This man had done her sister wrong. And Carrie should not be crying over him.

"No one liked Lucas," Jules said flatly.

Carrie blinked, and then glanced at Tess, who just grimaced in return.

"But...but you never said anything before!" Carrie frowned into her wadded-up tissue.

"What were we supposed to say?" Tess finally said. "You adored Lucas. And you were happy. And well, that's all we wanted for you. But—"

"But we didn't think Lucas really made you happy," Jules said. "You thought you were happy, but you weren't. You were desperate to hold on to him, Carrie. It shouldn't be that way."

Carrie grew silent for a few minutes as this sunk in. "I guess I was afraid of losing him. It felt too much like...Well, like losing Dad. I guess I just thought if I stayed close to him, I wouldn't have to worry. That he'd stay. That we'd have a life together. That we'd be happy." She started to cry again.

"Oh, Carrie." Tess frowned deeply, and if Jules didn't know better, she thought she saw a hint of forgiveness in her eyes.

"You were right." Carrie sniffed and looked straight at Tess. "I didn't leave Lucas last winter when you needed me. I could have. And I didn't. Because..."

"Because you trusted me enough to know that I would always be there, always love you. No matter what."

And she'd never trusted Lucas, Jules thought, knowing that Tess saw it too. But did Carrie?

Carrie nodded. "I hurt the person who mattered most."

Tess reached out and squeezed Carrie's hand. "You made your decision from a place of fear. I know. I was there when Dad left. I know how hard it was on you. On all of us." She glanced at Jules, who looked away and shifted in her seat. She didn't like hearing her sisters talk about their father. She was the only one who couldn't picture a memory of him, whose life felt no different before he'd left and after he'd gone. She'd just been a toddler—her entire life had been lived without him. He didn't know her favorite color. Or that she used to fill journals in her free time. He didn't know about the time she skinned her knee falling off her bike, and he wasn't in the audience when she'd won the writing award senior year. But he was there at some point.

And she couldn't even remember it.

"I'm sorry, Tess," Carrie said.

"I know you are," Tess said, giving her a smile.

Jules knew she should be relieved. After all, her sisters had made up. But she couldn't help wondering where that left her.

Chapter Sixteen

Tess

With the help of Carrie, Jules, and Phoebe, Tess managed to bake, decorate, and transport fifteen dozen cupcakes safely to the Winter Lake Town Hall the next afternoon. They were all exhausted from staying up late and waking early, but they were all smiling by the time they reached the stand reserved for her, complete with a tented piece of cardboard bearing her name: Tess Campbell Butler. Once the name had felt like her past and her future, all tied neatly in a bow. The two sides of her brought together. Now she didn't see two sides. She didn't see a future either. She saw a past only, in its entirety.

Tess smiled at her tablemates and carefully arranged the cupcakes in what she hoped was a pleasing presentation. She set the extras under the table, just in case she got lucky and needed to tap into her reserve stash. Grinning, she watched her daughter's eyes gleam at the display of cut-out cookies on the table next to hers. Mrs. Irwin, who taught piano here in town, outdid herself every year with her decorations. This year she'd managed to make ornament-shaped cookies that appeared to have a colorful stained glass in the center.

"Can you really eat that?" Phoebe asked, her eyes wide.

"It's pure sugar, so yes, you can!" Mrs. Irwin smiled.

Phoebe considered this for a moment and then shook her head. "They're too pretty to eat. I'd rather hang one on my tree."

The sisters laughed at that, even Tess, and for once she wasn't filled with that immediate instinct to tell Andrew what had happened, and the lonely realization that she couldn't do that anymore. She had her sisters to share the moment with. And that felt pretty darn good.

She pulled in a breath. Baby steps. One day at a time. That's what all the books said. She had made the cupcakes. She had even turned on the tree lights this morning, without Phoebe having to ask her to do it. She was here. She was even wearing a red cashmere sweater and gold earrings. And lipstick.

Tonight was going to be a good night. That was all she could hope for.

"Do you need any help?" Carrie asked, reaching down to take Phoebe's hands. She was one step ahead of Phoebe—she saw those curious hands reaching for an ornament cookie before Tess could even speak up.

She was a good teacher, Tess knew. And she'd make an even better mother. And now that she was finally free of Lucas, maybe she actually stood a chance at having some children of her own one day.

Tess pushed aside the twinge she felt when she thought of

her own future, which didn't feel half as promising at the moment.

Still, she thought, looking at Phoebe. She had her little girl. And that was enough. It would have to be.

"I think I'm all set here, but you guys might want to get a head start on the rounds before all the good items are taken," she said, giving Jules a knowing look. They could never forget the year they'd been late to arrive because their mother couldn't find her keys and had all but turned the house upside down looking for them, claimed they weren't going in a fit of frustration, while the girls sat near the door, in boots and coats and hats, waiting, and overheating. It was only once they'd finally taken off all their winter gear and wiped away their tears of disappointment that their mother announced she had found the keys. They were in the refrigerator all along.

They'd been stuck with what wasn't wanted, things that had been passed over again and again, like poor Mary Claire Keaton's fruit cake and Sabrina McBride's overly tart and seasonally inappropriate lemon bars.

"You'll have to rein me in," Jules said, her eyes lighting up as they always did anytime that sugar presented itself.

"Let's start with these," Carrie said, pointing at the ornament cookies. Tess knew that she wasn't just being polite either. The cookies were gorgeous, and she had no doubt that they tasted every bit as good as they looked.

"We deserve something special," Carrie said, looking over to give Tess a small smile. It was something that Tess used to say to her on the darker days when their mother hadn't emerged from bed, or Carrie was missing their father. Tess would be busy in the kitchen, of course, baking away her troubles, and she'd bring a plate of her creations to Carrie, even if it was late, or even if they hadn't had a proper dinner yet. "We deserve something special," she'd say. And no matter how bad they were feeling, they always smiled. And they always felt a little better after that.

Tess felt her eyes brim as she watched her sisters carefully help Phoebe pick the best cookies on the display table and then move on to scour the room for the rest of the offerings. Tess remembered the cranberry jam from Wilson's Farm that she always stocked up on and opened her mouth to call out, but it was too late. They'd walked too far and the room was filling up. They'd never hear.

"Well, look at this." Jeff walked up to her table and shook his head in awe at the display. It was one of her better offerings, even she had to agree. Last year she'd been too busy tending to last-minute shopping and Andrew's company holiday party and her volunteer hours at the school to make more than three flavors. This year, she had made five. Three dozen of each. Carrie had tasted all of them and given them her stamp of approval. Well, with the exception of the candy cane cupcake. Something to do with a new aversion to peppermint...

"I was busy," she admitted.

He met her eyes. They were blue and warm. So unlike Andrew's dark brown eyes, but somehow, recently, just as comforting.

"Good. I like to hear that." He held up a brown paper bag. "Before I forget. Something tells me you'll be too busy tonight to make the rounds."

Curious, Tess took the bag, aware of Mrs. Irwin's eyes on her the entire time. She looked inside, expecting to see a paper cup of coffee, judging by the weight of the bag, but inside were two jars of Wilson's cranberry Christmas jam.

"How did you know?" she asked, staring at him in disbelief.

He just gave a modest shrug. "I noticed a near-empty jar in your fridge last time I was over. And I remembered you picking up a few last year at this event."

"Wow. Well, thank you. Take a cupcake in return. Please." She proffered one of the plates, containing what she believed to be the best flavor of the day: cream cheese coconut, designed to look like perfect snowballs.

"I won't say no to that," Jeff said, taking one from the plate and putting it right to his mouth. Half the cake was gone in that single bite, whereas Tess knew for a fact that Carrie could make a cupcake last for half an hour, savoring every last morsel.

Tess laughed. She'd expected to wrap it up for him in the bakery boxes she'd bought just for the event, not have him eat it right here at the stand.

"You're welcome to another," she said, reaching for something else. The spice cakes perhaps. But Jeff just shook his head.

"You should be selling these, not giving them away." He polished off the cupcake with one more bite. "And I mean that, Tess. Not just about tonight's Holiday Bake Sale. You have a gift."

Tess gave him a look. "So do all the women here." He met her eyes. She thought of Mary Claire's chewy fruit cakes. She bit back a smile. "Well, most of the women here."

She heard Mrs. Irwin snort at the table beside her.

"I'm not just flattering you," Jeff said, raising an eyebrow. "If I was going to flatter you, I could think of other ways than through your cupcakes."

Her cheeks flared and she looked away, unable to respond to his words and not exactly sure how.

She straightened her already straight plates. She could see Mrs. Irwin watching this interaction as if it were a television show.

"I like to bake." She'd give him that.

"Good," he said, his eyes wide. "You should be doing something you like. You should be doing something that you enjoy. Something that makes you happy, Tess."

"A hobby and a career are two very different things," she said evenly. One paid the bills. The other did not.

"Think about it, will you? I can help, you know."

She considered his words. It was true that he could help. He was running his own restaurant, a successful one at that, and this meant that he knew a thing about the food industry.

But what was he even implying? A bakery? A storefront of her own? She didn't have that kind of collateral. And a catering business wasn't enough security. She needed steady work, not more worry.

And right now, she needed to tend to her stand.

She watched Jeff walk away and disappear into the crowd, wishing for a moment that he would turn around, come back and keep her company. Thankfully, she was interrupted by Sadie Johnson, who had grown up just down the road from the Campbell house and who had occasionally invited Tess and Carrie over to swim in their pool on humid summer afternoons. Now Sadie was married with four children and looked about as exhausted as Tess felt.

For one fleeting moment, she didn't feel quite so different than this woman who still, on paper, had everything.

"An assortment of six," Sadie said, admiring all the options. "You know these were gone from the school pageant before I could try one."

Pleased, Tess selected the six best and boxed them with a smile. She was still watching the crowd long after Sadie had walked away, until Mrs. Irwin leaned over across the gap between their stands.

"He's a catch," was all Mrs. Irwin said.

Tess had every intention of feigning confusion, asking who Mrs. Irwin was even referring to, even though the gleam in her eye was obvious. Tess had been caught. She had been looking into the crowd, and not for her sisters or even, she thought with a flicker of shame, Phoebe. She had been looking for Jeff. Thinking of Jeff.

And there he was, she noticed. Talking with Sabrina McBride, still single at age thirty-five, still beautiful too. Sabrina who had been head of the dance team in high school and now ran the studio in town and who now had a hand on his arm and was laughing at something he was saying.

Sabrina McBride couldn't bake, not like Tess, but Sabrina McBride was carefree and fun, whereas Tess...

She blinked. Tess was a married woman. At least, she had been.

Quickly, she adjusted the bands on her ring finger and pushed away a pulse of jealousy to focus on the items on her table. She looked down at the jams that Jeff had bought just for her. Yes, she thought. He was a catch. And she wasn't exactly sure what to make of that.

Ninety minutes later, Phoebe reappeared at the empty table, wearing a big smile. "We got so much stuff, Mommy! Like a hundred cookies!"

Tess looked over her daughter's head at her sisters, her eyebrows raised in question. "A *hundred*?"

"Well, not a hundred," Carrie said mildly at the same time Jules said, "Hey, you've got to support local business."

Interesting comment for someone who had left Winter Lake the first chance she had. Tess had often wondered over the years if she, too, would have settled down somewhere else if she hadn't gotten involved with Andrew when she was so young, but she hadn't been able to envision her future any other way. Now, she had no choice but to start imagining it differently. She rarely visited Jules or Carrie, but Phoebe might enjoy some trips to Boston and New York in the spring. And she would too, she realized.

"Did you save a cupcake for me?" Phoebe asked, searching the empty table hopefully.

"Sorry, kiddo," Tess said. "I sold out. But I'll make you another batch tomorrow. Though, something tells me we have more than enough sugar in those bags to last us through New Year's."

"A bunch of us were thinking of going over to Preston's for a bite," Jules said.

Tess knew that she had an easy excuse. She had a small child who needed to get to bed, even though there was no school tomorrow.

But the hope in her sister's eye was more inviting than the thought of going home and being alone again.

"That sounds like fun," she said, and Phoebe ran forward and hugged her tightly around the waist.

"Oh, thank you, Mommy," she said.

Tess's heart warmed at the sight. Since she'd sold out of her cupcakes, she gathered up her tote and empty containers and walked with her sisters to the car, where they deposited their purchased goods. She supposed that she should feel good about selling out, but the reality was that everything she'd earned had gone to pay for other people's cookies and cakes—something she didn't completely mind, considering it had all been part of the experience.

The restaurant was just a block away, and they hurried along. Tess holding Phoebe's hand, and Carrie and Jules linking arms. The Campbell women. Strength in numbers.

Just like they'd been as young girls, when then too, they only had each other.

Only *needed* each other, Tess thought. Because no matter what her sisters thought, or what she believed, she did need them. Always had. Always would.

Somehow, along the way, they'd each strayed, forgetting somehow how much stronger they were together.

They found the group easily, already seated at the table. Jeff and Cole were down at the end, having beers with one eye on the hockey game playing over the bar. Tess was relieved to see that Sabrina wasn't with them, and then, wishing that thought hadn't even crossed her mind, she settled into the chair farthest from Jeff, letting Phoebe take the one closest. He gave her a grin as she shrugged off her coat, and something in her stomach fluttered.

"I'm sorry about Lucas," she said to Carrie, once they'd ordered drinks—wine for Carrie and a hot cider for her. She meant it. Not that she was sad to see him go, but because Carrie had cared for him, even if she probably shouldn't have.

She'd always had a giving heart. Tess had decided not to remember that this past year.

Carrie's smile was wry. "No, you're not. But it's okay. You have a reason to not like Lucas, after all."

"It wasn't just because you didn't come last winter," Tess insisted. "He took you for granted."

"Maybe," Carrie said. "But now what do I have? No children. Maybe no hope of any. You know I always wanted a family." She folded a straw wrapper and tossed it to the side.

"Did Lucas want that too?" Tess asked. She already knew the answer, but she wasn't so sure that Carrie did.

"I'm not so sure that he did." Carrie sighed.

Tess squeezed her shoulder. "Then you're better off knowing. Better off without him. You'll meet someone. You'll be happy again. Happier."

Carrie looked at peace with this. She sipped her drink, hesitating before she asked, "And you? Do you think you'll ever be happy again?"

Tess thought about what Jules had said about Jeff. She looked over now to where he sat with Cole and Jules. He caught her stare and gave her one of his hundred-watt grins. She felt something in her stir. Affection. Gratitude. So many things.

"I have Phoebe," Tess said firmly. "And...I don't want to end up like Mom."

"You won't," Carrie said, and Tess wished she could

believe her. Somehow, hearing the words come from Carrie, she almost could.

"And you won't either," Tess encouraged her. "Wait for the right man to come along, Carrie. Don't just hang onto someone who will never give you what you want most, or treat you the way you deserve to be treated."

"I do feel better since coming back here," Carrie admitted. "It's strange to say that since I spent so much time away."

Tess knew she shouldn't care, but she couldn't help it. She needed to know. "Was the breakup with Lucas the only reason you came?"

"No!" Carrie's brows knitted. "I mean, yes and no. I wanted to get away, out of New York. And I felt...lonely. I could have gone somewhere, but when Jules said she was coming here, I realized how nice that sounded. All of us together. For Christmas."

"That does sound nice," Tess agreed. And Carrie was right: it sure beat being alone. "All of us together."

"Things will be different from now on," Carrie said as if she were reading a crystal ball, as if she were somehow certain of this. She'd always been the most optimistic of the three sisters, and Tess had relied on her for that. Now, she relied on it more than ever.

"Better?" Tess said. She needed to hear it.

Carrie grabbed her hand and held it tight. "Better."

Chapter Seventeen

Carrie

Carrie woke up to sunshine streaming in through the linen curtains, filling the small room with light. She felt light and free, and it took her a moment to remember what had changed in the past day.

And then she smiled to herself, remembering that she didn't need to feel anxious about going down the stairs to breakfast this morning. That she didn't need to worry about making eye contact with Tess and not knowing what to say, or changing the topic while blinking back tears every time one of her sisters mentioned Lucas. That yesterday had been spent baking and laughing and even listening to a little Christmas music, at Phoebe's insistence. That it was two days until Christmas and that she intended to enjoy it.

The only thing to dampen her spirit was the thought of Christmas coming and going. Of returning to her empty apartment in New York, where she no longer had much to look forward to, and maybe, never really had. Where she no longer had much of anything other than a low-paying job that she did at least enjoy, and Melody, of course. Still, thinking of going back made her feel empty and depressed. It reminded her more of what she'd lost than being here in Winter Lake did.

Refusing to feed into those worries right now, she pushed back the quilt and pulled open the curtains. The sun was bright in the sky and the snow on the ground seemed to glisten under its rays. If she craned her neck, she could see a view of the lake from this window—something that was typically hidden by the leaves of the big maple tree in the backyard.

She tossed on a pair of jeans and a turtleneck sweater and brushed her hair into a ponytail. As she emerged into the hallway, she heard the happy chatter of female voices down below. Jules was laughing at something, Phoebe was chiming in excitedly, and Tess—well, Tess sounded more and more like her old self. She'd been downright cheerful at the bake sale yesterday, and they'd shared a lot of laughs last night, remaining at the restaurant until Phoebe was too tired to keep her head off the table, and then Jeff had carried her to Tess's car and the three women had driven back to the house. They'd gathered at the kitchen table, drinking wine and chatting more once Phoebe was tucked into bed, about fond memories and antics they'd gotten away with, and about all the silly little things they used to do as girls like pulling the romance novels from the shelves in the libraries and then ducking into the farthest corner where they would devour them, scandalized.

"I missed this," Carrie had said to Tess when it was finally time to call it a night.

"Me too," breathed Tess, giving her a tired smile.

They were getting there, Carrie thought now. They'd get through this. Together.

"You guys are already dressed!" Carrie observed as she entered the kitchen. She glanced at the clock that hung on the wall near the table to see if she'd overslept. Back in New York, she was up at five every day, hitting the gym with Lucas before they both went off to work. Here in Winter Lake, she'd enjoyed not waking to the sound of her alarm, and last night, she'd actually slept through the night in a deep, dreamless sleep.

"Today's the Christmas Festival!" Phoebe announced.

Jules grinned. "Phoebe is counting the minutes until we leave. She wants to be the first one there so she can enter the sledding races."

Tess frowned. "So long as you're careful."

Phoebe disregarded the comment and smiled broadly. "We're having cookies for breakfast," she announced.

Carrie raised an eyebrow at Tess. That was rather relaxed for her.

Tess caught the look and hurried to say, "She had a banana already." But she seemed to manage a smile, finding humor in her own, rigid ways.

Sure enough, in the center of the table was a plate of assorted cookies that they'd selected last night at the bake sale. Carrie swiped a crinkle cookie and said, "Do I have time for coffee at least?" She supposed they would have some at the festival, but she knew she was in for a long day and needed all the help she could get.

"Only if you hurry," Tess warned. "Because—"

"Phoebe wants to do the sledding races," Carrie finished, grinning. She grabbed a mug and filled it within an inch of the rim.

"Don't forget!" Phoebe warned, wagging her finger sternly even as a giggle escaped her.

"You know, those sledding races remind me of when we were kids." Carrie added a splash of milk from the carton that was still on the counter. "Your mom and I used to race together," she told Phoebe, who responded with a look of astonishment.

"My *mother* entered the sledding race?" Phoebe looked at her with such shock, that even Tess laughed.

"Oh, sure," Carrie said, pulling up memories of Tess bundled up in her red winter coat she seemed to have worn for half her childhood before it was passed down, briefly, to Carrie, and then, later, to Jules, who probably wore it until it fell apart. "She was in charge of steering. I was in charge of the running start at the top."

"Sometimes you'd miss the sled when you tried to jump on." Tess lifted an eyebrow and they both burst out laughing. "Do you remember that time you face-planted at the top of the hill and almost got run over by Billy Harding and his brother on their toboggan?"

"I still have a scar under my chin as proof!" Carrie remarked, pointing to it, but she was laughing too. She turned to Phoebe, and Jules, who seemed to be listening with scrutiny. "We used to count down at the top, from three. Tess would even use her hands for the extra power to push off."

Tess's eyes lit up at that memory. "I think we got our technique from watching the luge event in the Olympics that one year."

"I wish I could remember that," Jules said, looking a little sad.

"Oh, you were there," Carrie said. "It wasn't like you had a bedtime or anything." None of them had. Their mother was overwhelmed at best, too weary for structure or discipline. Even when she was in a better mood, working, in her studio, she often got too immersed in her furniture making to think about practical matters. "You used to cheer us on from the bottom."

She caught Jules's frown and reached out to give her shoulder a little squeeze. "Everything okay?" Jules had been quiet last night too, saying little as they reminisced about the past.

"Just happy to see you two getting along again," Jules said lightly. She grinned up at her and took a long swig of her coffee.

Carrie looked over at Tess. "Just like old times," she sighed.

Jules didn't meet her eye as she stood up from the table. "Yep. Just like old times."

Carrie watched Jules leave the room, wondering what she meant by that, but one look from Phoebe told her that now wasn't time to ask.

"When can we go to the festival?" Phoebe asked impatiently.

Carrie glanced at Tess who shrugged and said, "Whenever you're ready."

"I'll just grab my scarf from upstairs," Carrie said. She swiped another cookie and popped it into her mouth.

"Don't forget your phone in case you want to take a picture of me winning the race!" Phoebe said, smiling broadly.

Tess shook her head, chuckling, and Carrie laughed. "Yep. Competitive." She left the kitchen and patted her empty back pocket. Normally she kept her phone in her hand or pocket at all times, always anxious to hear it ping, or check the screen just in case she'd missed the sound. In case Lucas was trying to reach her. But today she'd left it upstairs on the desk in the spare room.

She was present. And free. And...happy.

She went upstairs, grabbed her scarf, and picked up her phone, not thinking much of the blinking light in the corner. She clicked on the screen while she wandered back into the hall, and froze when she saw the message on the screen.

It was from Lucas.

He'd been to her apartment. He wanted to talk.

He missed her.

He missed her. Lucas missed her. She should be thrilled. She should be elated. She should be thinking, yep, she knew he'd come around. That four years weren't for nothing. That she wouldn't end up like her mother, miserable and alone. That he loved her. That she wasn't a fool. That she hadn't been dishonest with herself. That they actually wanted the same things out of life.

But all she could think of were her sisters' words. And that maybe, they were right. Sure, Lucas had committed to her for four years, as an adult, in his thirties, but what had he committed to? Weekends at coffee shops and brunch and walks through Central Park and late-night movies and Chinese take-out from that little place with the best egg rolls?

It would be so easy to fall back into that. It was her routine. Her life.

But was it her future? Because she was pretty sure that this was all he was offering.

"Everything okay?" Jules asked. She was handing a hot chocolate out to her expectantly; the steam was curling up in the chilly air. They were standing in the middle of the town square, shivering in their coats and standing as close as they could to one of the many bonfires that were set up around the snow-covered park. Tess and Phoebe were signing up for the sledding races, and in the distance, music was playing, the holiday variety, of course. They were in the middle of a sea of familiar faces, at a festival that she had attended year after year and had abandoned at some point in time.

Once this had been her life, her routine, too.

Carrie shook away the cobwebs and accepted the paper cup, letting it warm her hands. "Just lost in thought."

"You've been lost in thought since we left the house," Jules replied. She narrowed her eyes suspiciously. "You sure everything is okay?"

"I'm fine, really. Just tired from staying up so late last night," she added quickly. A convenient excuse but an untrue one. Really, what she had been thinking was that it was Friday morning, the day before Christmas Eve, and that Lucas was probably in his office in Midtown. She could slip away and call him, hear his voice, connect with her old life. But for some reason, the thought of it made her feel more agitated than relieved. What would it change? He hadn't suddenly decided he wanted marriage and children. Maybe, he hadn't even truly decided that he wanted her.

And she wasn't so sure she wanted him. Not when she thought of all the sacrifices it would require. Sacrifices like this town and all these traditions that he would find quaint and silly and boring.

That she had convinced herself she had, too.

"You know what I think? I think you're thinking about Lucas again." Jules wagged a gloved finger at her.

Carrie gave her a withering look. She couldn't hold it in forever, not with Jules pestering her like this. "Is it that obvious?"

Jules groaned. "You know he's such a terrible jerk, Carrie. Think about it. Did he encourage you to spend time with Tess last winter? Or was he too busy thinking about his big promotion party?"

Carrie frowned. She hadn't even thought about this. But no, Lucas hadn't encouraged her to go. In fact, his exact words were that he was sorry that she wouldn't be able to go since it conflicted with his big weekend. He'd answered the question for her. Looking back, she hadn't even found a chance to ask.

"He sent flowers," she said, but the gesture felt weak, even to her ears. At the time she'd thought that was so sensitive of him, that he cared about her feelings, cared about Tess and Phoebe. But now she saw it differently. He was covering his bases.

And she'd looked like the bad guy.

"It's my fault," she said firmly. "I should have come. Nothing should have kept me away."

"You were torn. Lucas didn't make your life easy, Carrie. I think you were too close to the situation to see that. Holding tightly onto someone doesn't mean that they'll never leave you."

A day ago, Carrie would have, reluctantly, agreed with this statement, but then she thought of Lucas's text, still unanswered, saved on the phone in her pocket. Maybe her sisters were wrong. They were mad. Rising to her defense. The way they always had. It's what sisters did.

"Not every man is our father," she said to Jules.

Jules looked surprised but didn't argue. "I didn't say that every man was."

They fell silent as they walked through the festival, stopping to admire some crafts for sale: knitted goods in thick wool, wooden ornaments painted in bright, primary colors that reminded her of her students and her life in New York, and handmade rag dolls that she would have loved as a child.

"And what about you?" Carrie was eager to get off the topic of Lucas and how terrible everyone had always found him to be. It didn't sit right with her. Not when she had spent four years with him. Not when she had wanted to marry him. Not when a part of her still did. And that was just the problem. "What's going on with you and Cole?"

"Oh. That." Jules gave a mysterious smile as she sipped her hot chocolate. "You know we always had chemistry."

"Chemistry isn't everything," Carrie replied. Still, it had always been there with Lucas. Even after four years, she still felt her heart race when she spotted him in the room. Still felt warm and fuzzy when he laughed at one of her jokes.

Did he feel the same? Or had it slipped, somewhere over the last few months, leading him astray, into the arms of the girl with the scarf?

It didn't matter now, she told herself. He'd panicked. He'd been confused.

But he'd come back. He missed her. And he wanted her back.

And Jules was right about that. She couldn't compare all men with their father. Because their father had never come back.

And eventually, she'd stopped waiting for the day that he would.

She'd thought she'd eventually get to that point with Lucas too. Hoped she would, at least. But now…Well, now Lucas had gone and turned the tables on her.

And it was just like Lucas to keep things on his terms, wasn't it?

"Lucas called," she blurted before she could even stop herself or consider the consequences of revealing this to Jules. Now she would be accountable, now she would have to take action, but maybe that's what she wanted. Maybe by telling Jules it was her head overriding her heart for once, keeping her on track.

Jules looked appropriately stunned. "What did he say?"

"He left a message," Carrie said. She hesitated. "He said he missed me."

Jules's eyelids drooped. "He misses you. Please tell me you're not going back to that, Carrie."

Carrie must have hesitated a moment too long. Jules swatted her arm—hard, nearly hard enough to slosh her hot chocolate—and cried, "Carrie! We talked about this! Have you learned nothing?"

"Maybe…" Carrie drifted off. The word felt weak, even to her own ears. Maybe what? He suddenly wanted two kids and a riding lawn mower?

"Maybe he's bored. Maybe that other girl didn't work out."

"Or maybe he really loves me," Carrie said firmly, and Jules sighed.

"He doesn't deserve you, Carrie. But I can't be the one to tell you that. You have to come to that decision on your own."

"You sound disappointed in me," Carrie said, stepping back.

Jules shook her head sadly. "If there's one thing I've learned recently, it's that love comes in all shapes, and that's complicated. And that even when you want to run from it, sometimes you can't."

Carrie stared at Jules, wondering if they were still discussing her own situation and suspecting that they were not. Could Jules really be thinking of Cole Dempsey of all people? They'd dated briefly, like, a decade ago!

Still, her words were what Carrie needed right now. No judgment attached. Just…good intention.

"So what are you going to do? "Jules sipped her drink and watched her carefully.

"I don't know yet," Carrie said honestly. "But I know that I don't want things to be the way they were."

Jules looked down at the snow. "Funny. I was just thinking that all I want is for things to be the way they were."

Carrie thought about that as they went in search of Tess and Phoebe. After all, it wasn't so bad, being back here. If anything, she was starting to think it might actually be hard to give it up again.

Chapter Eighteen

Jules

Cole Dempsey was giving her one of those looks. The kind of look that said a hundred words without saying anything at all. The kind of look he used to throw her way on those late summer afternoons when he pulled up to the front of her house, where she'd be sitting on the creaky old porch swing, a glass of lemonade sweating in her hand, a book in her lap, her sandals dangling from her toes. Her heart would skip a beat, and she'd manage to just barely suppress a smile as she opened the screen door to call out to her mother not to wait up. Not that her mother ever did. Her mother practically lived in that bed when the dark moods hit her. Other times, she'd be on the back enclosed porch that she'd turned into her studio, sanding and staining the pieces that she labored over, that kept her mind as busy as her hands.

Now Jules's stomach did the same little flutter it had ten years ago, and she bit down on her lip to hide her pleasure. So he was cute. Lots of guys were cute. But did they all know how to make her stomach flip and how to get her heart rate going?

Cole was exciting. He was fresh. And right now, he was the perfect distraction.

Jules glanced over at Carrie, deciding that it was safe to wander off without her. Carrie had found a group of friends from their school days, women who were now married and wrestling children wearing brightly colored snowsuits. Jules wondered if this bothered Carrie, what with Lucas not wanting kids, and all, but Carrie didn't look upset by this. She loved kids, but Jules could only hope that there wasn't more to it. That she wasn't going to fall into the Lucas trap again. That she would have better judgment this time. Not that Jules could really talk, she thought, as her eyes flicked back to Cole.

She pushed out a breath and made her decision. Carrie seemed okay where she was, laughing when one of the little boys picked a snowball off the ground and began to lick it like an ice cream cone. Tess and Phoebe were off doing their own thing. It would be best if it could all go unnoticed, then she wouldn't have to explain. Because there was nothing to explain. There was nothing going on with her and Cole. It was just a little fun.

After all, she was good at fun. Fun was fleeting. You didn't have to worry about it being anything more than that.

Jules stood up from the bench where she'd been sitting, sipping another hot chocolate and trying to stay warm near the bonfire. She'd been thinking about getting a few of those cider donuts for sale, but that could wait for now, as long as they didn't sell out first. Cole was waiting for her. If she stalled much longer, he might actually stalk over here, and wouldn't that raise a few eyebrows?

In a town this small, people knew everything about everyone. She walked over to Cole slowly, and not just because she was afraid of slipping on the packed-down snow that was warming under the dozens of lanterns that were set up in the square. She didn't want to appear too eager. It put you at a disadvantage. Opened you up for rejection and hurt.

Of all the guys she'd ever dated (and there had been many over the years, she supposed), she'd never called first. Sometimes she didn't even return calls. She'd never cooked dinner like the way she knew Carrie did for Lucas. Look how that had turned out! Jules hadn't needed a crystal ball to know that her sister's relationship was doomed.

Sure, she'd thrown a pizza in the oven for Aaron. And she called him pretty much all the time. But that was different. She and Aaron hadn't dated. She didn't have to worry about him.

Until now.

Her stomach heaved as her heart sank a little further. She blinked against the blinding white snow, wishing she had brought her sunglasses if only to cover the sadness that she knew was showing in her eyes. She lifted her chin and focused on Cole as she neared the picnic table at the southern edge of the square where he sat, away from the rest of the crowd. It was colder here, away from the lanterns and the people and the stands set up with food and drinks and games, and she shivered as she came to sit beside him.

"Move a little closer," he said, sliding her a grin. "I don't bite."

She cocked an eyebrow at him, still fighting a smile. "Never said you did." Still, she wasn't so sure that she wanted him to put his arm around her or anything. More and more, she wasn't sure what she wanted anymore, and that was just the trouble. Life was so much easier when you didn't want anything. When you were just content with what you had at the moment, not worrying about the future.

But now she was worried about the future. Sure, she'd get another freelance gig, and another after that, because she always did, but the thought of bouncing around filled her with uncertainty, and something else, something deeper. Something like…anxiety, she realized.

Cole was still grinning at her and she pulled in a breath and told herself to shake this off. She was just out of sorts. The week was winding down. Christmas was nearly here. She'd worry about what happened next in January. Like usual.

"Then why'd you stay away so long?" he asked, still grinning.

She frowned a little. She didn't like to think that she'd stayed away. She'd come back for the milestones, for the big, life-changing events. And she would have come back more often, too, if she'd thought she would have been helpful.

"I've been back to town. Besides, my life is in Boston now."

He scooted a little closer to her until they were shoulder to shoulder. "And what does Boston have that Winter Lake doesn't? Hmm?"

She was about to say Aaron, but stopped herself, blinked against the shock of that revelation. After all, what did Boston have? She had no job, no commitment to anything or anyone.

Her apartment wasn't anything to brag about; it could easily be replaced, and she had little attachment to it. It was small and functional. But it was all hers. And it was home.

"We have mountains. And a lake. And festivals." He elbowed her, and against the heaviness in her chest, she grinned.

Cole was handsome. He was exciting. He was fun.

But he wasn't Aaron. And that should be fine. Except that it wasn't.

Cole adjusted the hat on top of her head so that more of her face was exposed. "And I happen to know something else that Winter Lake offers that Boston doesn't," he said.

"Fresh air?" she asked, laughing a little. She readjusted the cap, pulling it down over her ears the way she liked it. The air was crisp, clear, and smelled faintly of pine. It was the smell of Winter Lake, she thought, smiling to herself. But somehow, it wasn't the smell of home. Home was where the heart was. And her heart...

She pulled in a breath, resisting a sigh.

Her heart was with Aaron. She could get up, right now, walk away from Cole, and not really care to look back. But she couldn't walk away from Aaron. And she couldn't bear the thought of him walking away from her.

Her biggest fear. She'd tried to avoid this exact situation. And yet she was facing it head-on just the same.

Cole arched an eyebrow at her. It was quite a devilish look and one that he no doubt practiced in the mirror starting around the age of twelve. A signature move that now seemed a bit overdone, really. He was trying hard. And so was she. And she was starting to think that it shouldn't be that way at all. She didn't want empty, flirty banter. She wanted…connection. Understanding.

Trust. Something she'd somehow had all this while, even when she thought she was running from it.

Cole was watching her steadily. That little smirk that used to make her perk up now left her a little flat. "I was thinking that Winter Lake has…me. You. You and me. I could show you what you've been missing if you hadn't skipped town."

She was about to say that she hadn't skipped town, that she hadn't run from anything, but that wouldn't be completely true. She'd run from a broken heart, she'd run from the pain.

And she didn't want to run anymore.

She opened her mouth to give an excuse, to leave, but she didn't have a chance. Cole leaned in, scooped an arm around her waist, and kissed her. His mouth was warm against the cold.

It was a nice kiss. A good kiss. A downright passionate kiss, if she was being honest with herself.

But as she looked up into Cole's eyes and then down to the curve of his lips and the invitation that was there, unspoken but mutually understood, she felt her body stiffen.

She didn't want to be seen sitting here, kissing Cole at the festival, or anywhere else for that matter. She'd much rather be walking from stand to stand, looking at the crafts for sale, buying gifts for her sisters and Phoebe, and eating a bag of those delicious cinnamon roasted nuts, talking to Aaron, knowing that he was by her side. That he always had been. And always would be.

That he loved her.

Because maybe, just maybe, she loved him too.

*

Jules made up her excuse. It was easy. She had to find Tess and Phoebe. They'd been waiting in line for Santa last she'd checked. Surely they have moved on to something else by now? She didn't react to Cole's look of disappointment. It was part of his game, his banter, and his persona. Something told her that by the end of the festival, he'd find another girl to cozy up with.

"You sure you have to run off so soon?" he asked, patting the empty space she had just occupied beside him. He waggled his eyebrows. Adorable? Maybe when they were eighteen. Now, she felt weary.

"I promised my sister," she said, tossing him an apologetic grin. Really, what had she been thinking, hanging around him this week? Oh, that's right. She'd been running again. But running into Cole's arms was not the answer.

"Well, find me if you change your mind," he said. He looked at her for a moment. "I've missed you, Jules. You and I, we're two of a kind."

She narrowed her eyes at him. "Two of a kind?"

He shrugged. "Oh, you know. Most of these people here take life too seriously. They want to settle down and live a boring routine life. Up at seven. Home for dinner by six. Sleepy town, sleepy life. No wonder you left. But you...you know how to have a little fun."

She took that in for a moment, let that sit there, and stew. He hadn't meant to insult her. In many ways, he was right. Saying all the things that her sisters said. This was the impression she had given off. To Cole. To Tess and Carrie.

Maybe even to Aaron.

219

She was the flighty girl, the one who was always up for a good time, but never one to stick to one situation for long. She was the first to leave. She was restless.

Only right now, she just wanted to stay put. She wanted to know that something was certain. That someone would stick around.

Because she was sticking around.

She reached into her pocket as she made her way back to the crowd. She spotted Carrie with her girlfriends, still talking, still happily accepting the snowballs that the children were handing her and admiring the angels that they were making in the snow.

Jules looked deeper into the crowd. She spotted Tess and Phoebe over near the craft stands, looking busy enough for the time being.

She ducked around to the back of the popcorn stand, where it was warm but quiet, and she dialed Aaron's number before she lost her nerve. He'd be in Maine by now, at his parents' house. He always went up on the twenty-second. Last year, the day before Christmas Eve they'd all gathered around the coffee table near the fireplace and worked on a jigsaw puzzle, sharing a bottle of wine and eating sugar cookies fresh from the oven. It was the kind of Christmas she had always wanted as a kid, the kind she had only ever read about in books until she'd had Christmas at Tess's house a few years back, but even then that had felt like Tess's Christmas, whereas with Aaron's family, it felt like...their Christmas. Like a tradition that she could count on, year after year after year. If she wanted to.

The phone was ringing now, each peal made her heart beat

even faster until she could practically hear it in her ears, and all other sounds from the festival felt washed out and muted. She licked her lips, waiting for him to pick up, to hear the sound of his voice, to know that everything was going to be okay. To tell him…What?

Panic set in. What would she say exactly? She'd never told anyone that she loved them. And was love even what she felt? Or was it longing, because she missed him? Would she cross a line, let him closer into her world, and then push him back out again? Or would he change his mind? Change his heart?

The voicemail clicked on. Jules glanced over at the table where Cole still sat, but it was too far a distance and she couldn't make out his face. And she didn't want to go back there. She'd rather be alone.

The phone beeped. She had to make a choice. To hang up, or to say something, anything.

"Aaron, it's me." She paused. She wondered if she would drain the storage or if she'd be cut off. "I'm in Winter Lake. And…it's Christmas. And…I miss you. And…I don't want it to be like this. I want…" What did she want?

It felt so complicated when really, it was so simple. She wanted Aaron in her life. Today and every day. She never wanted to miss him again.

"I think you know what I want," she said. She blinked rapidly, her mind racing. Did he know what she wanted? She thought of his reaction when she'd revealed she was going for the permanent position, how he hadn't even looked surprised, even when she had never shown interest in such a thing ever before.

He saw more to her than she saw in herself, she realized. He saw her potential. He saw straight through to her heart.

She swallowed hard. "You know me, Aaron. And I know you. And...I miss you."

The phone cut off before she'd said what she wanted to say. What she couldn't say and should have said. The three words that would have said more than all those other jumbled words.

I love you.

Because she did.

With tears blurring her vision, she pushed the phone back into her pocket and crunched over the snow to find her sisters who were now together, standing at the base of the sledding hill, waiting for the races that Phoebe had been so excited about to begin. She wasn't even sure they would notice if she didn't join them, now that they were both so chummy again, and she had half a mind to go back to the house, pull out a book and sit on the window seat in her room, trying to escape her own thoughts. Trying to push away the worry that she had messed up. That she'd used up her chances.

But she didn't want to be alone. Not today. Not tomorrow.

She needed to figure out her life, as Tess always liked to remind her. Only for once, it no longer felt within her control. She wanted more than she dared to allow herself in the past. And there was no doubt about it: it was scary.

But she was beginning to think that it was worth it.

Chapter Nineteen

Tess

Tess waited until the sledding races were over to slip away, even though it had been tempting to disappear sooner. The thought of her child speeding down an icy hill gave her chills that had nothing to do with the wind. It made her think of Andrew. And his final seconds on this earth.

But the look of sheer joy and exhilaration on Phoebe's face when she stood up had been worth a few moments of nervous agony. She was fine. Unscathed. Unbruised. And having the time of her life. The way she should be.

"Could you keep an eye on Phoebe for me?" She had directed the question at Carrie but it was Jules who answered first.

"Of course! I've been thinking of going down a few runs, too."

Carrie gave Tess a small smile. Only Jules would think to join the sledding race.

"I'll be back soon. Last-minute shopping," she explained.

There was a gift that she still needed to buy for Phoebe—the star necklace she had mentioned to Jeff. Surely Phoebe had spotted it at one of the shops. Maybe that was what had prompted the request. And she still had her sisters to think about, too. A nice scarf and hat set would be put to use.

She caught herself. Ever the practical one.

She left Phoebe in the company of her sisters with the promise to be back in time for the snowman building event and left the town square for Lake Street, where the shops were all lit up for the festival, many offering special sales or freebies to entice people to stop in: the toy store was offering hot cider and donuts, and the gift shop had a chalkboard outside that welcomed guests with hot chocolate. It had been a while since Tess had come down this way, since the fall, she supposed, when a Halloween event had lured Phoebe to the trick-or-treat event offered at all the shops.

Now she saw that the old barber next to Jeff's restaurant had finally closed its doors—business had been bad for years ever since Bruce Caparini started to give bowl-cuts that slanted on a forty-five-degree angle across the forehead, and that was back when he was around eighty. He had to be at least ninety-two now, Tess thought. The storefront was dark, the only one not lit by strings of lights. She wanted to see it lit by lights.

Tess didn't know why she was indulging herself like this, but she stopped and looked through the window, taking in the narrow space with the big windows that opened onto the heart of town. It could hold a long counter. A few tables near the window. More outside in the warmer weather.

She looked at the sign taped to the window advertising the lease information. She had no idea what the rent would be, likely unaffordable, but just in case, she took down the number in her cell phone, feeling silly as she did so.

Why was she even indulging in this fantasy? She was a single mother. She had a child to provide for. College funds and mortgage payments and little expenditures along the way were no joke. There was no fallback. No second income or inheritance. There was only her.

And, she thought, her sisters. Comforting, but not the answer to everything.

What she really needed was a steady office job. Only she'd never been good at computers and systems and all of those things. And going back to school was out of the question—more money and no time. She needed a job now.

And the one thing she was good at was baking cupcakes.

Slowly, she stepped away from the window, wondering if she should even call the number. But already her mind was toying with color schemes. Phoebe would want pink, of course. It was a happy color, Tess thought, warming to the idea. And a logo. That was something her friend Natalie could do for her. Something cheerful. Something that could lift even her spirits.

She grinned to herself, deciding that at the very least, it was nice to have something to dream about when she felt something smack her on the back. Not hard, but not exactly soft, either.

She frowned and turned, expecting to see some local boys having a good laugh at her expense, but instead she saw Jeff, giving her a look that was amused, but far from joking.

Her stomach tightened for one telling second at the way his smile lit up his eyes, and then, quick as she could, she bent down and scooped up some snow and flung it in his direction.

And missed. Instead, she narrowly skirted the awkward and slightly horrifying possibility of hitting old Hazel Ofman, once the town's librarian, in the head. But Mrs. Ofman hobbled along, oblivious, humming to herself.

Jeff stared at her with wide, gleaming eyes. Tess covered her mouth with one hand, but she was laughing.

"What did they used to call you on that softball team again?" Jeff said as he approached.

Tess laughed harder. It was a humiliating story, but it flattered her that he would remember such a thing. The only person other than her sisters who knew that story was Andrew, after all.

"Grandma," she said, grinning wider. She apparently had the arm of an old lady.

Jeff laughed, loud and strong, straight from the belly. "What are you up to, *Grandma*? I was just on my way to the festival."

"I had a last-minute gift to buy Phoebe," Tess explained.

"In the empty barber shop?" Jeff gave her an appraising look. "Or were you checking out that lease sign? Thinking about my suggestion?"

"Not in any seriousness," Tess said quickly. She felt a blush heat her cheeks. "Just...dreaming."

"It's good to have dreams." Jeff had caught up with her and now stood beside her, staring into the window of the storefront. He cupped his hands on either side of his face and pressed his fingers to the glass. "Wouldn't require much build-out. Just a kitchen, some paint, a counter."

"*Just* a kitchen?" Tess laughed.

"I've had my eye on it," he surprised her by saying.

Tess resisted the urge to frown. It wasn't her space, after all. She didn't have the funds to make an offer on it. But now, the thought of losing out on the possibility bothered her.

"The restaurant is packed," Jeff continued. "We could do with more space." He shrugged. He was standing shoulder to shoulder with her looking in the window, but she could feel him watching her.

"Huh." Tess nodded, unable to say anything more.

"Of course," Jeff eventually said, "if you wanted it, I wouldn't take it from you."

She glanced at him and scoffed. "Nonsense. You're the one in the business."

He gave her a little grin. "Only if you're sure."

"I'm sure," she said firmly, but her heart skipped a beat, leaving her with an uneasy feeling. If she didn't know better, she might call it disappointment.

His expression became strange, and he held her gaze a moment longer than friends probably should.

"I'm glad I ran into you, actually," Jeff said, roaming his eyes over her.

Her pulse quickened. Something in the way he was looking at her made her nervous, not necessarily in a bad way. But why should she feel nervous about Jeff? He was her rock. He was sweet. And kind.

And handsome.

"Oh?" Damn. Her voice was tight, locked in her throat.

"I have a present for Phoebe, but I wanted to run it by you first," he said.

Oh. She didn't know whether to feel disappointed or relieved by this. Relieved, she decided. Definitely relieved.

"I'm sure she'll love whatever you give her," Tess said, knowing that it was true. Phoebe adored Jeff. He was warm and funny and he'd filled a hole for her. He made her laugh. Made her almost forget about the pain of losing Andrew.

Forget. Tess drew a sharp intake of air, panic setting in. She couldn't let Phoebe just forget her father. And she could never replace him.

"Oh, it's not Phoebe I'm worried about," he said, laughing a little under his breath.

Tess gave him a hard look. She wasn't so sure that she liked the gleam in his eyes. "What did you buy her?"

He waved her in the direction of his building. "I'll show you."

Tess decided that she had a few minutes to spare to see what Jeff had in mind. "Please tell me it's not a puppy," she pleaded, her mind beginning to spin with the least appropriate gifts that Jeff could have bought. "I love dogs, and I know Phoebe's been after me for one, and maybe in the spring, but..."

"Relax," he said, stopping to set his hands on her shoulders. They were heavy and strong, warm and assuring. She met his eyes. She wanted to look away but she couldn't.

"It's nothing living then? No...vermin?"

He burst out laughing and dropped his hands. "Vermin?"

"You know...hamsters. Gerbils. Things that live in cages." Things that required clean-up and responsibility. It would be just like Jeff to feed into Phoebe's wishes rather than be practical about this.

"Noting living," he assured her. He led her over to his building, but instead of opening the door to the restaurant, he surprised her by unlocking the door that led to his apartment.

She hesitated on the street. This felt like a turning point in their relationship, and she didn't know why it should. It was just his apartment. He'd been to her house dozens of times—hundreds of times since she and Andrew had bought it.

But never alone. Phoebe had always been the chaperone. And before that, well, of course, there had been Andrew.

He glanced back over his shoulder. "You coming?"

She said nothing, seeing no reasonable excuse that wouldn't make her look paranoid and neurotic, and followed him up the narrow stairs to a landing on the second floor that contained one door. He opened it and she braced herself, expecting the worst kind of bachelor pad: a futon, crates from the restaurant for end tables, a television that took up three-quarters of a wall.

She blinked as she took in her surroundings. Polished wood floors. An oversized leather couch with actual throw pillows on either end. Framed prints of the Vermont landscape: she recognized a few of Winter Lake, a few of the mountain.

She looked away quickly. She didn't like looking at the mountains, not even in a photo. Hadn't been back on one since Andrew's accident. But she knew that Andrew would have still wanted Phoebe to ski, to do what he loved, what he couldn't do anymore.

She took in the rest of the space, not wanting to look too

curious, but still rather in awe of it all. A television that was unsurprisingly larger than her own was mounted above a fireplace and in the corner of the room was an actual dining table. With six chairs. She realized with shame that she'd assumed he ate sitting on the couch, or down at the restaurant, at the bar. But maybe he had dinner parties, or family over.

"Do you entertain?" she asked, motioning to the table. It seemed surprising that he would, given that she and Andrew had never been invited before.

He gave her a sheepish look. "Poker nights."

She gave a little smile. Of course. She'd forgotten about those. Andrew didn't go as much once Phoebe was older, and when he did, he stayed up too late and was tired the next day.

"He never wagered more than fifty bucks," she remembered. He was responsible when it came to things like that. He was responsible in general. And what happened on the mountain had been reckless, but it had been an accident. She knew that deep down when the anger faded and the sadness replaced it.

"Usually won, too," Jeff said ruefully.

Tess swept her eyes around the room once more. "This is really nice," she said.

"You don't have to sound so surprised," he said lightly.

Jeff tossed his jacket on the back of an armchair but she kept her coat on, not sure how long he intended to stay. The kitchen was open to the living room—all sleek stainless-steel appliances and open shelving stocked with canisters of dried pasta and grains and cereal.

He opened the fridge and peered in.

"Can I get you anything? Coffee? Water?"

She shook her head. "I'm fine."

"Well," he said, looking at her for a minute. "Let me get the present and see what you think. It's not every day that I give a gift to an eight-year-old girl, so I did the best I could."

Tess waited while he disappeared down a hallway, darting her eyes over the space again. On the shelves that flanked the tall window overlooking Lake Street were framed photos of candid shots. She walked over to them now, looking at photos of Jeff with his sisters and parents from last Christmas, another of Jeff when he was younger, jumping into the lake, his arms over his head, his body scrawny.

And another of Jeff and Andrew.

She felt the air leave her lungs as her eyes fixed on the photo, and gingerly, she took the frame from the shelf, almost afraid to touch it, as if she could drop it. It was a recent photo, taken the summer before the accident, during one of their picnics at the lake. She'd taken the photo; she remembered it now. Jeff was holding a beer and Andrew was standing beside him, manning the grill. The water glistened behind them. It was one of those picture-perfect summer evenings that you never wanted to end, the kind where butterflies flew until they were replaced with fireflies, and the sunset cast swirls of pink and peach and purple in the sky.

"I love that photo," a voice behind her said. She turned to see Jeff watching her, his expression serious, sobered.

She gave him a sad smile and set the frame back on the shelf, angling it exactly as she'd found it. "I remember that night. You brought Tiffany Chambers with you to the picnic. Whatever happened with her?"

He rolled his eyes skyward. "She started talking about babies and painting my spare room pink, that's what happened to her," he said, and they both laughed. He shook his head. "She wasn't the one for me."

Tess frowned a little. "I never knew you were looking for the one."

He shrugged. "Isn't everyone?"

"Not my sister Jules," Tess replied.

Jeff brushed a hand through the air. "Jules is young. When she finds the right guy, she'll change her mind."

Tess watched him closely, unsure why she felt the need to continue this conversation. "And is that how you feel?"

Jeff's stare was intense, as if he wasn't sure he wanted to answer the question.

"I think I've already found her," he said quietly. Tess blinked, wondering if she was misreading his signal and knowing from his serious expression that she wasn't.

Her heart was beating hard and she struggled for words to say.

Jeff was close, so close that she could feel his breath on her face, see the question in his eyes, and the bump on his nose from when he'd been hit by a hockey puck in the tenth grade.

She couldn't cross that line. She was Andrew's wife! And Andrew was gone. And right now, his loss had never felt more real.

She shook her head. "I'm not what you're looking for."

"You're exactly what I'm looking for," he said quietly.

She looked at him, really looked at him, and tried to imagine a future with him in it. And then tried to imagine one without him. And couldn't. Just like she couldn't imagine a future without Andrew.

"I don't want to hold you back," she said, swallowing hard. "I'm a downer."

Except that this wasn't true. Not really. Around Jeff, she felt upbeat, maybe even positive. "You want fun," she said firmly. "You want...variety."

"I want you," he said simply. He arched a brow, and his deep blue eyes hooked with hers. And just for a moment, she almost caved.

"You've gone through a rough time," Jeff said, inching closer to her. "Hell, we've gone through it together."

She stared at him, knowing how easy it would be to fall into his arms. To feel connected. And comforted. Forever.

But there was no such thing as forever.

"Think of what Trudy Flannigan said at the tree lot," she said, shaking her head.

"Who cares what that woman thinks? What anyone thinks?" Jeff paused. "What do *you* think, Tess?"

"I think..." But she didn't even know. Her head was muddled and her heart hurt from pounding so hard. From the thought of more change and more loss. She wanted to hold onto Andrew, as tight as she could, for as long as she could. But she couldn't lose Jeff. "I think you're mixing up your feelings."

He shook his head firmly. "I know my head," he said gruffly. Then, quieter, "I know my heart, Tess."

She looked at him, pressed down on her lips, and took one step back. "And I know mine." And her heart...was broken.

She picked up her bag, her eyes searching for the door. She had to go. She had to leave.

"I'm sorry," she said, blinking back tears, happy that her back was to him.

But the person she was apologizing to wasn't Jeff.

It was Andrew.

Chapter Twenty

Carrie

Carrie sat in the big armchair next to the tree, which was now lit, its branches filled with more ornaments thanks to Phoebe's insistence when they'd returned from the festival, cold and tired. A glass of wine was on the table beside her; her phone was in her hand. She reread Lucas's text over and over until she had it memorized, but even then, she read it again, to make sure that it was real and that she hadn't just imagined it.

So many questions. What had made him change his mind? Had scarf girl dumped him? And just how long had scarf girl been in the picture?

She reached for her glass and took a long sip, letting the wine warm her from the inside out. In the fireplace, the flames crackled, and in the distance, she could hear a Christmas movie playing in the family room where Jules and Tess and Phoebe were gathered. Her sisters had been quiet on the walk home, and she'd been grateful for it. Just like she was grateful to be spending the holiday here, in Winter Lake of all places. It was the exact type of Christmas she'd always longed for in so many ways: a big, country home filled with lights and greenery and ribbon, and a child's laughter. It was the life she had always wanted for herself, but one she'd never had with Lucas and, maybe, never would.

She looked at the screen again, at Lucas's words to her, wondering where to even begin. Which question to ask first?

She set the phone down on her lap. The truth was that she didn't know where to begin, or where it had all gone wrong. But Jules was right. Lucas had never encouraged her to be with her sister when she needed her most. And he'd never said he wanted children or a house in the suburbs either. He certainly never would have wanted to spend his Christmas here, in Winter Lake. And he never had. And so, neither had she.

So far, their entire relationship had revolved around what Lucas wanted, and she'd been fine with that. But now, she wasn't. Now, she wanted more. Or at least to know that more was possible.

At the festival, she'd seen families—husbands, wives, kids—made out of all the people she'd grown up with, gone to school with, and left behind. She thought she'd find a better life in New York. The life she wanted.

But now the thought of going back left her lonely and cold. And it wasn't just the thought of her cramped apartment. It was all of it.

She stood up and collected her wine glass to join her sisters in the other room. She'd reply to Lucas eventually, or maybe she wouldn't. But she wasn't getting back together with him or going back to that life.

All she'd wanted for so many years was a family of her own. But she'd tried to force a situation instead of opening her eyes.

She had a family. Right here. Under this roof.

And they'd been here all along.

After Phoebe went to bed, Jules disappeared upstairs to read. Carrie watched her leave the room; half wanting to ask if something was going on with her. But then, she shook the thought away. What could be going on with her? She had no boyfriend or desire for one. She seemed perfectly content with her lack of job security. She was usually in good spirits, sure, but maybe tonight she was just tired. It had been a long day. And an even longer week.

And more than a week had passed since Lucas had broken up with her. More than a week since Carrie had dared to think that her entire life was about to start.

Somehow, being back here in Winter Lake felt like a life-time ago. A different world. And not one she was sure that she wanted to go back to.

Carrie turned off the television as the movie credits wound down, and went into the kitchen, expecting to find Tess hard at work on the cupcakes she'd promised to make for Phoebe to leave out for Santa tomorrow night, but instead, she found her sister sitting at the kitchen table, cradling a cup of tea in her hands.

"The pot's still warm on the stove," Tess said.

Carrie took this as an invitation that Tess wanted her

company, like old times, before all that business of last winter, and she took a mug from the cabinet and added a tea bag. Decaf. She didn't need to be up all night. And tonight she had a feeling she would sleep straight through. The fresh air was doing her good.

So was being free of Lucas, she admitted to herself.

And so was being here with her sisters.

"Phoebe's so excited about Christmas," she said as she slid into the chair opposite Tess. "It's hard to believe tomorrow is already Christmas Eve." If she'd stayed in New York, and she and Lucas were still together, what would that have looked like? Sushi dinner, same as last year, no doubt. They'd exchange gifts on Christmas morning, but there would be no tree, no holiday music, no magic.

That's how Lucas liked it. And Carrie had always gone along with what Lucas liked.

She'd been afraid of what would happen if she didn't, just like her sisters had said.

Tess seemed to force a smile. "Christmas Eve was always my favorite day. I think it was the anticipation. Having something to look forward to."

Carrie wanted to ask what had changed, why she didn't love that feeling anymore, but she knew why. Tess had lost the ability to look forward to something. She just needed to find a way to rediscover it.

"Do you remember the Christmas when Mom bought us all ice skates?" Carrie could still remember the squeals of joy all three girls had let out when they unwrapped their boxes.

Tess laughed. "She let us go skating in our pajamas."

Carrie grinned. She'd forgotten that part. The best part. "That's what made her special, you know?"

"That's what made her irresponsible," Tess corrected, lifting an eyebrow. Then, after a pause, she said quietly, "But it did make her special. As much as I never wanted to be like her, there was a lot to learn from her."

Carrie leaned in across the table. "I remember that we had to teach Jules to skate. Or we thought we'd have to. But she was a natural. Do you remember how she barely fell, and when she did she just laughed?"

"She's a lot like Mom in many ways," Tess said. "I think that's what worries me so much about her. She's a free spirit. She doesn't play by the rules. She wears her heart on her sleeve but holds it back at the same time. She's afraid of getting hurt."

Carrie had never thought of it this way. She'd been too busy worrying that her own life would turn out like her mother's, but now she wondered if that would be so bad. They'd had their moments. And they'd had each other.

"I can probably say that I'm guilty of some of that myself. The fear of getting hurt part, at least," Carrie said softly.

Tess looked at her. "Me too."

Carrie was surprised by this rare admission and insight into Tess's feelings but said nothing. Tess had been so stoic for the entire length of her visit, just like she'd always been growing up, but something told her that she wasn't holding back anymore, that there was something on her mind. Something other than the problems that had kept the two sisters apart all this time, or Tess's secret intolerance for Lucas.

Lucas. Carrie took a sip of her tea. She idly wondered what he might be doing right now. Friday night. He was probably at the office. Or grabbing a beer at his favorite hotel bar down the street from it, with coworkers.

"I've been thinking..." Carrie ventured. She hadn't been thinking. Not with her head at least. But she'd always been one to play by her heart, hadn't she? And this time, she hoped that she could trust it to know what was best. "Maybe I'll move after the school year is finished."

Just saying it aloud filled her with relief. No more cramped apartment. No more noise. No more feelings of loneliness even when she was surrounded by hundreds, thousands of people. No more running away. Sure, she'd miss Melody, but they would visit each other.

Tess looked at her in surprise. "But you love New York."

"I moved there for all the wrong reasons," Carrie said. "I thought that by leaving this town, I'd have a better chance at the life I always wanted. But look at you. You stayed behind, and you got the life I always wanted."

Tess stared at her. "Have you forgotten that I am a widow?"

"You know what I mean," Carrie said. "And you have a community. People care about you. In New York, no one knows me. I've lived next door to my neighbor for over six years and I still don't know his name."

"So you think you'll move back to Winter Lake?" Tess looked so surprised that Carrie had to question her own decision, but only briefly. Going back to New York made her feel lonely. But the thought of staying here made her feel connected.

Carrie nodded. "I'd need a job, of course. But I'll apply to some of the local schools. See what happens. It's worth a try."

"I'd like that," Tess said, smiling. "I'd like that a lot. It's been easier with you two here."

"Oh, you don't give yourself enough credit," Carrie said.

"That's what Jeff says." Tess looked down at her tea. Carrie sensed that she wanted to say more, and stayed quiet. She was beginning to think that Jules was right, that there was something developing between Tess and Jeff.

"Jeff's a really great guy," Carrie finally said, watching her sister carefully as she sipped her tea.

Tess nodded thoughtfully. "He is. But…"

And there it was. There *was* something between them. Something that Tess was resisting, it would now seem.

"But Andrew—"

"Andrew will always have a place in your heart. And Jeff's too. I think that's what bonded you together. Maybe even…brought you together?" Carrie gave her sister a pointed look. "Andrew was special, I know," Carrie said quietly. "But learn from me. When a special guy comes along, don't push him away."

Tess looked over and Carrie followed her gaze. Jules was standing in the doorway to the kitchen, looking sadder than Carrie thought she had ever seen her before.

"Is everything okay?" she asked.

Jules's smile was wan. "Just tired is all. I was going to get a glass of water, but…I'd better get to bed. Christmas Eve tomorrow. I still have to do all of my shopping."

Carrie fought the urge to give Tess a knowing look. Of course, Jules had waited until the last moment to do her shopping, left to panic and pick through leftover items that weren't high on other people's lists. Last year, she'd received a pair of socks. Of course, it was the thought that counted, and well, that was what made Jules who she was.

"Jules, wait," she said before Jules was out of earshot. She didn't like seeing her so quiet like this. She wanted the old Jules back, the one who always smiled and who didn't let things bother her too much.

Jules reappeared in the doorway a second later. "Yeah?"

"I just wanted to thank you," Carrie said, smiling broadly.

Jules looked at her in confusion. "Thank me? I haven't bought your present yet, Carrie," she said, laughing.

"No, I mean." Carrie pulled in a breath. This was a long time coming. It was easy to see Jules as the kid sister. The free spirit. The one who fluttered through life without a care in the world. But she did care, didn't she? About Tess. And Phoebe. And about Carrie. "Thank you, for bringing me here this Christmas. Thank you for…making us a family again."

"All I did was suggest we visit," Jules said, but Carrie saw it differently.

"No," she insisted. "You encouraged me, and that's more than just a suggestion. And you gave me the courage I needed to keep trying, even when I wanted to give up."

"And here I thought I was the one you all saw as the quitter," Jules mumbled, but she struggled to fight off a smile as she looked at the floor.

"Maybe we did once, maybe we didn't understand. You may not live the most traditional path, but you're a hustler, Jules. When you want something, you go for it. And you wanted this." She gestured her arms around the table.

Jules's eyes went wide and she stared at her sisters for a long, silent moment, before a big grin spread over her face, all the way up to her shining eyes.

"I think I may join you after all," she said, walking over to grab a mug from a cabinet. "If you don't mind."

"Mind?" Tess said. "Oh, honey, we never minded."

"Really?" Jules looked from Tess to Carrie. "I mean, the two of you have your lives together and I—"

Carrie burst out laughing. "The two of us do *not* have our lives together, Jules. My boyfriend broke up with me after four years. After I told everyone I knew that we were getting married. After…" Oh God, the horror. She squeezed her eyes shut, just thinking of it now. "After my coworkers and class threw me a celebration party."

Tess's eyes were huge now and Jules was trying not to laugh. "With cake and everything?" Jules asked.

Carrie nodded miserably. "With cake. And a card."

Tess shook her head, chuckling, "Oh, Carrie." But she reached out and took her hand, squeezing it hard. No judgment. Just understanding. Because she knew Carrie. Knew her from the time she was a little girl who used to lie on her bed and daydream. It was easy to get caught up in fantasies sometimes.

"Well, you at least had a serious relationship. And you have a full-time job," Jules pointed out.

"I thought you never wanted a full-time job," Tess remarked.

Jules sighed. "I've realized that I do want that. I was just waiting for the right opportunity."

"It will come along," Tess assured her.

"I want to believe that. I…I don't really like the lack of security that comes with never knowing when my next paycheck will be. And, I liked getting to know the people at the last job. I liked having a routine. It was, well, reassuring. Here I always thought it would be the opposite."

Tess nodded. She pulled in a sigh and glanced around the table. "I found out this week I wasn't selected for the job I interviewed for, not that I'm surprised. I have next to no relevant qualifications. I'm a mom. I'm not even a wife anymore. And...I'm scared."

Her eyes brimmed with tears and Carrie was so astonished, it took a moment for her to react. It wasn't like Tess to break down or cry or admit any weakness. She was a fighter. She was scrappy. Maybe even scrappier than Jules. But it was all a front. A wall that was finally coming down.

"Oh, honey." Carrie stood up and crossed to Tess's chair, reaching down to give her sister a good, long hug. She dropped onto the seat closer to Tess, and Jules took the opposite. "You are an excellent mother."

"I worry every day that something will happen to Phoebe, but at the same time all I want is to give her a normal childhood, and I'm failing."

"We didn't have a normal childhood," Jules said. "And look at us. Sure, you're a helicopter mom and Carrie hitched her train to a guy who could never bring her happiness. And of course, I can't commit to anything without feeling like I'm having an anxiety attack. But we're trying. We're doing our best."

"And there were good parts," Carrie said slowly. They'd come back to her, one by one, ever since she got off the bus at the Winter Lake station. "We had some happy times. And...I'd like to think that what we went through brought us closer. I'd like to stay close. I've missed this. I've missed us."

Lucas missed her, she thought. But what she missed, what she'd needed, was this. Her family. Her home. Her life.

"I'm sorry if you thought we were hard on you, Jules," Tess said through watery eyes. "I just wanted to look out for you. Set you on the right path. Like I do with Phoebe. But...I could learn a lot from you. I already have."

"Learn from me?" Jules blinked.

Tess nodded. "You have a spirit to you, Jules. You know how to live. I think...I think that I'll step back and let Phoebe have a little more fun. When I think back to some of the crazy stuff we did...well, it's some of my fondest memories."

"Me too," Carrie said, grinning.

"I think we need to toast to more of those moments. And...more of these moments." Jules gave them a mischievous grin and grabbed a bottle of champagne from the back of the fridge. "It is Christmas, after all," she said.

"And what a Christmas it is," Tess said, grinning.

Chapter Twenty-One

Tess

It was going to be a white Christmas, not that there had been much doubt considering the snow had started before Thanksgiving and not let up since. Still, Tess couldn't help but feel a little skip in her pulse when she opened the curtains on Saturday morning and looked out onto the winter wonderland spread before her, as far as the eye could see.

Snowflakes swirled lazily from the sky, dropping onto the branches, creating a glistening blanket on the stretch of lawn.

When she was younger, Tess loved this day the most, Christmas Eve, even if the anticipation she felt was mostly only tied to the hope of a gift or two, there was always something under the tree and wrapped. Somehow, no matter how bad things got or how dark her mother's mood, she always managed to pull something together for the holiday—art kits or skates or a new sled, or pizza delivery, not exactly traditional but exciting all the same. It was one special day that

Tess could count on to be better than the others all year. It was a time of hope.

And even now, that hope still lingered, ingrained in her, even though she had thought that it was lost forever. But today, little bits of sadness crept in. She supposed it was inevitable, part of life. That somewhere along the way, even the best of days became bittersweet.

She stepped away from the window and walked to the closet to grab a sweater. She could have chosen black or grey, her signature colors lately, but she decided to push herself, just a little, and reached for a red turtleneck instead. It was the same sweater she had worn last Christmas Eve, which she'd spent baking and prepping for a big family meal the next day, even if it was just the three of them—Andrew's parents were staying in Arizona and her sisters were busy with their thing. Still, with only her and Andrew and Phoebe, they made the most of it, made it special, and that night when Phoebe had gone to bed and Andrew had eaten all of Santa's cookies, they set her presents under the tree and then curled up on the couch together, content, happy, fulfilled.

From downstairs she heard the peal of the doorbell, and she jumped, frowning as she considered who it might be. A delivery man with a package? But aside from Carrie, Andrew's parents were the only ones who ever sent anything, and their gifts had arrived two weeks ago. Carrie and Jules had taken Phoebe into town to buy "something special" for Tess, which was something that Andrew used to do, not that Tess shared that. It was a thoughtful gesture, and more likely than not an opportunity for Jules to hurry up and buy everyone something, of course. Maybe they had come back early? Maybe they had forgotten the key? Except Phoebe knew the back door was always unlocked. This was Winter Lake. The safest place to be.

Only right now she didn't feel very safe. She felt nervous and...scared. What if it was Jeff, coming back to continue their conversation, to take back everything he had said yesterday, or to say that he had meant it?

She considered this for a moment, not quite sure which would be worse.

This house was her world, her safe place, her haven from the moment she had first stepped inside. It had been her first real home, and it was where she had been the happiest.

And she wasn't sure that she could let Jeff inside right now. She just didn't know if there was room for him.

The doorbell rang again. It was cold. She should let him in. Hear him out. But all she wanted to do was hide. Barricade the doors. Never go outside. Stay safe and warm and untouched.

It rang again. Damn it! She hurried to the window, but from this angle, she couldn't see who was standing on the front porch. And from the sounds of it, they had no intention of going away.

With a racing heart, she hurried down the stairs, thinking of what she would say when she opened the door and coming up with nothing. She'd tell him that now wasn't a good time. Because it wasn't. No time was good anymore. Well, except for the time with Phoebe. And her sisters.

And Jeff. Their time together *was* good. Maybe even the best. There was no denying that.

She closed her eyes, her hand resting on the doorknob. And then, before she could lose her nerve, she pulled it open.

She opened her mouth to say something—what, she didn't know—except the man standing on her front porch was not Jeff at all. It was another man, slightly shorter, a little fuller in the face, with kind eyes and a slightly nervous smile.

He looked familiar, but she couldn't place where from.

"I'm sorry. Do I know you?" she asked. She hoped it wasn't one of those door-to-door salespeople she would have to let down gently. Honestly, it was a holiday weekend!

"I'm Aaron Taft," he said, raising his eyebrows. "I'm a friend of Jules?"

Of course! She'd met Aaron at Jules's college graduation, and taken a liking to his easy demeanor and quick wit right away. She hadn't had a chance to talk with him much. He'd been off to lunch with his parents, and Phoebe wasn't at an easy age, needing naps and snacks and distraction. But even then, from their brief interaction on the lawn before they'd all gotten on with their plans for the day, it was clear he was devoted to Jules. Clear in the way he looked at her, and smiled when she smiled. She'd asked Jules about him the moment he was out of earshot, but Jules had established quickly that they were only friends.

"Jules isn't here," Tess said, opening the door wider. The poor kid was cold. "I'm her older sister, Tess. We met once."

His smile was warm. "I remember. And Jules talks about you all the time."

She did? Tess felt touched by that. But then she thought of her situation, and she hoped the conversation didn't take a pitying turn. She glanced at Aaron, but his eyes were kind more than concerned, and she decided, just as she had the first time she met him, that she really liked this guy.

That maybe there were still good guys out there. That maybe she hadn't found the only one.

"She just went into town, but she'll be back soon if you want to wait?"

"Thanks. So long as I'm not putting you out." Aaron nodded and stepped inside the living room. "Nice decorations," he said as he removed his shoes and handed her his coat.

Tess looked around the living room, from the tree that was lit in the window to the other items that her sisters had set up, and smiled. "Thank you," she said.

Her heart sank as she closed the door, realizing that Jeff had not come over. That Jeff may never come over again. That it hadn't been him at the door at all.

And that suddenly, she wished more than anything that it had been.

"Coffee? Tea?"

"I'm fine," Aaron said, but he seemed nervous as he took a seat in the living room.

"Jules didn't mention you were coming," Tess commented, not that she minded. It was just, well, typical of Jules to not share her plans or decide something at the last minute, on a whim.

Aaron's cheeks flushed and he studied the apple-scented candle on the center of the coffee table for a moment. "She doesn't know I'm stopping by. It's sort of...a surprise."

Tess felt her eyes pop and he couldn't resist a smile. Was that so? Tess wanted desperately to ask him if he wanted to talk or share his reasons for coming all the way to Vermont, but she got the impression that he was nervous, if the endless tapping of his foot gave anything away, and so she decided to distract him instead.

"I have some old photo albums if you want to look through them while you wait," she offered. "I'm sure there are a few of Jules in there."

His face lit up and she walked to the built-in bookcase that flanked the fireplace, her eyes landing on the last family photo she and Andrew had ever taken, last February, at the town's annual Valentine's Day dance, and took one of the albums from the shelf. She opened it, just to be sure, and out popped a picture of Jules, about Phoebe's age, eating a slice of watermelon down at the lake.

"That's how I always think of her," Tess said, smiling fondly.

Aaron took the photo and looked at it, grinning. "That's pretty much how I think of her too. Even if I wasn't lucky enough to know her back then."

Tess watched Aaron for a moment, thinking of what Jeff had said just yesterday in his apartment. *When the right one comes along, you just know it.*

But did she know it? And was there more than one right one?

Suddenly, there was a loud noise from the back of the house and the sound of her sisters' laughter filled the air. Aaron set the book down and sat up straight, and Tess, a little flustered, said, "I'll go let her know you're here!"

She wasn't quite sure what sort of reaction this would spark, or what circumstances had led to this visit, and she felt a little nervous as she smoothed her palms on her jeans and turned toward the kitchen. But before she could make any sort of official announcement about their guest, Jules walked into the room and halted in the doorway when she saw Aaron, now standing beside the couch.

He thrust his hands into his pockets and then pulled them back out again. "I got your message."

Message? Well, this was interesting. It seemed that there was more going on with Jules than Tess had thought.

Jules's face was one of pure surprise, so much so that even Tess couldn't tell if she was happy or sad, and was even more baffled when Jules did the unthinkable and burst into tears.

Aaron, however, was smiling, all the way up to his eyes, that crinkled at the corners. And before Tess or Carrie could even steal their eyes away to glance at each other, Jules hurried across the room and planted a big kiss on Aaron's mouth.

"Don't tell me you just did that because there's mistletoe over our heads," Aaron said.

Jules was still crying. "I did it because I should have done it a long time ago."

Tess felt her own eyes brim and she looked over at Carrie, who was holding the hand of a mesmerized Phoebe.

"That's the way it's supposed to be," Carrie said quietly when Tess joined her in the kitchen. "You had it with Andrew. And Jules has it too. I can only hope that there's still a chance for me."

Tess thought back to her own rocky path that never could have been planned or expected and sighed heavily. She still didn't know where her path was leading. Or how it would end. She just knew that along the way there were choices.

"We should probably give them some time alone," she said.

"I'll take Phoebe upstairs to wrap your gift," Carrie said.

Tess nodded. She felt out of sorts, and restless, like there was an action she needed to take and she couldn't think of how to do it. "I think I'll use this time to get some of my shopping finished," she said, walking to the mudroom to grab her coat and push into her snow boots.

The walk to town was short, and for the first time all season, she was able to look around without feeling affronted—at the lights, the people, and the carolers who were standing at the intersection of Lake and Main, filling the air with holiday favorites.

She'd made it. She'd survived. And maybe, just maybe, she had even turned a corner.

The shops were open, and busy from what she could tell. It would seem that her family wasn't the only one partaking in some last-minute gift buying. She decided to try the gift shop on Main first—they sold everything, and they might even have a star necklace.

Candles were lit when she entered the shop, filling the space with a warm, spicy fragrance. She took her time, trying to enjoy a few moments of quiet, and peace, to clear her head and enjoy the beautiful objects around her. Maybe she *could* get a job in a store like this. Maybe it would actually do her some good to talk to people throughout the day, rather than staying home, alone, hiding from the outside world. Shutting out life. This last week, getting out, attending the festivals, and living again, had made her feel better. But it hadn't been easy.

She found a table with earrings and bracelets and heard her own gasp when she saw a single star necklace sitting in a box. She checked the price tag, feeling her heart sink in relief, and gripped it firmly. She couldn't even fight off her smile. She'd done it. She'd pulled it off. She'd managed to give her daughter a good holiday, and that felt good. Really, really good.

"You found it," a voice behind her said just as she finished paying and set the small box in her handbag, so Phoebe wouldn't get suspicious seeing her walking in the door holding shopping bags.

Her senses prickled. She couldn't avoid him forever, after all. Not in a town as small as Winter Lake.

She turned, expecting some level of awkwardness, but all she saw in Jeff's eyes was the same warmth that had comforted her these past ten months. They were the eyes of a person who had lived through what she had, every step of the way. They were the eyes of someone who knew her, cared about her, and was connected to her, forever.

And she wanted to believe in forever. She really, really did.

She pulled in a breath. "It seemed like a strange request, but if she wanted it…"

"Not a strange request," Jeff said, holding the door for her.

She passed through and tightened the scarf at her neck. "What do you mean?"

He was walking beside her, his step in time with hers, and from the looks of it, he had no intention of dashing off. And that, she realized, made her happy. They'd been through a lot, the worst, really, and they were still in this together. Whatever it was.

"I talk to Phoebe about Andrew sometimes," Jeff said simply.

Tess stopped, startled. She stared up at him, searching his face. Sure, she knew that Phoebe and Jeff chatted, but she assumed it was about school, how Phoebe spent her recess time, and other lighthearted stuff.

"You do? But…" She swallowed hard. She didn't know what to say, what to ask. "What does she say?"

She braced herself, unsure if she wanted to hear it. To know her daughter's pain. The pain that Phoebe didn't always show at home.

"She told me she misses him," Jeff said. There was a frown line between his eyebrows as if he wasn't sure he should be telling her this, but that he wanted to. Needed to.

"She doesn't say that to me," Tess said, blinking back her confusion.

"She's looking out for you." Jeff slipped her a grin. "Like mother, like daughter."

Tess shook her head, fighting back shame and regret. "I don't want her to feel that burden. I…I did everything I could to be different. To give Phoebe the childhood I never had."

Jeff set two firm hands on her shoulders, and she felt her anxiety sink away. He was looking her straight in the eye, and much as she wanted to, she couldn't glance away.

"You've given Phoebe an amazing childhood, Tess. She knows you're being strong for her. She sees everything you do for her. She's a smart kid, that one."

"Like her father," Tess said, giving a sad smile as she scuffed her toe against the salt on the sidewalk. She sniffed and looked up at him. "What else does she say?"

"Not much," Jeff said. "But one time I told her that every time she misses him, she should look up at the sky, and know that he's up there, looking down on her. I wanted her to know that he's always with her, you know. He's always with all of us, Tess. He always will be."

Tess felt the lump rise in her throat that she couldn't push back. The stars. Of course. "Thank you," she managed.

"I didn't have a chance to tell you yesterday that I sort of bought her a telescope. I don't know if a girl her age would like that sort of thing, but I thought she could look up and—"

"Are you kidding me? It's thoughtful. And generous. And…it's perfect," Tess whispered, swallowing hard. She shouldn't have expected anything less.

"I sort of got you a little something too," he said, giving her a long look.

Tess stiffened. She still hadn't bought gifts for her sisters. Or for Jeff.

"Jeff, you've given me enough," she started to say, but he held up a hand, stopping her.

He reached into his pocket and held out a piece of paper. He opened his mouth as if to say something and then thought better of it. He held it out to her.

She frowned as she took it. "I don't understand."

Jeff grinned, watching her expectantly. "Open it."

If this wasn't the day for surprises, Tess thought. She pulled in a breath and unfolded the paper, scanning her eyes over the document until she reached the very bottom. It was a lease. To a storefront.

"The old barber shop is yours. For a year. Consider me your silent partner. Your investor. Your biggest fan."

Tess stared at him. He couldn't be serious. But from the looks of it, he was.

"But, why?" she asked, knowing that she must have looked as shocked as she felt.

He shrugged his shoulders and gave her a lopsided smile. "Because I believe in you, Tess."

The tears streamed down her face now, thick and hot, and

she didn't try to hide them or brush them away. They were tears of relief. Of joy. Of despair and fatigue. But most of all, they were tears of gratitude.

"Aw, Tess." Jeff's grin was rueful. "It's just a store."

She reached down and took his hands. They were cold—he never wore gloves and she'd forgotten to put on her own after leaving the store—but standing here like this, she felt warm.

"You did more than give me a storefront," Tess said, smiling up at him. "You gave me a second chance. And you gave me hope."

Christmas Day

Tess took the foil-covered casserole out of the freezer and checked the handwritten instructions before setting the oven timer. That would be the last of them, and seeing as it was of the potato and cheese variety, she thought it would pair perfectly with the giant turkey that Jeff had brought over.

"I hadn't prepared for so many people," Tess said by way of apology to her sisters, who were gathered in her kitchen, Jules slicing the bread and Carrie stirring the gravy on the stovetop.

"You know we would have been just as happy with pizza," Jules said. The three sisters exchanged a grin. It was, after all, what they had grown up eating on Christmas Day.

"Yes, although the last time you all came for Christmas—"

"We're not focusing on *last* Christmas, Tess," Jules said. "We're focusing on *this* Christmas. And this Christmas, we're all pitching in. You don't have to worry about taking care of us, Tess," she added softly, giving her a gentle smile. "Let us help."

Tess blew out a breath and nodded her head. Jules was right. She didn't need to worry about taking care of Jules, or Carrie, or even Phoebe, at least not to the worrisome degree that she had for so long. Just this morning, she'd let Phoebe try out her new sled, and she hadn't even warned her not to go too fast as Phoebe ran to the top of the hill.

Carrie glanced into the other room where Phoebe was showing off her presents to Jeff and Aaron, who made a big effort to sound interested, even in the dolls.

"Aaron's a pretty special guy," Carrie said, giving Tess a little wink. "I didn't realize that you guys were more than friends."

They both looked at Jules and waited. Tess only hoped that Jules wouldn't shrug this off, say that there was nothing there, because there was something there. She could see it. And she knew that Carrie could too.

But Jules just bit her lip and looked at them shyly. "What can I say? He wore me down."

"So you're not going to let this one go?" Tess asked.

"Nope," Jules said with a little lift of her chin. "When you know, you know. He's right for me. And…he's not letting go."

She cut a glance at Carrie and frowned. "I'm sorry, Carrie—"

But Carrie just shook her head. "You don't need to apologize. No offense taken. Lucas was…well, he wasn't right for me. And I couldn't see that. But now, being here, being home, I do. I have an entire future ahead of me, and between us, I'm really ready for some changes in the New Year."

"Me too," Jules said.

Tess was quiet as her sisters finished preparing the dinner. She knew that they were right, that there was an entire future ahead of her, too. And she was ready for change. Ready to embrace it.

"There's just one thing I need to do before we eat," Tess said.

She slipped out of the room and walked upstairs to her room, fishing the phone out of her pocket. Andrew's phone was still in his bedside drawer, the power off, but the service activated. Maybe someday she'd bring herself to cancel the plan and save herself the monthly payment, but for now, she had no intention of stopping it. Sometimes, she just needed to hear his voice.

But today, she had something to say.

She pulled his name up from her contacts list, just like usual, only this time, she didn't dare to dream that he would answer. His voicemail came on right away, and she listened to his voice, so familiar, so comforting. A memory that was seared in her heart and would always be there.

She swallowed hard, knowing what she had to say, and knowing that he would understand. That maybe, just maybe, this was what he wanted for her.

"Hi, Andrew," she said, feeling the familiar lump rise into her throat. "I wanted to hear your voice. And I wanted to wish you a Merry Christmas. Phoebe got everything she asked for, and…she's happy. That's a good thing. And…it made me realize that maybe it's okay for me to be happy too. That it wouldn't be a betrayal. That…you would understand. So, I wanted to let you know that I might not be calling for a while, but that doesn't mean that I don't think of you every day. That I don't cherish our time together. That I'm not grateful. Or heartbroken. That I don't miss you or every single second we had together. That I don't love you. Because I'll always love you, Andrew. All of us will."

Tess felt the tears roll down her cheeks, hot and thick, and this time she didn't try to brush them away.

She sat on the edge of the bed, holding the phone to her ear, until she heard a beep, and she knew that their time was over for now.

She set her phone on her own nightstand and walked to the door. When she opened it, she heard the sounds of laughter and music from below. A full house for Christmas. And, hard as it was to believe, a full heart.

ABOUT THE AUTHOR

Olivia Miles is a *USA Today* bestselling author of women's fiction and contemporary romance. She has frequently been ranked as an Amazon Top 100 author, and her books have appeared on several bestseller lists, including Amazon charts, Barnes and Noble, BookScan, and *USA Today*. Olivia lives on the North Shore of Chicago with her family.

Visit www.OliviaMilesBooks.com for more.

Lightning Source UK Ltd.
Milton Keynes UK
UKHW041638271122
412931UK00004B/170

9 798986 262437